"What's to keep you from marrying me?"

Luc was furious. "And if you aren't staying here, then why can't you come to Brazil?"

"Because I don't want to!" Emily glared at him.

He sank down on the sofa, staring at her in disbelief. "I thought I'd made myself clear," he said. "I want you for my wife. I can give you security, even wealth. You will want for nothing. Now that I've seen you again I realize how very suitable you'll be. You're poised and adult now, attractive, a very good mother—what more could a man wish?"

"I'm not concerned with how I fit your specifications," said Emily bluntly. "I don't think joining our lives together now is a good idea." She hesitated, then sighed. "I don't love you, Luc."

CATHERINE GEORGE

gilded cage

Harlequin Books

TORONTO • NEW YORK • LONDON
AMSTERDAM • PARIS • SYDNEY • HAMBURG
STOCKHOLM • ATHENS • TOKYO • MILAN

Harlequin Presents first edition November 1983
ISBN 0-373-10640-8

Original hardcover edition published in 1983
by Mills & Boon Limited

CHAPTER ONE

EMILY stood gazing out of the small casement window in Lady Henrietta's bedroom, her eyes absently on the last of the day's visitors as they left Compton Lacey. One man paused to take a photograph of the ancient house in the fading sunset light, and Emily smiled, knowing precisely the picture he saw through the viewfinder. Encircled by the green waters of its moat, the house had stood almost unchanged for the past six hundred years, dramatic, dreamlike, the embodiment of an illustration for some long-forgotten mediaeval romance.

This was the time of day Emily liked best, when left to itself again the old house seemed to relax and settle for a while before it was locked up and left to the solitude of the night. She stared dreamily down at the swans preening themselves on the moat, unaware that she was observed. To the man who stood silently in the doorway the girl looked like some wraithlike former occupant of the house, insubstantial in her grey dress, her long pale hair and finely chiselled profile only dimly visible in the gathering dusk of the small room. He held his breath, reluctant to disturb the girl's reverie, but something in his very stillness communicated his presence to her. She turned sharply, immediately reaching to switch on the lamps on the mantel as she saw him standing there.

She received a swift impression of a lean, darkly-tanned face with a prominent nose, and heavy-browed dark eyes beneath black hair that curled down into the upturned collar of a white trenchcoat.

'I'm sorry!' Emily smiled apologetically. 'Please come in; I thought everyone had gone.'

'I hope I didn't startle you.' White teeth gleamed in an answering smile as the man ducked his head to enter the room. He spoke with a trace of accent Emily found hard to place. She hesitated.

'Would you care to know about the contents of the room?'

'Very much.'

However, her companion seemed to take more interest in her face than the treasures surrounding him, and Emily found it more difficult than usual to concentrate on the details that were automatic to her by now from long practice. Deliberately brisk and prosaic, she launched into her account of the Charles I chest, the Queen Anne kneehole desk and the George IV toilet mirror, the man listening intently to her low, clear voice as she indicated the heraldic panes in the windows, the exceptional quality of the panelling and the ornate splendour of the fourposter bed.

'The lady in the painting,' asked her visitor, when she paused, 'is that the Henrietta for whom this room is named?'

'Yes.' Emily moved over to the fireplace to look up at the smiling beauty in full court dress. 'She's Lady Henrietta Compton, who married Sir Giles Lacey in the reign of George IV, bringing with her a very large dowry which enabled her husband to make extensive restoration to various parts of the house.'

'If the artist was accurate, rather than flattering, Sir Giles was a very fortunate man.' The deep, rather harsh voice, with its faint elusive accent, held a mocking note. 'Heiresses seldom had beauty to accompany their fortunes, if one may believe all one reads.'

'No,' said Emily consideringly, looking up at the confident, beautiful face below the powdered curls. 'It hardly seems fair, does it?' Then she collected herself hurriedly. 'The other guides have gone from this floor. Would you like me to show you through the upper rooms? It's very nearly time to lock up.'

'You must do that?'

'No. Colonel Hammond, the custodian, closes up the house after he makes his final check-up. If you'd follow me.'

They moved slowly through the rest of the rooms, Emily's voice cool and concise as she pointed out features of interest in the chapel and the sacristy, also the barrel-vaulted ceiling in the great parlour, smiling at his expected amused reaction when she showed him the 'modern' improvement of closing in the upper gallery from the elements, its modernity dating from the time of the first Elizabeth. The approaching dusk invested the house with an even greater charm than the broad light of day, but she was not sorry when they reached the final room, the solar. The silent presence of the man beside her, listening with attention to her every word, was unnerving, different from her normal lecture, delivered impersonally to a room full of people.

'This is the final room, which, apart from its very fine collection of books, has a rather famous stain on the floor— over there near the fireplace. This is reputed to be where the owner of the house killed a priest he found making advances to his wife.' Emily smiled suddenly up at her companion. 'I suppose these days his reaction might be considered somewhat extreme.'

He shook his head, smiling.

'I think his reaction was perfectly justified. I would do the same if any man made advances to *my* wife.'

'Really?' Emily was determinedly impersonal as she led him down the narrow stone stairs and through the oak door that gave on to the formal Elizabethan garden. 'That's the lot, I'm afraid. It's quite a small house compared with some of the other National Trust showplaces.'

'Small, but perfect. A jewel in a beautiful setting.'

Some inflection in the deep voice made Emily's colour rise, and her manner was rigidly formal as she bade the stranger goodbye. Resisting the urge to watch the tall figure out of sight, she retreated to the gatehouse to say goodnight, and hand over her National Trust Warden badge.

Mrs Hammond, the custodian's wife, looked up, smiling.

'A bit late tonight, Emily dear. I'm sorry the rather exotic-looking gentleman held you up, but he appeared at the last minute and I hadn't the heart to turn him away.'

'No problem, Mrs Hammond. I had nothing better to do.' Emily smiled cheerfully as she collected her coat.

'Well, you should have. An attractive girl like you with nothing to do on a Saturday night—it's a crime!' Mrs Hammond's kind face wore its usual look of concern.

'Oh well, Mrs H., you know I'm a home bird.' Emily said goodnight quickly, promising to be back the following afternoon, then escaped before the other woman could expound on her favourite theme.

The shadows were lengthening as Emily crossed the bridge

over the moat, and a chill evening breeze eddied among the branches of the gnarled old trees in the parkland surrounding the house. Centuries before there had been a real drawbridge, and Emily liked to picture knights on brightly caparisoned horses riding gaily over it, though she smiled wryly to herself as she walked rapidly along the drive. These days girls were more likely to require their dream man at the wheel of a red Ferrari than on a white charger! Immediately she thought of the big dark man in the white trenchcoat. Emily had hardly liked to examine his face more than fleetingly, but the impression remained with her of dark good looks and strength, in both physique and personality. She wondered idly what sort of car *he* would drive—something long and fast, probably, certainly not a family car, despite the allusion to a wife. It was difficult to imagine him with little ones clustering at his knee. Emily's involuntary giggle changed to a gasp of fright as a figure detached itself from the gloom of the shrubbery leading to the car park.

'I startled you for the second time,' he said, standing foursquare in front of her. 'I am sorry, but when I saw no other car in the car park besides mine I waited to drive you home.'

Emily regarded the subject of her thoughts with mixed feelings.

'How kind,' she said coolly. 'I normally cycle back and forth, but I had a puncture this morning, so I walked.'

'Far?'

'No. A mile or so. I live in the actual village down the road, Compton Lacey; the same name as the house.' To her irritation Emily could hear herself beginning to chatter, put out by the way he stood so still and immovable, looking down at her. 'It's no distance—I don't really need a lift. Thank you just the same,' she added belatedly, wishing he would stand aside.

'Surely it is not a good thing for a child like you to walk alone along such a deserted road in the dark?' he asked harshly.

'I'm not a child—I'm almost nineteen.' Even to her own ears this sounded ridiculous, and Emily was hardly surprised to hear his soft laugh.

'So old! But in some ways that makes it even worse.'

'But it would be safer for me to accept a lift from a strange man, I suppose—a foreigner, I might add!' Emily was aghast momentarily at her own rudeness, relieved to hear him laugh again.

'You are quite right to be cautious. I applaud it.'

I *am* glad, she thought irritably, as he searched in his inside pocket and produced something it was too dark for her to make out.

'If you will come over to my car I will put on the lights and show you my passport,' he said persuasively. 'Then we may introduce ourselves formally and perhaps you will then allow me to drive you this mile or so to your home.'

Emily gave up. After all, there was little point in complaining about the dull monotony of life if one didn't take advantage of the smallest of diversions when it occurred. She inclined her head regally and walked with the man to his car, which was just as she'd imagined, long and speedy-looking.

'Not a red Ferrari, though.' To her horror she said the words aloud, and could have bitten her tongue in vexation. Her companion unlocked the car door and opened it, looking enquiringly into her face as the interior light shone on it.

'You accept lifts only in red Ferraris?'

'I never accept lifts at all,' snapped Emily, aware of the suppressed amusement in his voice as she unwillingly inspected his proffered passport. It showed his photograph, unmistakable and stern, giving his name as Lucas Antonio Jaime Guimaraes Fonseca, nationality Brazilian, age twenty-nine, hair and eyes black, no distinguishing marks. Stiffly she handed it back.

'How do you do, Mr—Fonseca.' She hesitated over the unfamiliar name. 'I'm Emily Harper.'

He took her hand solemnly, shaking it with grave formality.

'*Encantado*, Miss Harper. Now may I take you home?'

Emily had begun to feel more than a little ridiculous by this time.

'Thank you.' With dignity she settled herself in the comfortable passenger seat while he held the door for her and showed her how to use the seat-belt. She leaned back in luxury as he started the car, enjoying the way it glided slowly over the uneven surface of the long drive that wound its way for half a mile through the grounds of the house before reaching the narrow road that ran past the main gates in the direction of the village.

'Where do you live, Miss Harper?' asked her companion.

'It's the cottage just past the church.'

'Do you live with your parents?'

'No, they're both dead.'

'*Coitada!* How sad.' He was obviously affected by her words. 'But surely you do not live alone. You have relations?'

'Not many.' Emily wondered fleetingly whether she should be telling him all this. 'I have two old aunts in Scotland on my mother's side and I'm related, in a very distant way, to Major Lacey who used to own the big house. He's some sort of connection of my father's, and he lives in the Dower House now. He also owns the cottage I live in—there it is.'

Lucas Fonseca brought the car smoothly to a halt outside the gate of the cottage Emily indicated. Standing back from a small front garden, the house had obviously once been two separate dwellings, though the conversion had been effected with a care that did nothing to alter the charm of the black and white half-timbered building. A brass coach lamp was alight on the outer front wall.

'Someone is inside?' he asked, looking at the light.

'When my mother died I took in a tenant, Mrs Crawford, a widow with a small son. She's the local district nurse, a super lady and popular with everyone. Mrs Crawford—Lydia—lives in one half and I have the other, so although we're quite separate neither of us is really alone; a very convenient arrangement. Now I'll say goodnight, Mr Fonseca, and thank you for bringing me home.'

He put out a hand and caught hers as she turned to open the door.

'Wait a moment, Miss Harper, please. Now that we have formally introduced ourselves could you not take pity on a lonely visitor to your country and have dinner with me?' His dark eyes probed hers intently, and Emily felt suddenly shy, then she remembered something he'd said earlier and frowned.

'I believe you're married, Mr Fonseca, which is only one of the reasons why I can't accept.'

The dark face took on a baffled expression and one eyebrow raised in enquiry.

'Why do you think I'm married? I can assure you in all truth that I am not!'

It was Emily's turn to be confused.

'But when I told you the priest was killed for making advances to the owner's wife, you said you would do the same if it were *your* wife.'

He threw back his head and laughed, looking sideways at her with a wicked grin.

'I was speaking hypothetically—is that the right word? Alas, I have found no one willing to have me up to the present.'

Against her will Emily smiled back.

'Have you asked many?'

'None. I have never met anyone I wished to share my life with yet. Have you?'

'No,' said Emily regretfully, 'I haven't. I'm not likely to meet many likely contenders in Compton Lacey, either.'

'Well then, now that we have cleared up that point, I repeat: will you dine with me?' he said persistently.

'I said it was only one of the reasons. The other one is that I'm babysitting—Lydia's son.'

'Perhaps you merely do not wish to dine with me.' He frowned.

'Oh no, not in the least,' said Emily candidly. 'I would have enjoyed it very much; dinner invitations are few and far between. Never mind. Thank you very much for asking me. Goodnight.' She got out of the car quickly, but he was before her, opening the garden gate as she reached it. Lucas Fonseca loomed tall as he took her hand and raised it unexpectedly to his lips.

'*Até logo*, Miss Harper.'

'What does that mean?'

'The same as *au revoir* in French,' he said, smiling briefly before turning away to get in the Jaguar, waving a hand in farewell as he accelerated away from the curb.

Emily watched the vanishing tail lights thoughtfully before hurrying up the garden path and round to the side entrance to Lydia's part of the house. She knocked and went in, to find

Lydia laying the table, dressed in all the glory of what she called 'the good frock', which was a well-cut silk shirt-dress in dark green.

'Hello, love, you're late tonight—come on in.' She looked up smiling, her serene face made up with unusual care beneath greying dark hair which had obviously recently enjoyed the ministrations of the hairdresser.

'I haven't held you up, have I, Lydia?' asked Emily anxiously. 'The bike had a puncture this morning——'

'And you've had to walk home? What a shame—not to worry, I'm not due at Celia's for a couple of hours, so I thought you could have tea with Tim and me and take the weight off your feet. Thank God it's my weekend off. How do you like my hair? Here, give me your coat.'

Surrendering to Lydia's forceful personality, Emily abandoned explanations and did as she was told, gratefully accepting a cup of tea and stretching out her feet to the blaze.

'Your hair looks gorgeous, Lydia, but why are you eating now? I thought it was a dinner party.'

'It's expanded and turned into a buffet supper; ergo, I'm lining my stomach with a little alcohol–absorbent insulation, otherwise the first glass of sherry will knock me flat.' Lydia grinned, then patted the generous curves of her hips. 'Not that I need the calories. You don't think this silk shows up the bulges too much, do you, Em?'

'Of course not,' said Emily firmly, 'you're tall enough to carry it off—not a shrimp like me.'

Lydia eyed her militantly.

'Don't put yourself down, Emily Harper. Your looks are the type to appeal to the discerning——'

'Which breed isn't exactly thick on the ground in Compton Lacey,' said Emily, giggling, then stopped, a faraway look in her eye. 'Mind you, I met someone today who was definitely different.'

Lydia was immediately all attention, settling herself in the armchair on the other side of the fireplace.

'Tim's still watching some programme on his television upstairs, so we'll wait a moment or two before eating,' she said comfortably, 'so tell me who you met.'

'He was late, after all the others had gone, so I showed him through the upper rooms on his own.' Emily paused.

'Go on,' said Lydia expectantly.

'When I'd finished he was waiting near the car park to see if he could give me a lift home. I wasn't too keen——'

'Why ever not?' Lydia looked at her in despair.

'Well, I didn't know him, did I? He could have been Jack the Ripper,' said Emily reasonably.

'But he obviously wasn't, so carry on.'

'He showed me his passport as identification, and he's a Brazilian called Lucas Fonseca—I think that's how you pronounce it, he's twenty-nine and quite good-looking, in a dark Latin sort of way.'

'Goodness!' breathed Lydia, impressed. 'Did he give you a lift home—what sort of car?'

'Yes, he did, in a white Jaguar XJS, very nice indeed. A whole lot better than my bicycle!' Emily laughed outright at the expression on Lydia's face.

'Well, surely that's not all, Emily!'

'Almost. He asked me to have dinner with him.'

'Then what on earth are you doing sitting there, you idiotic girl! Go and get ready,' said Lydia, exasperated.

'Oh, I didn't accept,' said Emily lamely. 'After all, I was babysitting for you. I could hardly let you down, especially on a Saturday night.'

Lydia jumped to her feet in frustration.

'I could have found someone else, silly. Or even have carted Tim along to Celia's party. He could have watched television there if necessary. You are the absolute end, Emily Harper! Too high-principled by half.' Lydia stopped short, then grinned at the younger girl. 'But then you wouldn't be you otherwise, I suppose. And after all, he knows where you live. Where's he staying?'

'I didn't ask him.'

'Oh, Emily!'

Later on that evening, after Lydia had departed for her soirée, and two games of draughts had been played with Tim, Emily shepherded her charge to bed and returned downstairs to make herself a cup of coffee and sit by the replenished fire with a book.

The fictitious characters in the novel fought a losing battle with thoughts of the man from Brazil, however, and Emily gave up trying to follow the story after a while. She sat daydreaming, her eyes on the flickering flames, wondering if Senhor Fonseca was dining alone, or whether he might have found some other companion to take pity on his loneliness. Not that he seemed the type to be disturbed at being left to his own company. A singularly self-sufficient type of personality, thought Emily, forceful even, and obviously used to having things all his own way. It was flattering, but scarcely credible that she could have had much interest for him. Emily had no illusions about her own attractions. As Lydia said, she had the sort of looks that would appeal to the discerning, or to anyone with the patience to take a second look, but at first glance she knew very well she lacked impact. Her hair was glossy and thick, hanging to her shoulders where it curled slightly at the ends, but it was a muted ash-blonde, though where it grew away from her forehead there were several lighter streaks, legacy of an unusually warm summer. Her skin was fair and transparent, all too inclined to show the ready colour that rose easily at moments of stress. Her features were all straight lines as though drawn by a delicate hand with a very fine brush and her eyebrows flared away in straight strokes from her delicate nose, the only curve in her face the lovely line of her mouth above a rather square, resolute chin. Added to this in her disfavour, as far as she was concerned, was a lamentable lack of what her mother used to term as 'presence', as Emily was only a little over five feet tall and her figure was slight and fine-boned.

Altogether not exactly front page stuff, she thought ruefully, overlooking the one vivid note of colour she possessed. Beneath the straight brows her eyes were a light, bright, translucent blue, a feature inherited from her remote connection with the Lacey family.

Wistfully Emily wished she were beautiful, fascinating, that at this very moment she was drinking champagne at some exclusive restaurant with Lucas Fonseca, dazzling him with her wit and charm. . . . Oh, come on, Emily Harper, she told herself crossly, forget about him. It's most unlikely you'll meet him again, so put him out of your mind. It was easier said than done, and irritably she jumped up and went upstairs to have a peep at the now sleeping Tim, then went back down to the fire, thinking for the hundredth time how fortunate she was to have Lydia to share the house with her.

Emily's parents had been surprised when after long childless years their daughter had arrived when Mrs Harper was in her forties and Professor Harper some fifteen years older. Already retired from lecturing at the local university, he had died when Emily was small, leaving her mother sufficient income to live very quietly in the cottage owned by Major Lacey and scrape enough to send Emily away to school. Laura Harper had herself been an only child and was in no way gregarious, content in the secluded life she led, only to succumb to cancer shortly before Emily was due to leave school. The disease had been arrested for a while, but six months ago she had slipped quietly out of life after a long, stoically borne illness, during which Emily had nursed her devotedly, with the aid of the district nurse, Lydia Crawford. The latter had been Emily's saviour during this time, with her cheerful common sense and compassionate nursing expertise.

Initially Emily was panic-stricken at being left virtually alone in the world, but a visit from Marcus Lacey after the funeral, assuring her that the house was hers rent-free for as long as she wished, did much to restore her balance. He advised her to divide the cottage again and find someone to live in the other half, using the rent to help support herself. Lydia had lit up with enthusiasm when she heard. Herself a widow with one small son, her present house was too big for her to maintain, and sharing Church Cottage with Emily was an ideal solution for all concerned.

Emily was still staring absently into the dying fire when Lydia returned home just before one, and after listening to a vivid account of the party over a cup of tea she retired to her own quarters and went swiftly to bed, still regrettably preoccupied with thoughts of the handsome Brazilian.

CHAPTER TWO

SUNDAY was the busiest afternoon at Compton Lacey and Emily, stationed in the Great Hall, had no time for thought as she supplied a constant stream of visitors with all the details of the Aubusson tapestries, the intricately beamed ceiling, the various paintings on the walls. She enjoyed answering the countless questions put to her, especially from overseas visitors, who were always impressed by the sheer antiquity of the building, which was one of the oldest fortified manor houses in the country. Its survival was largely due to its extremely remote location, deep within the Forest of Arden, where it had escaped the attentions of Oliver Cromwell. Emily considered herself very fortunate to have a job of such absorbing interest, especially as her expensive education had been cut short by the need to look after her mother, leaving her ill-equipped to find work of a more commercial nature.

Hard put to it to find a spare minute for a cup of tea, she found the afternoon flew by with no time to think of her foreign visitor of yesterday. Today the sightseers were mainly family groups and elderly couples, with the odd sprinkling of students here and there. The weather had turned colder, and Emily was glad of her black and white wool kilt and blue mohair sweater. Thick ribbed tights and knee-length black leather boots were a further precaution against the draughts that eddied through the old house, despite the modern central heating system. When the last of the visitors had finally gone Emily was decidedly weary and none too charmed at the prospect of walking home. Making a resolution to get her bicycle mended next day, she bade the Hammonds goodnight and huddled into her old sheepskin jacket. Twilight was rapidly giving way to darkness as Emily walked briskly along, her hands deep in her pockets, shivering slightly in the cool evening breeze. Her heart gave a great leap as she saw the tall figure waiting near the car park, instantly recognisable despite different, darker clothes. He started forward as she came into view.

16

'Good evening, Miss Harper.' The slightly harsh voice with its faint accent was unmistakable and, surprisingly, familiar. Emily made no pretence of a surprise she didn't feel.

'Good evening, Mr Fonseca. What brings you to Compton Lacey again so soon?'

He took one of her hands from its hiding place in her pocket and held it between both his own. Hard, almost rough hands, Emily noted absently.

'The need to see you again,' he answered simply, his unvarnished statement silencing her completely. Without a word she allowed herself to be installed in the white Jaguar, eyeing him cautiously as he came round the front of the car and sat in the driver's seat. Lucas Fonseca turned towards her, making no effort to start the car.

'You are not on the telephone,' he stated, frowning at her.

'Lydia has one in her half; for use in her job. I can't afford a separate one for me,' said Emily. 'Besides, it isn't necessary.'

'I could not reach you by telephone, so I came to see you.'

Her eyes widened.

'You came to the house?'

'At about four this afternoon. Your friend Mrs Crawford took me in and gave me tea until it was time to fetch you.' He grinned at her infectiously. 'We had quite a chat.'

'I'll bet you did!' Emily chuckled. 'She called me several kinds of idiot for refusing your dinner invitation last night.'

'So I gathered. So I hope very much you will give her no cause for complaint and consent to dine with me tonight.'

It was too dark to see the expression on the dark face turned towards her, nevertheless Emily was left in no doubt as to the urgency of his whole attitude, his body overtly tense.

'Well?' he prompted.

Emily threw caution to the winds.

'Yes, thank you, I'd be delighted.'

He relaxed visibly.

'I am glad,' he said quietly, switching on the ignition. 'Now tell me about your day.'

To her surprise Emily found it amazingly easy to do just that, and gave him a spirited account of the afternoon's visitors, including the American lady who thought the beams in the ceiling of the Great Hall should be replaced because they were 'warped and kinda rotten, honey, they must be dangerous'. Her companion told Emily gravely that she must make allowances for the opinions of misguided foreigners, and they laughed together, though Emily felt bound to add that the lady in question had been very charming, insisting on taking her photograph against the background of the imposing stone fireplace.

When they reached the gate of Church Cottage, Lucas Fonseca left the car idling and glanced at the thin gold watch on his wrist.

'It is now six-fifteen, Miss Emily Harper. May I come back for you at seven-thirty?'

Emily nodded, frowning a little at a sudden doubt.

'Is it somewhere very grand? I'm afraid my wardrobe is a bit limited.'

His face held a curiously protective look as he smiled down at her.

'I am staying at the White Hart on the Birmingham road, and they do a reasonable meal. I am certain that anything you choose to wear will be appropriate.'

Reassured, Emily smiled at him and got out of the car.

'See you later, then.' With a little wave she ran up the garden path, practically colliding with Lydia, who had obviously been lying in wait and appeared round the corner of the house with suspicious promptitude.

'What happened?' Her face was alight with anticipation.

'Come and chat while I get ready, Lydia.' Emily unlocked the door, switching on lights recklessly and galloping up the stairs at a speed that left the other woman behind. 'I hear you had a visitor this afternoon!'

Lydia arrived in Emily's bedroom panting, and subsided on the bed, while Emily dashed to and from the bathroom, tearing off her clothes while the water was running.

'Can you imagine my reaction, love, when this gorgeous male rang my doorbell this afternoon, enquiring as to your whereabouts?' There was a giggle from the bathroom as Emily began soaping herself. 'You know, Em,' went on Lydia, a faraway look in her eye, 'I took one look at him and twenty years melted away like magic. What a smile, and that tan— did you see the quality of the suede jacket he was wearing?'

'Didn't notice,' was the blithe response.

'You're hopeless! Anyway, presumably you've actually consented to dine with him tonight—where's he taking you?'

'The White Hart,' called back Emily. 'That's where he's staying.'

'Nice and handy. What are you wearing?'

Emily came into the bedroom in a short towelling wrap, her hair pinned up in a knot on top of her head.

'Now that, Mrs Crawford, is a very good question. I just don't own the right type of clothes for wining and dining.'

Lydia bounced off the bed to inspect the contents of the wardrobe Emily was gazing into without much hope.

'You don't have to be done up too much, especially on a Sunday night,' she said practically, clicking hangers along the rail. 'What about this?' She drew out a plain slim skirt in fine black wool.

'I had that when Mother died,' Emily said doubtfully. 'I haven't worn it since. There's a black sweater I wore with it.'

'You must have something a bit more festive than that—here, what's this?'

Lydia produced a hanger from the end of the rail, inspecting the blouse on it with approval. Fine creamy silk with long full sleeves gathered into wide lace-edged cuffs and a yoke with lace-edged pin tucks below a high collar made a perfect accompaniment for the severe black skirt.

'I feel a bit guilty about that—I kept it for myself when someone brought it for me to sell on the Nearly New stall at the church fête—I put some money in, of course.'

Emily's confession amused Lydia inordinately, but she merely handed the garment to the guilty-looking girl and told her to get a move on.

'Now's your time to wear it, then—do you have any decent tights?'

'I think I still have the ones I wore with the skirt,' said Emily, searching in a drawer. 'Yes, here they are. "Black Coffee", extra fine.'

Well before the appointed time Emily was ready, her face made up with great care and her hair swept smoothly into a loose knot on the crown of her head. One slender leg, in its sheer dark covering, swung backwards and forwards nervously as she perched on the arm of a chair as she waited, wishing Lydia had stayed to shore up her confidence, but that lady had departed in good time, leaving Emily to wait alone, suddenly beset by all kinds of doubts about the approaching evening. Feeling jittery, Emily heard the slam of a car door with a feeling of doom. Looking wildly around the room as the doorbell sounded, almost wishing she could hide, she sternly took a deep breath, steadying herself forcibly before opening the door.

Lucas Fonseca, wearing a dark grey suit and dazzling white shirt, regarded her with open appreciation.

'*Que beleza!*' he said softly, taking her hand.

'Good evening,' said Emily a little stiffly. 'What did you say?'

'Merely how beautiful you looked. Are you ready to leave?'

She nodded, then collected her handbag and the crocheted black shawl Lydia had lent her before locking the door and following her escort down the path to the car. He handed her in with ceremony before getting in the driving seat.

'Are you nervous of me, Miss Harper?' he asked as the car moved off silently.

'Yes,' said Emily baldly, her fingertips white where they clutched her small handbag convulsively.

'I won't eat you, I promise.' The chuckle in his voice relaxed her a little, and she stole a shy look at his profile as they left the village and turned on to the Birmingham road.

He leaned down and switched on the car radio, finding some pleasant background music and turning the volume low.

'Now then, Miss Emily Harper, I am a lonely foreigner who is much honoured to have the company of such a charming young lady for dinner. I will behave with the utmost propriety, I assure you, and will bring you back home at whatever time you wish. Does that reassure you?'

Emily felt immediately sheepish, and relaxed in her seat with a sigh.

'Yes, of course. I'm sorry—it's just that I've always been a bit shy. In the beginning I found my job very difficult from that point of view, but I am improving—it's been very good for me.'

'Please, do not apologise. I find such diffidence very appealing.' He shot a brief smile at her. 'It is more than a little unusual in this country, also, where the ladies are reported to be all liberated.'

Emily thought this over.

'I rather think that being liberated is pursuing the course one wishes to follow. I do just that—so perhaps even I am liberated in a way. I suppose in your country things are different?'

'Many women follow professions, of course, but in the interior where I live some of the old customs still prevail. Some families adhere to the rule that a young lady of good family should not go out alone with a young man before she is married, not even her *noivo*—fiancé. She must be accompanied by a sister, or some other relative, or a maid.' He grinned at the expression on her face. 'You find this archaic?'

Emily nodded.

'I do, I'm afraid. I consider myself a bit of an anachronism, but, as you see, I'm out for an evening with you alone, and you're a complete stranger. What's more, you're a bird of passage. I hope. . . .' Her voice trailed off as they arrived in the forecourt of the White Hart, which was set back from the road in an attractive garden.

Lucas Fonseca was immediately out of the car and round to open her door, putting a hand under her arm to help her out.

'What do you hope?' he asked softly, looking down searchingly into her face. 'Do you hope you have not made a big mistake?'

'Yes,' said Emily honestly, 'and now that sounds extremely rude put into words.'

He led her through the hotel entrance, whispering into her ear:
'I promise—it is not a mistake.'

Seated in a secluded corner of the oak-beamed dining-room, Emily began to relax. By the light of the rose-shaded lamp on the table she looked up with undisguised curiosity at the planes and angles of her companion's face.

'Why are you looking at me like that?' he asked.

'Well, I haven't really had the opportunity before to see what you actually look like,' she admitted frankly. 'I didn't like to stare when we were up at the Manor House, and otherwise it's been too dark to see properly.'

His teeth and eyes gleamed in amusement.

'And now that you have made a study, do you like what you see?'

She nodded.

'Yes. You're extremely good-looking. But of course you know that.'

His smile changed to a startled frown.

'Why should you say that? I do not care for the sound of it.'

Emily examined him consideringly, head a little on one side, surprised and a little touched to see him shift slightly in his seat.

'I didn't mean to suggest you're conceited; but you have a certain aura about you.' She hesitated as his eyes narrowed. 'You're so—self-confident, absolutely in command of yourself. The way you dress, carry yourself; they're the mannerisms of a man sure of his reception, I think.'

Whatever he might have replied was forestalled by the arrival of the waiter, and it was only when they were both eating smoked salmon and tasting the dry white wine that accompanied it that he answered her.

'I do not think it is my looks that—engender this aura that you speak of.' He broke off and smiled at her persuasively. 'I would be very pleased if you would allow me to call you Emily?'

She nodded, smiling shyly.

'My family and friends call me Luc,' he went on, 'perhaps you will do the same?' Taking her acceptance for granted, he returned to his original statement. 'If—and I do not totally agree with you in this—I appear sure of myself it is more likely to be due to my circumstance in life than an accident of how my face is arranged. My family owns a gold mine in Minas Gerais in the interior of Brazil, and although I work hard in it and take my responsibilities seriously I have been brought up with total security, both in my family's wealth, and in my own place in life. This probably sounds feudal to you, but I am trying to be honest.'

Emily was very thoughtful as the main course of roast beef was set in front of them, accompanied by a different wine, a full, red Portuguese Dão. She sighed.

'You are pensive, Emily,' Luc said softly, filling her glass.

'I was thinking how very different our backgrounds are. We come from entirely different worlds rather than countries. Also,' she added, 'I'm not accustomed to drinking anything alcoholic at all, so forgive me if I'm a bit doubtful about all this wine.'

'Then do not drink any,' he said instantly. 'I have no wish to make you uneasy. And I do not see why our different backgrounds should prevent us from enjoying each other's company.'

'No, of course not.' Emily smiled and applied herself to her roast beef with appreciation. 'When you say "family", does that mean brothers and sisters?'

'Alas, no. I am an only child. My mother died at my birth and my father has never remarried, so my early upbringing was supervised by my grandmother, who is an English lady from Camborne in Cornwall.'

'So that's how you speak such good English!'

'I also received some education in England,' he answered.

'Oxford or Cambridge?'

'Neither, little—snob, I think you say.' He laughed as she flushed. 'I spent a year at Camborne School of Mines, otherwise I went to M.I.T. in the States.'

'Then you should have an American drawl,' said Emily, abandoning her plate half full.

'My grandmother would never allow it.' Luc regarded her plate with disapproval. 'Surely you can eat more than that!'

'Sorry.' Emily looked at the succulent meat with regret. 'My normal Sunday supper is something like cheese on toast, so I've done relatively well.'

He leaned across the table, his heavy brows drawn together in concern.

'You are too small, Emily, you should eat more and put curves on those fine bones of yours.'

She drew back instantly, the ready colour high on two of the bones in question, her clearly defined cheekbones.

'I hardly think I'll grow any more now,' she said distantly. 'Do tell me more of your home in—where in Brazil is it that you live?'

Obediently he abandoned his personal remarks and began to talk of Campo d'Ouro, high in the mountains of the state of Minas Gerais, where his family had mined gold for over a hundred years. He described the beautiful garden full of exotic plants and flowers where the palm-shaded house seemed to grow out of its environment, at one with its colourful surroundings where macaws screeched in the courtyard in the sun. The house was called Casa d'Ouro, and Luc lived there with his father and grandmother, and had come to Britain to inspect a new type of pneumatic rock drill manufactured in Cornwall.

'I was told I would consider the Cotswolds worthy of a visit,' he concluded, 'so I am spending a few days' holiday here before returning to Brazil.'

Refusing dessert, they both lingered over coffee while Luc asked Emily about her life in return. She found it surprisingly easy to tell him about the sorrow of losing her quiet, unassertive mother, and how her new way of life was just beginning to crystallise into routine.

'Of course, if it weren't for Marcus Lacey,' she told her attentive listener, 'I would have had quite a problem. My parents paid him rent for our cottage, but he insisted I live there free of charge when Mother died, or I don't know quite what I should have done; also he got the job up at the Manor House for me, so as things are I can manage quite well. Apart from boarding school, which I didn't enjoy very much, I've never been anywhere other than Compton Lacey.'

'Do you never have the urge to explore the world, do all those things other girls find so necessary?' he asked.

'Of course I do. I'm perfectly normal! But I like the tranquillity of the country, and to be honest, the glimpses of other people's lives afforded by television are alarming rather than attractive. I expect I seem like a timid rabbit to someone like you.'

'And what is your idea of someone like me?'

'Oh, someone cosmopolitan, travelled, highly educated—sophisticated, I suppose. But that's a very general sort of observation—after all, I hardly know you.'

Luc stretched a long-fingered brown hand across the small table and captured the restless fingers fiddling with her coffee cup as she talked.

'I would very much like you to know me better, Emily; just as I would like to know you very well indeed.'

'That's hardly possible,' she said coolly, disengaging her hand. 'You'll be leaving the country shortly, while I shall carry on here, firmly established in my bucolic routine. Which I enjoy very much,' she added defiantly.

Luc stood up abruptly, holding her chair for her, and they left the food and tobacco scents of the inn's warmth, to emerge into a cold, starry night. Emily shivered involuntarily as the wind cut through the thin silk of her blouse, submitting to Luc's swift ministrations as he wrapped the shawl securely round her and kept his arm round her waist as they walked swiftly to the car.

The drive back to Compton Lacey was accomplished in almost total silence, apart from an enquiry as to whether she were warm enough. Emily sat, tense and uneasy, stealing an occasional glance at the jutting profile of the man who drove swiftly and expertly, his expression hard to see in the darkness. When eventually they turned off the main highway down the twisting narrow road to Compton Lacey she slowly began to relax. This feeling was shortlived as the car continued past Church Cottage and through the village, almost to the gates of the Manor House itself, where Luc brought the car to a halt in a narrow layby near the entrance.

Before Emily could voice the startled protest that he obviously expected, Luc undid his seat-belt and turned towards her, capturing her cold hands which had suddenly grown icy with apprehension.

'Please, Emily,' he said huskily, 'do not fear me. I wished us to talk a little longer and I knew you would not care to invite me into your cottage as you live there alone. Please—do not tremble, I beg.'

'I don't seem able to help it,' she said irritably, staring down at their clasped hands. 'I'm not used to this sort of situation.'

'I did not think you were, *carinha*.'

The caressing note in Luc's voice did nothing at all for Emily's peace of mind, and she swallowed dryly, wishing herself safely home and in bed.

'What thoughts are hurrying around so frantically behind

those beautiful blue eyes?' Luc freed her hands and unfastened her safety-belt. 'There, now you are free.'

Emily's nostrils flared and she took a deep breath.

'Have you brought me here to—to make love to me?'

'I will do nothing against your wishes, *carinha*,' he answered obliquely, taking one of her hands and smoothing his thumb rhythmically backwards and forwards on the smooth skin. 'If you say to me now, "Start the car, take me home and go away for ever" I will do so, I promise.'

Emily found it quite impossible to say anything of the sort, and after a while he slid an arm very gently behind her, bringing her head down on his shoulder, his chin on top of her hair.

'I hope so much that you will not say this, Emily,' he went on quietly, 'because I want to stay here with you a little while, to come and see you tomorrow and the day after that, and every day until I leave.'

Emily lay against his chest, quiescent, all her instincts for flight lulled by the sincerity of the quiet deep voice she could feel vibrating against her shoulder.

'But if I let you do that,' she said doubtfully, 'If I do see you every day for a while, and then you disappear out of my life altogether, as you're bound to do, that same quiet existence of mine may not be so attractive to me afterwards. I shall perhaps be less content with my lot.'

'We shall write letters, and I shall come back before Christmas to see you again,' he said positively, his arm tightening. 'I do not intend to allow the mere fact of distance to be any obstacle. You will write to me?'

Emily turned in his grasp so that she was looking up into his dark eyes, intent on hers beneath the frowning black brows. She could feel the warmth of his breath on her cheek, and marvelled secretly at the wonder of being held so close to a muscular, male body, aware of the tautness of the arm around her, and the scent of him, compounded of some elusive male cologne, also tobacco, she thought, and something else, which could only be the particular personal aura of his own skin.

'You are very silent, Emily,' he said softly. 'But you are not trembling, at least. Does this mean you are not unhappy to be close to me like this?'

Luc's wide, well-cut mouth was only a small space away from Emily's and the nod she made in agreement reduced the distance to nothing. His lips touched hers almost imperceptibly for the space of a heartbeat, then, to their mutual surprise, both took fire, feeling blazing up in both of them simultaneously as their mouths fused and clung, parted momentarily as Emily gasped in wonder, then there was no more hesitation as both bodies sought closer contact, his mouth seeking, and finding, a response from hers that made her heart hammer as if it were trying to escape through the silk that covered it. She drew back momentarily, pressing her hand to her breast, but he replaced it with his own, holding her against him so fiercely it should have hurt, but she felt nothing except a wild gladness that sang through her veins in a triumphant paean of joy. Suddenly Luc tore himsef away, taking her face in both hands and staring down at her in a way that did nothing to decelerate her pulse.

'Has anyone ever kissed you like that before?' He sounded almost hostile, his breath coming unevenly, his accent more pronounced than usual.

Emily shook her head wordlessly, her eyes staring back wildly into his, which closed involuntarily as he brought her hard against him once more and they held each other tight, awkward in the confines of the car, until some semblance of calm began to return to them both. Eventually Emily disengaged herself and sat back in her own seat, noting vaguely that her hair hung around her shoulders in a wild tangle. Luc put out a hand and captured a lock of it, bending to kiss it as it slithered through his fingers, then he took her hand to his mouth and kissed each finger one by one, finally pressing his mouth into her palm, closing her fingers over it as he took his lips away.

'My hair came down,' said Emily faintly.

'I prefer it like that, leave it that way,' he said possessively. 'Now then, Emily Harper, there must be something else going on in that mind of yours besides the state of your hair?'

'Yes, there certainly is. So much I don't know how to put any of it into words.' Emily slid a sidelong look at him. 'Luc, do you always feel like that when—well, when you kiss someone?'

His shoulders shook slightly.

'No, *carinha*, I do not. Do you?'

'I've only been kissed a couple of times, at parties we used to have with the neighbouring boys' school at Christmas. And there was no comparison with—I mean it was nothing like—like the way you kissed me just now.'

Luc put out a hand and turned her face towards him, looking down into her questioning eyes with a tenderness that disarmed her completely.

'Emily, I kissed you because I could not resist the urge to do so. I had no idea that it would be such an explosive experience. You may take it from me that what we felt is not an everyday occurrence. Kisses can be very gentle and undemanding, I assure you—just like this.'

He bent his head to hers to show her. As a demonstration it was a failure, for as soon as their mouths made contact precisely the same reaction occurred as before. A great wave of heat enveloped them both simultaneously until they were clutching each other in a kind of desperation when their lips parted, both of them breathing in great painful gasps as they stared at each other blankly.

'*Deus!*' he panted, his hands bruising her shoulders, though Emily was totally oblivious to any discomfort. 'I should say I'm sorry, but I am not. You have an annihilating effect on me. It frightens me, almost.'

'It frightens me completely,' said Emily definitely, and detached herself firmly from his grasp. 'Please take me home right now, Luc Fonseca, while I'm still approximately in my right mind!'

Luc took a deep breath, running his hands through his hair, then he switched on the ignition.

'I suppose that now you will not let me see you tomorrow,' he asked, as they returned the way they had come.

'I don't think I should, in fact I know very well that I shouldn't,' she said, sighing. 'But I—I would like to see you again very much.'

At this touchingly honest little statement Luc crushed one of her hands convulsively in his, only releasing it as they drew up at the cottage.

'What time do you finish at the house tomorrow, *carinha*?'

He tucked her shawl round her shoulders and smoothed back her frankly untidy hair.

'It's my day off—no, don't get out.' Emily turned to leave.

'Spend the whole day with me then, Emily!' His hand held her captive.

Emily turned and looked at him for a long moment, then, reassured by what she saw in his eyes, she nodded. Luc smiled brilliantly, leaning instantly to kiss her, but she dodged, opening the car door and turning to laugh at him impudently from the pavement.

'Oh no, you don't!' she whispered, mindful of disturbing Lydia.

His teeth gleamed by the light of the street lamp, his eyes dancing with devilment.

'Coward!'

Emily nodded vigorously in agreement.

'*Até amanha*, Emily,' he said softly.

'What does that mean?'

'Until tomorrow, *carinha*. Goodnight.'

Emily lay awake for a long time in a state of excitement that refused to subside. The curtains were drawn back so that she could see the stars, wondering if Luc were watching them too, then laughing at herself for being so pathetic. As if he would! No doubt this was just a pleasant little interlude, a means of idling away his remaining time in Britain. After all, one evening together hardly constituted the basis of a relationship, by any standards. The problem was how little she knew of the opposite sex—the very minimum of experience would come in handy at the moment.

At school the staff had guarded their charges' purity with relentless fervour, and here in the village the few young people of her own age tended to treat her with caution because of her stay at boarding school. It would be nice to have a confidant, she thought wistfully, if only to talk things over and ask one or two pertinent questions. Much as she loved Lydia, somehow she was not quite the person to ask about Luc. Emily had a feeling she would disapprove strongly of some of the evening's events. Had her own behaviour been extraordinary, or was it normal to feel that overwhelming excitement? Luc had felt it too,

that was patently obvious, but perhaps that was because he
was male. Luc's maleness was something better banished from
her mind altogether, she concluded, or it was more than
probable she'd get no sleep at all.

CHAPTER THREE

ALL Emily's nagging doubts had vanished like magic next
morning, and she was ready and waiting when Luc drew up in
the Jaguar just after ten. She threw open the door and smiled
shyly at the tall, athletic figure as he came swiftly up the
garden path, his camel cords and silk shirt, both a shade or
two darker than the supple suede of his jacket, making Emily
very much aware of the shortcomings of her own chain-store
skirt and sweater.

'Good morning.' She gave him her hand. 'I don't know
quite what you had in mind for today; will I do as I am?'

Luc bent his dark head and kissed her fingers, then looked
at her in surprise as though her question was unnecessary.

'You are quite perfect, Emily,' he said in a matter-of-fact
manner that restored her confidence immediately. 'And in a
quite different way, so is this room. Your parents had great
taste.'

Emily looked around the room, following his gaze, trying
to see it with a stranger's eyes.

'They were fond of antiques, and took great pleasure in
tracking down various finds. I believe the sofa table is quite
valuable, according to Mother, and the two matching velvet
chairs are late Regency, but I'm not very knowledgeable on
the subject myself. I just love this room because it's home, I
suppose.'

She became aware of Luc looking down at her with such an
air of amused indulgence she was annoyed.

'Am I boring you?'

'Not at all, little one. But I think you are trying very hard
not to let the events of last night embarrass you in the cold
light of day, am I right?' Luc put an arm round her waist and

lifted her reluctant face to his with the other hand. 'Let me reassure you, Emily. Today we will explore all the beautiful places you can think of, and we shall talk, and learn about each other, find somewhere interesting to eat, and try to forget that very special something that occurs when we kiss. I shall not lay even one finger on you again, unless you say I may.' He stopped, looking down enquiringly into her troubled face. 'What is it?'

Emily released herself deliberately and backed away a little, smiling at him ruefully.

'Well, I thought perhaps you might think that I—well, that it——'

'That last night was a common occurrence for you, *carinha*?' Luc laughed outright. 'Not at all. It was very obvious that it was not.'

'Why?' demanded Emily, inexplicably nettled.

'Because, my innocent, coupled with the warmth of your response was an unmistakable sense of astonishment. You were very surprised, I think—don't be upset, *carinha*, you were no more surprised than I!'

'Why should *I* surprise *you*?' she asked quietly.

'Not you, Emily, it was I that surprised myself.' Luc's teeth gleamed white in his tanned face. 'I don't think that sounds quite right, but you must be lenient with my English. It is not the language that comes easiest to me.'

Suddenly happy, she put on her coat.

'You speak English perfectly—as you well know. That trace of accent is just enough to be fascinating.' She grinned at the look on his face. 'Well, it is; I'm sure it's an enormous asset as far as the opposite sex is concerned.'

Luc opened the door for her.

'But does it affect you that way, Emily?' he murmured into the back of her neck as they went down the path.

'Oh yes,' she said carelessly, 'but I'm working on it. Oh, Luc, isn't it a lovely day?'

'It is a perfect day,' he agreed gravely, settling her into the car seat. 'And it's going to stay that way all day,' he added as he started the car. 'I shall personally ensure that it does.'

He was as good as his word, and took her for a leisurely drive through narrow roads leading to little Cotswold villages that basked in the light of a mellow autumn sun. They had lunch in Moreton-in-Marsh and then wandered around the small town for a while before driving to Broadway and Chipping Campden and exploring the very different attractions of each. Finally they came back to Stratford for dinner and Luc booked seats at the Royal Shakespeare Theatre for 'Much Ado About Nothing' on the following night, lucky to get two cancellations.

'I have never been to the theatre here,' he told her as they lingered over coffee in the riverside restaurant. 'Have you?'

'Only when I was in school,' said Emily. 'They used to organise at least one trip a year; more if one was doing A-level English.'

'You studied English, Emily? What did you wish to do?'

'English and History were my particular thing. I wanted to teach History, actually, but as you know, fate took a hand and I had to leave school early.' Her eyes dropped, then she raised her chin resolutely and smiled at him. 'However, I do impart quite a lot of historical knowledge about Compton Lacey to anyone who'll listen, so I could have been a lot less fortunate.'

He stretched out a hand to take hers.

'*Coitadinha!* Poor little one, you have been left alone very young.' He frowned at her, his eyes full of concern. 'Is there no one you can turn to should you need help?'

'Well, I have Lydia close at hand,' Emily smiled reassuringly. 'And Marcus is in constant touch. You should meet him, he's a very charming man, though he doesn't enjoy the best of health.'

'Is he young?'

'In his forties. Why?'

'I wondered if he might have more than a cousinly interest in your welfare.' Luc's frown deepened.

Emily withdrew her hand swiftly and stood up, leaving Luc no choice but to do the same.

They left the restaurant and walked back towards the theatre in silence for a while.

'I have offended you, Emily?' Luc's hand held hers captive, even though she made an attempt to free it.

'It just seems so tawdry to reduce everything to this

man/woman thing,' said Emily distastefully, leaving her hand where it was rather than wrestle childishly. 'Marcus regards me as merely a distant connection in awkward circumstances who needs a helping hand, nothing more.'

Luc stopped in his tracks, bringing her close against him. The narrow pavement opposite the park was deserted in the limbo when most people were at home in front of the television, or out wining and dining, and before the end of the performance when Stratford would be thronged with the after-theatre crowd. Emily stared up mutely into Luc's scowling face, aware that the contact of their bodies, though they barely touched, was producing the same effect as the night before, and she resented the fact that her physical responses were functioning in total independence from her mind, which was furiously trying to remain aloof.

'I'm jealous of the thought of any man in your life,' Luc said through his teeth, his nostrils flaring as he felt her instant recoil, his hands biting into her upper arms through the sleeves of her coat. Emily swallowed, her breath quickening as she looked up at him in disbelief.

'That's ridiculous,' she said jerkily. 'We've only just met. I don't know you. You don't know me. Besides, I'm not—not exactly Helen of Troy. Hardly the type to bowl a man over at first glance. I'm too ordinary——'

'Be quiet,' he said forcibly, and cut off any further protests by stopping her mouth with his own and taking her wholly into his arms. After only a moment or two he raised his head at the sound of approaching voices, and in silence they began to walk again, his arm close round her waist as they wandered slowly back to where the car was parked.

In a trance Emily got in the Jaguar and watched Luc walk round to seat himself beside her. He leaned over to fasten her seat-belt, kissing her nose as he did so, and started the car without a word. For some reason the tender little caress made Emily wildly happy, and she leaned back in her seat perfectly relaxed while the car ate up the miles on the road to Warwick where they bypassed the lovely old town and took the Birmingham road for Compton Lacey.

It was still comparatively early when they reached the cottage, and Emily was racked by indecision, eventually giving a mental shrug as she turned to Luc when they drew up outside the gate.

'Will you come in for a cup of coffee, Luc?'

He gave her a surprised look.

'Is that wise, Emily? Apart from your fear of my intentions, would you not mind that my car is at your gate for all to see?'

'It's only half-past nine—hardly the middle of the night,' she pointed out. 'I should think my good name could stand it if you stay an hour. And, of course, you did promise not to lay a finger on me without my permission!'

'Then I accept with pleasure, before you change your mind.'

Once indoors Emily lit the small gas fire in the living room and retired to the kitchen to make the promised coffee. Luc lounged in the doorway, watching her graceful, economical movements with pleasure while she chattered away to him happily.

'It's only instant, Luc—can't afford the real stuff, I'm afraid,' she apologised as she set a small tray.

'Now that is a commodity we can offer in abundance in my country,' he laughed. 'You must come and see my home and taste our coffee, feel the warmth of the sun.'

Emily giggled as he took the tray from her and placed it on the beautiful old sofa table.

'Now that really is an unlikely proposition—unless I win the pools.'

He looked blank.

'What are these "pools"?'

They sat close together while Emily explained the complications of filling in football coupons and the rewards it was possible to reap. The coffee in their cups grew cold while she talked, her small face animated until she realised that her companion was silent, watching her changing expressions with unwavering eyes.

'I'm boring you,' she broke off abruptly, shifting a little further away from him.

'On the contrary, Emily, I am fascinated by every word you say, even more by the way the expressions on your face change by the second, like the kaleidoscope my grandmother has at home.' Luc's smile faded as their eyes met and held, but he remained where he was, tense and still. 'Do you not consider me admirable, little one? I am keeping my promise, and a very difficult one it is to fulfil.'

Emily made no pretence of misunderstanding him.

'I had noticed,' she said, turning away, 'and as I've no intention of giving the requisite permission perhaps I'd better bid you a fond farewell and see you off the premises.'

Luc rose to his feet instantly, his manner a shade formal as he raised her hand to his lips.

'I will be waiting at the Manor House at five-thirty tomorrow, Emily, to take you to the theatre; will that be convenient?' He kept her hand in his. 'I will bring you back here to change, if you wish, of course.'

'That's not necessary, Luc—I'll wear something suitable to the house.' Emily smiled up at him gaily. 'I warn you, none of my clothes really suit your sort of life.'

He smiled down indulgently into her face.

'You know nothing of my normal life, *carinha*. I spend the greater part of it in dusty drill trousers and shirts, heavy boots. Not in the least elegant, I assure you.'

Emily studied him deliberately, head on one side.

'I think it's very possible that you look elegant whatever you wear, Senhor Fonseca.'

He drew in his breath and reached for her instinctively, but checked himself sharply and made for the door.

'That's not what you English call "cricket", *carinha*. If I am to keep to the rules, so must you.'

'Spoilsport,' said Emily impenitently, and waved him goodbye vigorously as he strode rapidly down the path. After he had gone she closed the door behind her dreamily, then suddenly seized one of the sofa cushions and did a mad polka with it all round the room before sedately washing up the coffee cups in a less zany frame of mind.

For the next few days Luc waited for her to emerge from Compton Lacey each evening and took her to the theatre in Stratford, the cinema in Leamington Spa, to a French restaurant in Kenilworth. Emily felt like Cinderella before the fateful stroke of midnight, and did her best to treasure each moment they spent together without thinking that shortly he would be gone and her life would revert to its former uneventful routine.

How am I going to bear it? shrieked a strident mental voice. She closed her mind to it frantically and spent some of her special hoard of savings on a new outfit she saw marked down in a very select dress-shop in Warwick. Lydia had given her an early lift into the town on her rounds and Emily was really supposed to be buying groceries, but instead of concentrating on baked beans and breakfast cereal she was irresistibly drawn to the elegant window where the creation lay cleverly draped against 'a wicker screen. Basically little more than a skirt and sweater, really, she told herself, but her hand was pushing open the door even as she thought. The charming lady who owned the shop looked at the size while Emily held her breath, and, sure enough, it was a size ten. A very small fitting, she was warned, which was why it was reduced, but when she had hastily scrambled out of her jeans and sweater to try the suit on it had quite obviously been made with Emily in mind, a Mary Farrin model spun from yarn fine as a cobweb in a mulberry shade that threw up Emily's fairness and brought a glow to her cheeks. The skirt had been knitted to give the impression of countless tiny pleats which swirled at the hem, and the top was short-sleeved with a deeply slashed neck opening.

'Should it have a button or something?' Emily eyed the faint hint of cleavage visible with doubt, but was assured that it was meant to look just like that.

Without further persuasion she consigned caution to the winds, paid for the suit, then rushed round the shops at top speed buying food in record time in order to catch the bus back home early enough to start a casserole. Tonight she intended to entertain Luc at home in some small return for the past few evenings. Taking her courage in both hands, she rang the White Hart from the callbox in the village, and asked for Mr Fonseca, praying he would be there. He was, his voice tense when he answered.

'Emily? What is it? Is something wrong—are you ill?'

'No, no, Luc, nothing like that. I just wanted to make a suggestion,' she explained apologetically, touched to hear his audible sigh of relief.

'Of course, *carinha*—or do you mean I may not see you tonight?'

'No—or rather yes,' said Emily wickedly, making a face at herself in the small mirror above the telephone.

'Emily, please make yourself clear!' Luc's voice was satisfactorily anxious, and she hurried to explain.

'You've been entertaining me royally all week, so I thought it would only be proper if I cooked dinner for you here tonight.'

There was a lengthy pause.

'Do you think that wise?' he said at last.

'Probably not. My repertoire consists of only three recognisable dishes, so you're probably taking a great risk,' she said flippantly. 'I'll expect you at eight, Luc.'

She rang off before he could protest any further, and ran home to start the recipe she liked best, humming happily as she browned succulent cubes of beef in a heavy pan, seasoning them with a teaspoon each of curry, ginger, sugar and salt, adding sliced onions, Worcestershire sauce and stock and transferring the lot into a cast-iron casserole to simmer in the oven while she tidied up and gave some of the lovely old pieces of furniture a loving polish. The garden yielded some branches of bright beech leaves to arrange in a copper pot with the last few rust-red chrysanthemums. When these were placed with care on the sofa table Emily ran an eye round the room, sniffing the fragrance of lavender-scented polish mingled with the tantalising aroma from the kitchen, and, satisfied, decided it was time to turn off the oven and cycle to the Manor House for her afternoon stint.

It was a fairly quiet afternoon, and she was jubilant to get home by five-thirty to switch on her casserole to finish cooking while she washed her hair. As she blew the long pale strands dry the thought of drinks suddenly struck her. She opened the sideboard without much hope to see one bottle of sherry, of excellent brand, but half empty, and the remains of another of brandy, kept for emergencies by her mother. Emily shrugged. Luc would just have to slum it for one evening, she decided, and turned her attentions to her casserole. The meat was fork-tender by this time. Adding a generous dollop of creamed horseradish and a carton of sour cream, she left the pot to sit on top of the stove to blend its flavours together while she dressed.

She was quite pleased with herself when she was ready. The new outfit clung and swirled simultaneously, giving her a look more sophisticated than usual, added to by her hair, which she left down, on Luc's instructions, but caught at the nape of her neck with a tortoiseshell comb. Her one expensive pair of black slender-heeled shoes had to do, though she yearned for something strappy and frivolous. Making a face at herself in the mirror, Emily ran downstairs to envelop herself in a large apron while she prepared the rice, mushrooms, corn and green beans to accompany the main course.

Fifteen minutes before Luc was due to arrive everything was ready, and Emily stood in the kitchen checking on her fingers that all the tasks she had set herself were done. There was no table to lay, regretfully, as the dining room had been in the other half of the cottage and was now Lydia's sitting room. They would have to eat from trays on their knees in front of the fire, which Emily had lit earlier, and was now flickering invitingly round the two huge logs arranged carefully in the cowled stone fireplace. No way could she fit someone of Luc's dimensions at the table in the minuscule kitchen. Besides, it would be a change for him, decided Emily—picnicking off trays would hardly be routine in his life-style at home. Wondering what Brazilian food was like, she checked the contents of the various pots and pans, then halted at the sound of the old iron knocker on the front door. Luc was five minutes early.

Emily opened the door to find him standing there with his arms full of bottles, a smile of warm admiration on his face as he examined her from head to foot.

'How very elegant you look, Emily—or should I say Miss Harper? May I please put these down somewhere, *carinha*, or I shall lose the lot.'

Emily swiftly relieved him of two of the bottles, scolding.

'It isn't a party, Luc—you shouldn't have brought so much; but thank you anyway. I'm afraid I was too engrossed in providing the food to give a thought to the drinks.'

As Luc came into the firelit room Emily looked at him with undisguised pleasure. Instead of the more formal clothes he had worn previously he was dressed in tight-fitting black cord jeans, a shirt in fine cream wool and a black suede waistcoat.

'You look elegant too, Luc,' she said, smiling happily at him.

'But not nearly enough to match that very charming dress, Emily.' Luc raised her hand fleetingly to his lips. 'I thought something casual would be appropriate for an evening at home—but I see I was wrong, you look like a princess.'

'It's new,' said Emily candidly. 'I saw it in a shop in Warwick this morning when I was supposed to be buying food, and I couldn't resist it. So I was extravagant. I'm a bit fed up with my usual things.'

'To me you are enchanting whatever you wear—but you know that.' He was purposely brisk as he turned to the array of bottles. 'I had no idea what you were cooking, so I brought one red, one white, one rosé, a bottle of dry sherry and one of champagne.'

Emily looked at him ruefully.

'You do realise that we shall be eating from trays, Luc Fonseca? Our erstwhile dining room is next door with Lydia, and somehow I just couldn't picture you in my little kitchen!'

'Just to be with you, Emily, is of infinitely more importance than what I eat, or where I eat it!'

There was silence after his words, broken only by the crackling and spitting of the logs in the fireplace.

'We're having beef in horseradish sauce,' said Emily finally, her eyes held fast by his.

'Then perhaps we should drink the red wine,' he answered softly, moving closer.

She turned abruptly, blinking, and opened the sideboard to take out two crystal goblets.

'Will these do?'

'Perfectly. Perhaps you can find two sherry glasses also and we'll have an aperitif.' He was deliberately casual as he helped her to her feet. 'I like my sherry dry, but perhaps you do not?'

Emily shook her head vigorously.

'I warn you now,' she said gaily, 'I have absolutely no palate, so I'll have some of my own bottle in the sideboard. I shall drink it while I put the vegetables on.'

Luc stationed himself in the kitchen doorway while Emily put the finishing touches to the meal, watching her as she tasted and seasoned, his eyes indulgent as she carefully brought the casserole to the correct heat without curdling its creamy contents.

'No first course,' she said cheerfully over her shoulder, 'and no serving dishes. I'm just putting everything on your plate, so if there's something you don't like just leave it.'

'*Carinha*, from the heavenly smell coming from that pot that will be highly unlikely,' he assured her. 'Besides, I'm starving. I didn't have any lunch.'

'Neither did I.'

Without further ado Emily drained the vegetables and filled two plates generously. Settled on the comfortable rubbed leather sofa in front of the fire, they both fell on the food avidly, Luc flatteringly extravagant in his praise. In a gratifyingly short time he had cleared his plate, insisting that he help himself to more, his mouth inelegantly full.

'Did you learn to cook at school, Emily?'

'Yes, but not things like this, really—more in the Sole Véronique and Chicken Florentine style. Sort of upmarket, but not what my mother considered suitable for a hungry man. This dish was my father's favourite. I enjoy cooking, but my usual cuisine alone is more in the mince and bacon and egg area, and lots of salads. I'm not terribly good at puddings either, I'm afraid, but I've noticed you don't eat sweet things.'

'I am touched that you remembered.' He smiled at her tenderly. 'You are quite right. Creamy concoctions are not at all to my taste. But you are, little *cozinheira*.'

'What's that?' Emily's colour was high as she took his empty plate with hers and whisked them off to the kitchen. 'No, stay where you are—I'll just put the coffee to perk while we have our next course.'

Luc leaned back against the velvet sofa cushions, watching her indolently as she came back with a cheeseboard and a bowl of crisp apples.

'*Cozinheira* merely means "cook", suspicious one.' He grinned at her and looked appreciatively at the fine piece of Stilton she offered him. 'Now *that* really is to my taste, Emily. No biscuits, thank you, just one of those tempting apples and a large slice of that noble cheese. *Gostoso*—delicious, to you.'

Emily found she was drinking a third glass of wine as they

finished their cheese, and felt rather alarmingly weightless as she got up to collect the coffee tray.

'I've had much more to drink than I should have,' she said solemnly as she poured two cups of black coffee with infinite care. 'It's a bit risky serving coffee at all to a Brazilian, I suppose, but if you don't like it you'll just have to lump it.' She grinned at him cheekily over the rim of her cup.

'What is this "lump it"?' Luc frowned ferociously.

'Never mind.' Emily patted his arm condescendingly. 'I forget you're a poor misguided foreigner!'

Without warning he took her cup from her and put it down on the tray with a bump that threatened the delicate china's safety, then pulled her roughly into his arms, looking down into her startled face with an evil smile lifting the corners of his mouth.

'Misguided foreigner, am I?' He was almost too quiet for her to hear. 'Tell me you're sorry.'

'I'm sorry,' said Emily instantly.

'How sorry?'

'Very sorry, Luc.'

'Show me,' he demanded.

'How?'

He closed his eyes, his voice unsteady as he held her close. 'You know how, *carinha*. Put me out of my misery.'

Emily's mouth reached his before he finished speaking and there was silence in the small room as their lips came together, clung, opened, welcomed, and communed with each other in a frenzy of delight that was at once an immense relief and a sweet torture. Luc pulled her across his lap and sank back with her against the velvet cushions, never taking his mouth from hers as Emily gave herself up joyfully to the insidious warmth that lapped them both, enclosing them in a cocoon of pleasurable sensation. Sensation soon became much, much more than pleasurable, as his hands slid slowly into her hair, removing the comb and playing with the long shiny strands, winding them round his wrist to bind her to him, as the other hand smoothed rhythmically over her back and shoulders, lulling her hypnotically into something approaching a trance. When Luc lifted his mouth from hers she sighed, turning her face blindly into his neck as he released her hair and slid his hands over the gossamer fabric covering her small, pointed breasts. The convulsive shiver that ran through her at his touch was purely sensuous, no thought of rejecting his hands entering her head. With a gasp Emily sought his mouth urgently with her own, the ardour of her untutored response driving him wild. He crushed her to him, burying her head against his chest murmuring incoherently into the tangle of her hair.

'*Querida*, forgive me—I promised, but it is almost impossible—I should not have come—*Deus*, Emily. . . .'

Luc trailed into silence as she pushed herself away from him and stared up into his eyes, her face transformed from its usual delicate aqua-tinted charm. Colour flared along her cheekbones and her eyes burned with a brilliant, lambent blue, their expression blank and unfocussed as she pushed her hair from her face with a careless hand. Something in her unwavering stare was causing Luc's breath to come faster, his nostrils to flare, and as the signs of his disturbance became increasingly more evident, her mouth curved in a smile as old as Eve. Whatever shreds of self-control Luc had left deserted him suddenly and completely. Teeth clenched, hands trembling, he threw the velvet cushions on the floor and drew the silent, unresisting girl to lie full length before the dying flames of the fire. Taking her face between his hands, he began to kiss her again, his whole body trembling in an intense effort to be gentle as he laid his lips on her eyes, her cheeks, her throat, returning to her parted lips again and again as though he would never be satiated by their sweetness. Emily curled her body against his, instinctively arching against him to get closer and closer, to soothe this new burning ache that was consuming her, possessing her, so that nothing in the world mattered but the assuagement of her longing. She pushed her hands inside his shirt, wanting the touch of his skin, putting her open mouth against his chest, kissing all of him she could reach, while his hands grew frantic, removing her clothes, then his own, with an awkward haste she barely registered until their bodies came together, skin against skin, the dim light of the fire the only illumination as it washed over the dark copper of Luc's body against the fair, pale fragility of hers. There was no one to hear as Luc's English deserted him and a torrent of Portuguese poured into Emily's ear as, caution engulfed in raw need, he initiated her into the first painful pleasure of love. The faint, hoarse cry of pain she gave was lost against his mouth, and her struggles stilled by the sheer superiority of his body as it subdued hers, then all was utter silence as he lay, still holding her tight, his face pressed against hers in an agony of immediate remorse.

After a long, long time Luc felt a shudder run through Emily's body and he raised his head. Her eyes refused to meet his and she kept her lids lowered. He swallowed.

'You are disgusted with me, Emily?' Bleakly he turned her unwilling face up to his. 'You shuddered. Am I abhorrent to you, *carinha? Deus*—say something!'

Emily surprised him with a little sidelong smile.

'It's only that I'm shy, I think, Luc—and a bit cold. Not very romantic, I know, but I'm not used to lying about without any clothes on.'

With a sound suspiciously like a sob he got to his feet, jerking her up with him.

'Forgive me, little one—shall I dress you first, or put more logs on?'

Emily began to laugh.

'I think it's best if I put my own clothes on, if you'll just turn your back—oh, and if you'd just let me go for a moment.'

He relaxed a little.

'Then you are not angry?'

'No.' Her eyes slid away from the urgency in his. 'How could I be? It was every bit as much my fault as yours—more. You did try to fight against the inevitable, after all. I just let it knock me flat without a struggle.'

His dark face still troubled he turned away and pulled on his jeans, then made up the fire, his eyes averted as Emily tried unsuccessfully to locate various items of clothing.

Luc stood staring down into the fireplace, resolutely keeping his eyes on the flames beginning to curl round the fresh logs.

'You are very slow,' he said gruffly at last, then turned at the sound of a smothered giggle, to see Emily standing barefoot in a brief half-slip, clutching the top half of her new suit to her chest.

'For pity's sake, cover yourself, Emily!' A reluctant grin spread over his face.

'Well, I would,' she said apologetically, 'but you seem to have disposed of my clothes with such energy that I can't find some fairly vital items. They're all over the place.'

Luc laughed outright and joined in the hunt, discovering her bra tangled in the folds of his shirt, handing the beribboned trifle to her in apology.

'I have behaved in a very barbarous fashion, Emily—you have every right to throw me out here and now.'

She had her back to him and was struggling in vain to do up the clasp of the offending item of underwear.

'Not before you do this thing up for me,' she panted in frustration.

Luc bent his attention to the small task, frowning as he discovered the problem.

'To add to my sins, Emily, I'm afraid the—the hook?—has come off. I must have torn it in my—my——'

'Enthusiasm?' suggested Emily, abandoning any efforts at modesty and turning to face him, her sweater still bunched in front of her, an irresistible smile lighting her whole face. Luc's teeth gleamed in an answering smile, a light growing in his eyes that resembled the flames beginning to flicker in the fireplace.

'I love you, Emily,' he said simply, and held out his hand.

Without hesitation, ignoring her dishevelled state, she walked into the circle of his arms and he stood holding her quietly, his chin on top of her head, one arm close round her waist while the other hand stroked her hair.

'I hurt you, *carinha*?' he whispered.

She nodded her head vigorously.

'It will not hurt like that the next time.'

Emily trembled at the note in his husky voice, her vibration communicating itself to Luc and his grasp grew tighter, her arms going round his waist in response as he held her fast against him, her face against his bare chest, his buried in her hair.

'Is this the next time?' she said, her voice muffled.

He took a deep breath.

'Only if you want, *querida*,' he said unsteadily.

'Oh yes, I want!'

All thoughts of modesty were cast to the winds as this time it was Emily who threw her remaining garments to fall carelessly where they would in her haste to be close to Luc, glorying in the touch of his mouth and hands that were leisured and lingering in their quest to give her all the pleasure that his previous frantic haste had not allowed. She twisted and turned beneath his caresses, responding to him with all the untapped warmth of her nature, returning kiss for kiss, learning to caress and touch him so that some of his unhurrying care was abandoned and his mouth and fingers became urgent as their bodies surrendered to the force that overwhelmed them both.

Some time after, when their breathing had finally slowed to something approximating normal, Luc said roughly,

'Do you love me, Emily?'

'I think I must,' she said honestly. 'I can't imagine doing what we did unless I loved you.'

'Oh, Emily!' He cradled her to him protectively. 'One does not need to love to want to *make* love.'

'You may not. I do.'

He shook her hard.

'You know that was not my meaning. My English is not colloquial enough. But you must believe I love you, Emily. From the moment I saw you——'

'That was only five days ago,' she said practically.

'Five days—minutes—years—what does it matter? Will you marry me and come to live in Campo d'Ouro with me?' Luc's face was deadly serious, his dark eyes glowing and anxious as he took her face in his hands. 'Are you willing to leave your life here and come to live in Brazil?'

Emily gazed back unflinchingly.

'Yes, I am. But for the moment I think I should put my dressing gown on and you should get dressed too. I feel extraordinarily vulnerable like this.'

Luc drifted his mouth down over her eyes and nose, lingered a moment on her mouth, then deliberately dropped a kiss on each small breast before lifting her to her feet.

'I prefer you like this,' he said, eyes glinting, 'but I would not wish you to catch cold.'

Emily grinned back, then a sudden wave of colour washed over her face and she shut her eyes.

'What is it?' he said, alarmed.

'It just swept over me,' she said faintly, 'that my behaviour tonight was not precisely what I was taught as fitting at the school I went to.'

'What behaviour?'

'Well, standing here like this and doing—well, doing what we just did.' Emily kept her eyes closed tightly, to Luc's amusement. 'And—well, I've never seen a man without any clothes on before.'

Luc threw back his head and roared with laughter, a joyous sound that instantly drove away the embarrassment that had suddenly overtaken Emily. He turned her round, gave her a gentle slap on her bottom and proceeded to make himself decent again while she rounded up her scattered garments and went upstairs for her robe. Then they went into the kitchen and washed up the dinner things together and made coffee again, eventually settling themselves in front of the fire to drink it and make plans.

'I must fly back on Sunday,' he told her, holding her close in the crook of his arm. 'Then I shall tell my father and grandmother and make some necessary arrangements. I shall return here for you in about a month, *carinha*. Will that be suitable for you?'

Emily gazed into the fire with bemused eyes.

'I can hardly take it in, Luc,' she said hesitantly. 'Won't your family think that this is all a bit sudden?'

'All I am concerned with, Emily, is whether *you* think I am in too much of a hurry. If I lived in this country I would take more time to court you properly, let you become accustomed to the idea more slowly; but as things are I must—what is the phrase—sweep you off your feet.' His voice dropped a little, roughened with sincerity. 'I cannot chance losing you, *querida*.'

Emily twisted in his hold, throwing her arms round his neck and pressing her face hard against his.

'No chance of that,' she said unsteadily. 'I'll be ready and waiting when you come back. And anyway, this is not goodbye tonight, Luc, we've another day tomorrow.'

Emily was wrong. She woke to knocking on the front door early next morning. Pushing her tousled hair out of her eyes she threw on her dressing gown and ran barefoot down the stairs to find a white-faced Luc on the doorstep, formal in dark suit and tie.

'Darling, what is it?'

Emily drew him hastily into the living room, her arms going round him as he took her into a bonecracking embrace.

'It's my father,' he said, swallowing hard. 'I received a cable an hour ago. He has suffered a major heart attack—I must go at once. I was able to get a cancellation on a plane today.'

Emily looked at him with aching compassion, longing to give him comfort yet at a loss to know how.

'Let me make you coffee——'

'No, *carinha*,' he interrupted, refusing to let her move. 'I must go now. I'm driving down to London where I will take back the car, and there are several things I must see to while I'm there before I catch the plane. I do not have much time. Now. I must be practical.' He released her for a moment and took a leather-covered diary from his breast pocket. 'You said Mrs Crawford has a telephone. She will not mind if I ring you at her home?'

'No, of course not.' Emily manfully battled with the lump in her throat and give him the number, which he noted alongside her address.

'I will ring as soon as I have seen my father, Emily,' he said, taking her by the shoulders and looking deep into her eyes. 'I will write also, and when—when my father recovers I shall return for you. Until then, remember that I love you, I love you, Emily.'

Tears began to trickle down Emily's face, and he pulled her roughly against him, murmuring comfort in a mixture of Portuguese and English, none of which registered. The stark fact of Luc's departure dominated her completely for a moment until her natural common sense began to return. Emily drew away from him a little, her eyes on a pulse that was beating violently in Luc's throat. She gave an inelegant sniff and smiled damply up into his strained face.

'I hope you won't carry a picture of me in your mind the way I look at the moment,' she said, striving to lighten his despondency. 'My dressing gown is a relic of schooldays.'

Luc bent his head and kissed her quivering mouth hard, his hands bruising her shoulders.

'I shall hope to see you many times like this,' he said huskily, 'with your hair untidy and your body warm from bed—our bed, *carinha*. Soon I hope there will be no more painful goodbyes.' He broke off, looking at his watch. '*Deus*, Emily, I must go. *Até logo, carinha*.'

'Goodbye, Luc.' Emily's hand clung to his as she saw him through the door. 'I hope very much you find your father recovered when you arrive home. And please drive carefully down to London.'

They stood for a long moment, hands clasped, while Emily fought to keep back the tears and they looked at each other in anguish. Then Luc bent and kissed her swiftly, literally tearing himself away, striding down the path to the gate, his head bent. He turned once before he got in the car, and Emily smiled valiantly in response to his wave, then he was gone.

The next couple of days went past like years. Emily did her stint at the Manor House, glad of something to pass the time, spending the rest of the day listening for Lydia's knock to summon her to the phone. By the end of the fourth day after Luc's departure Emily was hollow-eyed from lack of sleep, and beginning to lose weight from lack of appetite. She attacked the garden, reducing it to neatness for the winter with a violence that helped a little to relieve the pent-up state of anticipation mixed with bitter disappointment that was her waking state of mind. Lydia was very concerned, but Emily refused all offers to spend time with her next door, as she couldn't bear to be in the house where the phone rang frequently, but the caller was never Luc.

Frantic with anxiety, she rang the airline to see if the plane Luc took arrived safely in Rio, and after a momentary feeling of relief on learning it had, she was beset by a new anguish as to the cause of his silence. Every morning she ran downstairs to see what the postman had brought, but no airmail envelope ever dropped through the letter-box. In the haste of his departure Luc had forgotten to give her his address. Besides, she thought proudly, no way am I going to write to ask why he hasn't contacted me. And, to be fair, heaven knew what sort of situation had waited for him on his return. His poor father could have been worse, or even have died. His grandmother would need looking after. Luc himself would be worried out of his mind, utterly grief-stricken, if the worst had happened. On and on went the list of possibilities in Emily's mind, giving her no respite from the endless speculation as to the reasons for Luc's silence.

Of course, thought Emily, after two agonising weeks had dragged by, it is very possible that he is a consummate actor, and our pitifully brief time together was merely a pleasant way of whiling away his holiday. All that line about coming back to marry me was probably a bit of sugar to sweeten the fact that he had relieved me of my much-vaunted virginity. No doubt a commonplace occurrence to him, but he was considerate enough to try and infuse a little respectability into the incident by conning her as to his intentions. Emily laughed silently, her face mirthless. 'Intentions' was rather an outdated word, used in that context. It was more than possible that Luc Fonseca had intended nothing more than a diverting little interlude, and the marriage bit had been a sop to her sensibilities.

'Look, Emily, I think it's about time you had a square meal,' said Lydia severely one morning, as she saw her yanking up weeds viciously in the front garden.

'I'm all right, honestly,' said Emily, smiling brightly as she sat back on her heels.

'Well, you don't look it, to be frank. Come in and have some lunch.' Lydia helped Emily to her feet with a peremptory hand. 'No excuses, now. It's Monday, so you don't have to dash up to the Manor House, and you'll just have to try to ignore that blasted phone.'

Emily gave in and allowed herself to be fussed over and cossetted, plied with shepherd's pie and trifle and all the latest news from the neighbourhood. She ate obediently, though less than her hostess wished, and sat docilely by the fire with a cup of tea afterwards, somnolent with warmth and food. Lydia noted her pale face and shadowed eyes with a professional eye.

'Not sleeping too well, Em?'

'No, not too well at all, to be honest.' Emily sighed, staring into the cheerful crackling fire. 'Silly, really—sort of arrested development, I suppose. I should have been nursing a broken heart a lot earlier than this, judging by the girls at school.'

'Very understandable, love,' said Lydia. 'If this is your very first stab at romance you did rather choose a high-powered subject to cut your teeth on.'

Emily frowned, nibbling her bottom lip.

'I didn't choose, Lydia. Luc just happened. And after all this time without hearing from him I imagine I can just write him off to experience.'

'It's only just over a fortnight, love.'

'It may be a fortnight to you, Lydia. To me it's been a little private eternity.' Emily heaved herself up out of her chair. 'I'll wash up so you can get back to work.'

'Thanks, love.' Lydia put on her blue overcoat and the matching uniform cap, looking at Emily with troubled eyes. 'It *will* pass, Em. All hurts heal in time. I thought I'd never get over Tom's death, but I did. You've had a rough time, losing your mother and trying to sort your life out for yourself. I could ring Mr Fonseca's neck for him!'

Emily smiled wearily.

'That makes two of us. I've just about reached the stage where I'm angry instead of—well, desolate is the word that springs to mind.'

'That's the spirit,' said Lydia approvingly. 'Try to put him out of your mind.'

'That's going to be difficult.' Emily sighed, then grinned. 'Not impossible, of course. I shan't allow a few short days in my life to ruin the rest of it. One thing I'm resigned to, though.'

Lydia turned, her hand on the latch.

'What's that, love?'

'I know I'm not going to hear from him now, somehow. This morning as I was fighting with the weeds a feeling of certainty took over, so I'll stop looking for the postman, and I'll make friends with your phone again.'

When Lydia had gone Emily turned to the lunch dishes

with a sigh. Her last assurance to her friend had been sheer invention to reassure Lydia. And now, by some means, she would have to make it come true, banish Luc from her mind and forget the fateful few days that had been such a colourful interlude in her humdrum existence. And perhaps Colonel Hammond would be kind enough to let her avoid Lady Henrietta's bedroom in future. It had no record of being haunted, but for Emily it had acquired a very personal ghost, tall and dark, with a glinting smile she found impossible to erase from her mind.

CHAPTER FOUR

ON a cold, blustery March day, some eighteen months later, Emily closed the door of the Dower House on the last sorrowful, sympathetic face and leaned against the heavy oak panels for a moment, limp and drained. For the count of ten she stayed where she was, eyes tightly shut, then pushed herself upright, irritated by the melodrama of her pose. As she crossed the polished wood floor of the hall her face brightened at the faint sounds of exuberant bathtime coming from upstairs, and she hurried to join in. She was barely past the newel post when the doorbell rang yet again. Emily slumped against the banister rail in despair. Surely there was no one else to come? It was past six o'clock on this endless, harrowing day, and human nature could only stand so much.

Sighing, she retraced her steps, automatically smoothing a stray strand of hair back into its smooth chignon, schooling her pale face into a polite, social expression. She switched on the porch light and shot back the great iron bolt, opening the door for what seemed like the hundredth time that day. The light from the ancient, wrought-iron porch lamp fell on the dark, sombre face of the tall man who stood, silent, waiting for her to speak. The polite smile on Emily's face died, the last vestige of colour in her face dying with it. Her visitor's face was instantly familiar, and she stared up at him in incredulous hostility. She struggled to take a deep breath and failed. Her hands fluttered in a feeble effort at warding him off, then she gave an odd, stifled little moan and crumpled abruptly into the outstretched arms of the man who sprang forward to catch her.

Luc Fonseca shouldered the door closed behind him and stood looking down at the fine-drawn face that lay so still and white against the dark cloth of his coat. His lips tightened as he estimated the weight of the small limp body in his arms, his head jerking up as he heard a horrified exclamation from the stairs. Lydia Crawford came running down into the hall, her kind face worried.

'Mr Fonseca! What happened? Poor child—I suppose it was the shock of seeing you. Bring her in here.'

She directed him through an open doorway into the rather shabby elegance of the drawing-room, motioning him to lay the still girl on one of the faded brocade sofas flanking the marble fireplace, where a log fire gave out light and warmth into the high-ceilinged room.

'Why is she taking so long to come round?' Luc's voice was harsh with anxiety, the social niceties ignored. 'What has happened to her, Mrs Crawford? *Deus*, she looks so thin and exhausted!'

Lydia poured some brandy from the tray on the low table between the two sofas, handing the crystal tumbler to him.

'Try to get that down her if you can,' she said, then looked over her shoulder, forehead furrowed. 'Look, can you cope on your own for a moment—there's something I must see to upstairs.'

'Of course.'

Luc put down the glass while he shrugged himself out of his coat, oblivious to Lydia's departure, all his attention for the alarmingly quiet figure which lay as though lifeless. With infinite care he slid his arm behind Emily's shoulders and gently began to stroke her cold white cheek with his other hand, holding her close and talking quietly in a soothing monotone.

'Wake up, *carinha*. Open your eyes. I know you are not pleased to see me, but wake up so that I may talk to you, explain . . .'

To his relief Emily gave a faint sigh and stirred a little. Luc held the brandy to her lips and trickled a little of the spirit into her mouth. She swallowed, gagged, opened her eyes and stared blankly into the face bent over her. Her lids shut instantly and she turned away from him in repudiation.

'No, Emily,' Luc said urgently, refusing to loosen his grasp. 'You must drink just a little more of this. You will feel better.'

He tilted the glass against her lips and automatically Emily swallowed some of the brandy before pushing the glass away and struggling to sit upright.

'You may take your arm away,' she said, her voice barely above a whisper, but its icy distaste unmistakeable. Silently the man obeyed and rose to his feet, standing over her with sombre eyes fixed on Emily's face, where the leaping flames reflected a slight, borrowed warmth. She refused to look up.

'I don't know why you're here,' she went on, with complete composure, 'or how you knew I would be here at the Dower House. Nor am I interested. So perhaps you would leave. At no time would you be welcome, but today is inopportune in the extreme. Please go.'

Her head fell wearily back against the sofa, as though the effort of her frigid, stilted speech had drained her of her last resources.

Luc Fonseca looked about him for the first time, noting trays with half-empty plates of canapés and sandwiches, the remains of an enormous fruit cake and a number of sherry glasses still bearing traces of their recently consumed contents. He looked down into Emily's withdrawn face.

'You were entertaining?' He frowned. 'I had not thought—I mean, it is so soon after your husband's——'

'Death, you mean.' For the first time Emily looked directly at him, her blue eyes glacial as she swung her feet gingerly to the floor and sat upright with care. 'I know nothing of customs in your country, but in Britain it's normal courtesy to offer refreshment to those people civil enough to come to a funeral on a cold March day. This afternoon my husband was laid to rest with his ancestors in the family vault.'

Luc stared down at her in disbelief.

'But I was informed of his death a week ago. I assumed all

would be over by now. In Brazil burial takes place in twenty-four hours.'

Emily rose to her feet, looking at him with suspicion.

'How did you know about Marcus's death?'

'I read the notice in the paper.'

'You said you were informed.'

'A slip of the tongue, no more.'

'Even so, how did you know he was my husband? My name wasn't mentioned.' Her breathing became agitated and Luc pushed her gently back down on the sofa, where she sank unresisting against the cushions, her eyes cold and questioning as they tried to pierce the armoured expression in his.

'For the time being just let us say I knew. I have always known. But now is not the time for explanations which can only add to your distress.' Luc dropped to one knee in front of Emily and took one of her flaccid hands in his. 'Please believe me, Emily. I would not have come today if I had realised it was such an unsuitable time to choose. I will go away now, with the hope that you will allow me to return tomorrow.'

Emily shook her head immediately, but her protest was halted as Lydia came back into the room, and she brushed Luc aside, getting to her feet anxiously.

'Is—is everything all right, Lydia?' Her eyes communicated silently with the other woman and Lydia smiled cheerfully.

'All settled in happily for the night,' she said reassuringly, then cast a professional eye over Emily. 'You don't look too marvellous, though, young lady.'

'I fear the blame is mine. I gave her a shock,' said Luc grimly.

Emily ignored him.

'Are you in the neighbourhood for long, Mr Fonseca?' asked Lydia hurriedly.

'My plans are uncertain. I shall stay at the White Hart for a short time.' He turned and bowed formally to Emily. 'Allow me to offer my condolences. Perhaps you will spare me a few minutes tomorrow afternoon? I hesitate to intrude at such a time, but my time in England is limited.'

'No!' Emily bit back the violence of her protest. 'I mean,

would you make it tomorrow evening, if you really feel your visit is necessary.'

'I do,' he said formally, picking up his coat.

'Seven-thirty, then,' said Emily, unsmiling.

There was silence for a moment as the two looked at each other like antagonists, the pale slender girl in the stark black dress and the tall, grim-faced man in the dark, formal suit, his shirt-collar startlingly white against the dark tan of his skin.

'Thank you, Mrs Lacey,' he said gravely. '*Até amanha.* Goodnight, Mrs Crawford.'

'I'll see you to the door,' said Lydia swiftly, and ushered him into the hall while Emily sat down again abruptly, her legs unable to support her any longer. Head in hands, she tried to assimilate this additional shock. For eighteen months she had heard nothing at all of Lucas Fonseca; vanished from her life as though dead, or departed for another planet. As well he might have done for all she had known. She had regarded him as dead. Almost she had accustomed herself to the idea. To see him standing there this evening, like a spectre from the past, had been an affront, an outrage. Dead he was out of her life, alive he was a challenge, a threat. I refuse to allow it, she thought fiercely. My life is mapped out. Marcus helped me make a future. I will *not* let Luc come back and ruin everything a second time.

She looked up earily as Lydia returned.

'I must go up to Jamie.' She rose unsteadily to her feet.

'No need,' said Lydia firmly. 'Sit down and put your feet up, he's fast asleep. I gave him his supper early and he went off quickly. He's a good little lad.'

Emily's face softened, and she sank back thankfully on the sofa, motioning Lydia to sit down. They both sat staring into the flames in silence for a while before Lydia sighed and looked across at Emily, her kind face troubled.

'It's no good, Em. There's no point in trying to ignore the fact that Luc appeared tonight.'

'No. How right you are.' Emily's mouth curled. 'Right little melodrama, one way and another, wasn't it? Stupid, passing out like that—quite the Victorian heroine! But Lord, Lydia, the very sight of him standing there like an apparition was just too much after the rest of today.'

'It was perfectly understandable, I would say. You've eaten practically nothing since Marcus died, and there's been such a lot to see to. After all, love, you're very young to have all this on your plate. Luc should never have reappeared like that without warning.'

'I don't feel young,' said Emily wearily. 'I feel old, ancient, as though I mislaid my teens somewhere.' She paused, eyes narrowed, considering Lydia in speculation. 'Do you know, Mrs Crawford, I have this strange feeling. Somehow or other Luc's dramatic reappearance wasn't quite the cataclysmic shock to you that it was to me.'

'Well, it wouldn't be, would it?' Lydia said reasonably. 'He was your pigeon, not mine.'

'Mm,' Emily was by no means satisfied. 'Nevertheless I rather think you knew he was coming.'

Lydia sighed.

'Yes. At least, I knew he would some time. I really had no idea it would be today. He should have waited a bit.'

A strange feeling was creeping over Emily, as though the ground were shifting beneath her feet.

'Lydia!' Her blue eyes were dark and enormous in her white face, as she stared at her friend incredulously. 'You've known what happened to Luc all along, haven't you? No——' as the other woman started to speak, 'don't bother to deny it. My God, why didn't you say something? You knew the agony I went through ...' Great tears started to roll down Emily's face, the first since Marcus's death, and at the sight of them Lydia jumped to her feet.

'Now for heaven's sake don't upset yourself, Emily. It was agony for me, too, to keep quiet about it, but he swore me to silence—oh dear—look, love, let's be sensible. I'll tell you everything, I promise, but not until you've had something to eat.'

Emily jumped up, wavering a little on legs that were still unsteady.

'How can you bother about food——'

Lydia put up an inexorable hand, and began to gather up the used plates and glasses, quick and efficient as always.

'I'm going to wash these while that pan of soup in the kitchen heats up,' she said firmly. 'Then I shall make a pot of tea, set a tray and we'll have a little snack in here. In the meantime you can go up and check on your son, change into your nightie and dressing gown, and not a word will you hear from me until then.'

Recognising the finality in Lydia's voice, Emily helped clear the debris of the funeral refreshments, carrying trays out into the big old-fashioned kitchen. Leaving Lydia up to her elbows in suds, Emily climbed the shallow treads of the oak staircase and entered the nursery, which, unlike the rest of the house, was completely modern, with Winnie the Pooh wallpaper and white-painted furniture with nursery-rhyme stencils. Her son lay in an untidy heap at the foot of his cot, and Emily felt her usual surge of love at the sight of his rosy, sleepy face. She straightened him out gently, tucking the covers round him. His eyes opened drowsily and looked straight up at her in the soft dim glow of the nightlight.

'Mum—mum,' he muttered indistinctly, his mouth curving in the smile that rendered Emily helpless. She bent over him and kissed him and he sighed, turning over to settle into sleep once more. She tiptoed from the room to her bedroom next door, averting her eyes from the closed door of the room where Marcus used to sleep. He had left that for ever. She dashed the tears away from her eyes and concentrated on taking off the unbecoming black dress and brushed out her hair from the confines of the severe chignon.

When Emily returned to the kitchen, snug in high-necked nightgown and fleecy aquamarine wool dressing-gown, Lydia turned away from the pan of soup she was seasoning and looked at her with approval.

'That's better. You look terrible in black.'

'I'll never wear it again if I can help it,' said Emily fervently. 'Let me do something to help.'

'You take the tea-tray with the bread and cheese, etc., I'll bring the soup bowls and the cutlery.'

Before they settled down to their simple meal Emily added a couple of logs to the drawing room fire and they sat opposite each other, the trays on the long low table between them.

'Right, Lydia, I'm eating, so fire away,' said Emily, finding she was hungrier than she'd thought after the first appetising mouthful of onion soup.

Lydia ate for a while before starting to speak.

'I've known that Luc was all right since just after you married Marcus,' she began without preamble.

Emily stared at her blankly, opening her mouth to interrupt, but Lydia held up a hand.

'I think it's best if I tell you the whole story, Em, then you can have your say afterwards. Not that I have much to tell.'

Emily heard her friend out in silence, as advised, and poured out tea after they finished their soup, cutting two slices of fruit cake to eat with it. She remained surprisingly calm throughout the little tale, though inside she felt a burning rebellion at the callous way the gods take up poor mortal lives and tangle up their destinies with all the carelessness a kitten might bring to snarling up a ball of wool.

'It was only about a fortnight after you came back to Compton Lacey with Marcus and announced that you were married,' began Lydia. 'The phone rang one night and it was Luc, from his home in Minas Gerais. He was very agitated and his accent was much more pronounced than usual, also the line wasn't too clear. One way and another we had quite some difficulty in getting a clear picture of events on either side. To be brief, when Luc went back to Brazil the taxi taking him from one airport to the other in Rio was involved in an accident. Luc suffered concussion from a blow on the head, and though not unconscious for long, was the victim of temporary amnesia when he came round in hospital. He could remember things in the past, more or less right up to his trip to England, but the time immediately prior to the accident had been wiped clean from his memory.'

Emily stirred restlessly at this.

'Sadly,' Lydia went on, 'he was not in time to see his father alive. Senhor Fonseca Senior died from a second coronary before Luc was well enough to return to Campo d'Ouro. The experts had predicted that Luc's recall would be total in time, and little by little everything did return to him—hence the frenzied telephone call to me for news of you. I had to tell him that you were married, of course. He—well, he took it badly, to say the least. I heard no more for quite a while, then he wrote to me, asking me to write to him regularly, giving him reports on you and to let him know should you need help in any sort of way.'

Emily was dumbfounded.

'Do you mean that all this time you've been sending off bulletins about—about everything that's happened to me? My God! Something like a school report, I suppose. "Emily tries hard, but needs more application" used to be a favourite comment. What were yours, Lydia?'

'Don't be too hard on me, love, I was sort of pig-in-the-middle,' begged Lydia. 'Luc made me promise faithfully I would never tell you. I could never decide whether he was right.'

'He wasn't,' said Emily bitterly. 'Is there anything else I should know?'

'When I wrote about Jamie's birth there was complete silence until three months ago, when he began writing again. I subsequently told him Marcus was terminally ill, and eventually informed him that he had died. I admit I knew he was here in the country, but I had no idea he would turn up today, of all days.'

'They bury people within twenty-four hours in Brazil,' said Emily dully.

'I see.'

There was silence while they both sipped tea, staring into the fire. Lydia sighed.

'When he comes here tomorrow are you going to freeze him out like you did tonight, Em? To be fair, it wasn't his fault things happened as they did.'

'I realise that. Or at least, one part of me does, the sensible, logical side. But the other part feels a terrible, burning resentment. The fact that it's entirely unmerited doesn't seem enough to send it away.'

'Do you resent my part in it, Emily?' asked Lydia anxiously.

'No, of course not, Lydia.' Emily smiled in reassurance. 'How could I? You did what you thought was best. Besides, you know very well that I could never have survived these last months without your help and support, I don't know what I would have done without you.' She yawned suddenly, exhaustion finally overtaking her like a tidal wave. 'God,

Lydia, I'm tired! I think it's time for bed. I know it's early, but it's been a long, long day.'

Lydia rose, piling up the trays.

'I wish you'd let me stay here tonight, Emily. I could easily have packed Tim off to one of his friends.'

Emily smiled gratefully as they went into the kitchen.

'You've done quite enough in having Jamie all day and putting him to bed for me. Besides, I'm not nervous. And anyway, you're back to work tomorrow. Thank you for everything, Lydia, I don't know what I'd have done without you.'

When the sound of Lydia's departing car had died away the old house seemed very empty and still. Emily locked up hurriedly and went upstairs to peep at her soundly sleeping son before settling herself down in her wide bed in the adjoining bedroom. Despite her weariness it was a long time before she could stop her mind from going round and round on an endless treadmill of speculation about Luc's reappearance. She wondered how he would have got on with Marcus, then the thought of her husband's kind face with the weary eyes opened the floodgates and she turned her head into her pillow and wept bitterly in a storm of pity, and a futile rage against the injustice of life.

CHAPTER FIVE

JAMIE was a very good little boy about settling down to sleep at nights, but he was equally good at waking up bright and early. Emily was glad of her early night when she heard him banging against the bars of his cot at six-thirty next morning, reiterating his usual litany of 'Mum—mum' until she went in to him.

'Who needs an alarm clock with you around?' she said ruefully, as the little figure in the red stretchy sleeping suit held up his arms, confident of being picked up, his mouth wide in an irresistible grin that displayed his six milky-white teeth. 'O.K. Out you come!'

Thank heavens it would be just a normal, peaceful day today, thought Emily, as she stripped and changed Jamie. She dressed him in warm sweater and dungarees and carried him down to the kitchen where the big Aga stove was still alight, filling the room with warmth against the raw chill of the morning. She installed the wriggling little figure in his highchair and gave him a rusk to occupy him while she made porridge and boiled eggs, joining Jamie in making a good breakfast for the first time in months. Towards the end she had been too involved in nursing Marcus to have much appetite, and had become noticeably skinny, even to herself. Her daily woman, Mrs Giles, would be in at nine to help clear up after yesterday, so for an hour or so she could actually read the morning paper in comparative peace while Jamie played in his playpen. The only abnormality about the day would be the meeting with Luc this evening.

Emily sighed. What was she going to say to him? What could he want to say to her, if it came to that? Their brief relationship had blossomed and died a long time ago. The Emily who had been hit for six by the charm of the handsome Brazilian just didn't exist any more. She had been transformed into the chatelaine of the Dower House of Compton Lacey, a very different proposition from the naïve, inexperienced girl whose defences had been unequal to Luc's charm. Poor man, she thought dispassionately. He'd had a hard time of it too, losing his father like that coupled with his own traumatic experience. She had thought of many reasons for Luc's complete disappearance from her life, but had never come within any distance of the truth.

After Mrs Giles arrived tand they had worked together to set the old house to rights, Emily wrapped Jamie up well and took him for a walk in the grounds of the Manor House in his pushchair. The day was grey and blustery and she walked briskly, trundling the chair along at a fine pace, to Jamie's delight. Emily felt uneasy. She wished Luc weren't coming tonight. She should have put him off for a day or two, even if his time were limited. She had every excuse, after all. And now she came to think of it, seven-thirty was an idiotic time to suggest. Perhaps he thought she'd asked him to dinner. Emily's 'dinner' usually consisted of something like scrambled eggs or soup eaten with her son before she put him to bed. Not really the sort of meal she could offer Lucas Guimaraes Fonseca. Still, there was a well-stocked drinks cabinet. Perhaps his visit would be brief. Emily bent to retrieve the woolly rabbit Jamie had hurled from his chair and turned for home. At least Jamie could be depended on to settle down to sleep promptly, and with luck should be well away before Luc's arrival. Emily felt suddenly depressed. Not so long ago the prospect of seeing Luc would have transported her into the seventh heaven. Now it was merely another chore to be disposed of as painlessly as possible.

'Come on, Jamie,' she said brightly. 'Let's go and have lunch.'

The rest of the day was taken up in writing acknowledgements of all the letters of condolence on Marcus's death. She played with Jamie for some time afterwards to restore her balance, then gave him his supper. While Emily fed her son with fish in cream sauce she became nervous about whether she would have to offer Luc a meal. Depositing Jamie in his pen for a while, she rummaged in the freezer and produced a quiche Lorraine, setting it on the rack above the Aga to thaw. There was no lettuce, but she found a firm white cabbage, shredding it and mixing it with sweetcorn, onion and sliced red pepper for salad. Finally she put some potatoes to bake in the oven after making up the fire and checked on the contents of the pan of soup at the back of the hotplate. Mrs Giles always 'knocked up' a pan of soup when she came to clean, and today it was vegetable, thick with winter roots, celery, leeks and onions. That should do, thought Emily, then if he doesn't stay nothing will be wasted.

By this time Jamie had tired of his blocks and was beginning to droop, so Emily scooped him up and cuddled him in her arms as she took him up to the cheerful, brightly lit nursery. He went down without a murmur, hugging his rabbit, and Emily gave thanks, as she did most nights, for such a sunny dispositioned child. She stood looking down at him lovingly for some time, then tiptoed out, leaving only the nightlight to keep him company.

Emily had a swift bath and thought dispiritedly what to wear. Not the black dress of yesterday; Marcus had hated black and she had worn it merely as a sign of the respect she knew the mourners at the funeral would consider mandatory. Marcus had bought her quite a lot of clothes, and had appreciated the subtle, muted colours that suited her best. She took out a dress of ginger-pink suede, draped cleverly across her breasts, the skirt bias-cut to swing gracefully as she moved. She brushed her hair back from her face and let it hang loose, screwed small pearl studs into her earlobes and made up her face with care. She might as well meet Luc with all flags flying. The pathetic creature of yesterday was ousted by a poised young woman who looked back from the mirror with confidence. Marcus would have approved. Her full lower lip trembled for a moment, then she held her head up high and went down to turn on all the lights and make up the drawing-room fire.

Emily had just finished setting a tray with sherry decanter and glasses when the doorbell jangled. Her stomach muscles contracted for a second and she took a deep breath, annoyed with herself, before crossing the hall to open the heavy door to her visitor.

Luc Fonseca came into the hall carrying a sheaf of pink roses, which he handed to Emily as he closed the door.

'Good evening, Emily,' he said gravely. 'I trust I find you recovered today.'

She accepted the flowers and took his sheepskin jacket.

'Thank you, Luc. They're very beautiful. And yes, I'm perfectly well today.'

They exchanged looks for a long moment before Emily turned away.

'Please go on into the drawing room while I put the roses in water. Help yourself to a glass of sherry; oloroso or dry, whichever you prefer.'

'Thank you.' Luc bowed his dark head formally and did as she suggested while Emily laid the coat on the settle in the hall and took the flowers to the kitchen. Her pulse was more rapid than usual. Which was only to be expected under the circumstances, after all, hardly the result of realising how very attractive Luc still was, especially in the black velvet jacket and silver-grey trousers and shirt he was wearing. When she went back to the drawing-room he was standing before the blazing fire, a glass of sherry in his hand.

'May I pour one for you?' he hesitated. 'I'm sorry, I should refer to you as Mrs Lacey. I'm afraid I forgot when I arrived.'

'No,' said Emily quickly. 'I'd rather you didn't. Emily will do. I'll have the oloroso, please.' She took the glass he filled for her and drank deeply, glad of the warmth of the wine, which had an immediate calming effect.

'There is something very comforting about an open fire,' he remarked quietly, leaning against the mantelpiece. 'Something we rarely have in Campo d'Ouro, except on the coldest of nights.'

'It's a necessity here.' Emily seated herself in the corner of one of the sofas. 'We do have central heating, of course, but the rooms are large and high-ceilinged—in winter we need the fire to make this room habitable.'

There was silence for a while, prolonging and stretching until the room was filled with tension.

'This is a very difficult situation,' said Luc finally. 'I came to give my reason, Emily, for what happened and did not happen, after I left you that last time. It is not easy. You were a shy young girl then, and now you are the poised lady of the Manor.' He looked at her searchingly. 'Though I sense none of the hostility you displayed last night.'

'No,' she admitted. 'I—well, I suppose I bullied Lydia into telling me a few pertinent facts after you left. Apart from that I was not precisely myself, as you can appreciate. I'm sorry if I was unreasonable. After all, you weren't to know it was the day of the funeral. Also I'm not the "lady of the Manor", as you put it. This is merely the Dower House, where Marcus lived after he handed Compton Lacey to the National Trust.'

'Will you continue to live here?'

'No. It was part of the bequest to the Trust. Marcus had an agreement that he would stay here until his death, then the Dower House becomes Trust property too.'

Luc frowned.

'But what will happen to you and—your son?'

'We're moving away from the district.' Emily held out her glass to be refilled and Luc did so abstractedly.

'Should not the child have inherited this house?' he asked, his heavy brows meeting in perplexity.

'The arrangement was made before he knew of Jamie's advent, and I wouldn't allow him to alter it in any way.' Emily stood up quickly and changed the subject. 'Will you have dinner with me, Luc? It's the simplest of meals, but you're quite welcome to share what I have.'

Luc was plainly taken aback.

'If you are sure I do not intrude. I had expected to return to the White Hart to dine, but naturally I would prefer to remain with you.' He paused, holding her eyes with his. 'I remember with utmost clarity the last time we dined together.'

Emily kept her face blank.

'I'm afraid I can't remember what I gave you to eat,' she lied, smiling politely. 'Tonight it's what we call "pot luck" in this country.'

He gave an oddly formal little bow.

'As a foreigner I am hardly likely to understand, but am more than happy to find out by sharing this "pot luck" with so charming a companion.'

With the feeling that Luc was deliberately turning on the Latin charm, Emily led the way to the dining room, which by day gave a splendid view of the Manor House from the long windows, but tonight was elegant by candlelight, its atmosphere very much that of the third George when it was built. The dead white of the paintwork on the pilasters and cornices was in direct contrast to the soft mushroom-brown paint of the walls, and the straw-coloured heavy satin curtains drawn against the chill of the night.

Emily waved Luc to the chair opposite her at the oval table and went to fetch in the tureen of soup. Luc watched her ladling the savoury mixture into Royal Doulton bowls, her delicately cut face closed and concentrated on her task.

'You do not have servants?' he asked, as they began their meal.

'Not in the way you mean. I have a daily woman who comes in some days, otherwise I manage alone.'

Luc accepted a piece of the crusty French loaf she offered.

'And your son? You have no help with him?'

'I don't need any. In this country one looks after one's own children, unless the mother has a career. My career at the moment is bringing up Jamie.'

'Does this content you?'

'Yes, indeed. He's a happy little soul, which is—only to be expected.'

Luc obviously noticed her hesitation but said nothing, applying himself to the soup and merely commenting on its excellence.

'Do have plenty,' urged Emily brightly. 'The second course is not over-exciting.'

However, when she set the piping-hot quiche on the table, flanked by the crisp winter salad in a crystal bowl and a platter of baked potatoes, their skins slit and stuffed with sour cream and chives, Luc was adamant that the White Hart could not have provided anything more delicious than Emily's pot luck.

They chatted generally while they ate, both deliberately avoiding every subject which might become emotive. Gradually Emily began to relax and recapture some of the ease she had felt with Luc during their brief time together long before, and by the time they were once again seated in front of the drawing room fire, drinking coffee, the atmosphere was a great deal more cordial than prior to the meal. Emily scanned the contents of the drinks cupboard and brought out a bottle of Remy Martin fine champagne cognac, handing the fragile balloon glass to Luc with no constraint when she told him the brand had been Marcus's favourite.

'You are brave for one who must be grief-stricken,' said Luc, finally deserting the impersonal and plunging back into the sphere of relationships.

Emily sipped the very small quantity of Grand Marnier in her glass and considered a little before she answered.

'I don't think bravery comes into it,' she said reflectively, then impulsively leaned over to touch his hand, 'and please don't think I'm insulting your command of the niceties of the English language!'

Luc's hand tensed beneath the touch of her fingers and Emily removed them hastily, taking refuge in refilling their coffee cups.

'I became accustomed to the fact that Marcus would die, because I was aware from the first that this would be sooner rather than later in his case. He had leukaemia, and there were several recessions in the progress of the disease before the final, terminal stage, which made it easier to be resigned to the eventual fact of his death when it finally occurred. I did a lot of my actual grieving in the days before his death, which makes my present behaviour possibly more explicable to you.'

Luc was sitting with one long leg crossed over the other, displaying the fine black leather of the half-boot he wore, one elbow on the arm of the settee, his chin on his supporting hand. The brooding look he turned on her hinted at an inner disquiet at odds with his outer appearance of relaxation.

'He was fortunate to have you by his side at the end,' he said quietly. 'He must have taken great delight in his son, though you must be very tired after coping with an invalid and a baby. You are very thin; motherhood has not changed you much.'

Emily flushed, ignoring the last part of his comment.

'Jamie was always a source of happiness to Marcus, though, of course, towards the end it wasn't possible for them to be together for any length of time. More cognac?'

Luc declined and there was silence for a while.

'Emily,' he said eventually, sitting up straight, bracing himself for what he was about to say, 'I have come six thousand miles to talk to you, and though I began badly by presenting myself on the day of your husband's funeral, I would be glad if you could bring yourself to hear me out.'

'Of course,' agreed Emily, settling herself to listen. 'That was the reason I allowed you to come tonight, as I imagine your time in this country is restricted.' Silently she marvelled at the formality of their conversation. No one listening would ever have suspected that for a fleeting few days they had once been so close.

'When I left you that morning, Emily,' he began huskily, 'I was torn apart I was—shattered at the news about my father, agonised at leaving you so precipitately when we had just—just——'

'Become lovers,' suggested Emily calmly.

'As you say,' he agreed. 'The flight back to Rio was one of the least enjoyable experiences of my life, to make an understatement. My mind was in a—turmoil?—the whole way, half of me frantic with concern for my father, the other half unable to forget the moments when I held you in my arms, when——'

'Perhaps you could cut out the more emotional bits,' interrupted Emily restlessly.

'I'm sorry. I have no wish to offend you.' Luc took a deep breath before continuing. 'In Rio I took a taxi from the one airport, Galeao, to the other, internal airport, Santos Dumont, and the cab was involved in an accident. I was thrown against the window and hit my head. I remember nothing else until I woke up in hospital with no recollection of my trip to the U.K., or that my father was ill. My amnesia was temporary. Little by little things began to return to my mind, but only in fragments. I knew there was something wrong—badly wrong. When I found that my father had died before I even reached hospital I thought that this was the cause of the terrible feeling of anxiety that consumed me. But back in Campo d'Ouro, with all the aftermath of my father's death to deal with, my grandmother to console in the loss of her beloved only son, this feeling, this almost insupportable feeling, still persisted. My grandmother was highly sensitive to my distress and did her best to help me remember the missing gap in my time in England. One day she remembered the name of the hotel they cabled to call me home, and as soon as she mentioned the White Hart everything fell into place.'

Luc took out a fine lawn handkerchief and passed it over his forehead. Emily got up and fetched the bottle of Remy Martin.

'I think you'd better drink a little more of this, Luc.' She looked at him levelly. 'There's no need to go on. Lydia put me very loosely in the picture last night. I mean, she just gave me the bare details.'

'I am being too Latin and undisciplined for you?' he said, a wry smile at the corners of his mouth. He pushed a hand through his crisply curling hair, accepting the cognac Emily offered him with appreciation.

'I'm not knocking you, Luc, but it was a long time ago, and it's all over now. I was bitter at the time, but not now.'

'You were bitter yesterday,' he reminded her, frowning.

'I had no idea you were even alive until yesterday,' she retorted, sitting down again. 'You could have been in orbit round the moon for all I knew—that is until I pressurised Lydia into telling me about your little arrangement.'

'Then I think I should put you "in the picture", I think you said, even more accurately,' he went on relentlessly, his emotions obviously now well in hand. 'I immediately telephoned Mrs Crawford, not even remembering the time difference. Did she tell you it was in the middle of the night for her?' Emily shook her head. 'I could hardly take it in when she told me you were married. It was impossible to believe that you had married your cousin so short a time after we had—we had——'

'Had sex together?' said Emily brutally.

The colour left Luc's face, leaving him grey beneath the tan. He stood up slowly, setting his glass down on the tray with great care, his mouth compressed, rigid with distaste.

'I do not feel——' he began, but was interrupted by a sharp cry of anguish from upstairs.

Emily tore out of the room with a muttered apology over her shoulder, running upstairs at top speed to the heartbroken sounds coming from her son's room. Jamie was sitting up in his cot, his arms held out in piteous supplication, the reason for his distress immediately obvious. He had been very, very sick. Emily grabbed a towel from the low chair she used to change him and enveloped her sobbing little son in it, cradling him to her fiercely while she looked for somewhere to lay him down for a moment.

'Mum—mum—mum,' hiccuped the flushed little boy, clutching her convulsively, his sobs beginning to subside.

'Never mind, my lovely boy,' she crooned, 'it was that nasty old fish, I expect.' She laid him gently on the furry rug beside his cot, still in his cocoon of towel, while she gathered up the sheets from the cot and ran into the bathroom to dump them in the white pail kept for nappies. She flew back into the bedroom and gathered up her son, taking him into the bathroom to remove his sleeping suit and sponge him down. When he was comfortable and dry Emily stood irresolute for a moment.

'I'm going to have to put you down for a moment while I

do your bed,' she said to the drowsy baby, then jumped as a voice spoke from the doorway.

'Perhaps you had better give him to me,' said Luc softly, holding out his arms, his eyes on the child's face. Emily clutched Jamie to her breast instinctively.

'No, really, he'll ruin your jacket—I can manage.' She was breathless with embarrassment, and something else, which could only be fear.

'Emily.' Luc spoke without inflection, and silently she surrendered the relaxed little body of her son to him. She turned away sharply and began to sponge the plastic-covered cot mattress, drying it energetically and fetching fresh sheets and blankets from the white chest of drawers beneath the window. In complete silence she remade the little bed, then turned back to Luc for Jamie, who was now fast asleep. Without a word he brushed past her and laid the little boy on the mattress, tucking the fleecy blanket gently round him. They both stood in silence, looking down at the mop of black curls against the white sheet. The child gave a great sigh, then opened bright dark eyes amd smiled up at Emily.

'Mum—mum,' he murmured, then his thumb went into his mouth and he settled down in his usual little curled-up ball, fast asleep before the two looking down at him turned away to tiptoe quietly from the room.

They went downstairs still enclosed in the same chill shell of silence until they reached the drawing room, where Luc pointed out a silver-framed photograph on a glove table between the two long windows.

'Marcus Lacey, I think,' he said quietly.

Emily nodded, looking at the coloured photograph of the slim man in a tweed jacket and riding breeches, his labrador alongside him gazing up in adoration at the man who smiled at the camera, his eyes narrowed a little against the light, but their colour perfectly visible for all that. They were the same shade of light, bright blue as the girl who looked up in apprehension at the man staring fixedly at the photograph.

CHAPTER SIX

THAT night Emily lay twisting and turning in the grip of a terrible cold anxiety that sent her several times into the next room to hover over Jamie's cot, looking yearningly down at the soundly sleeping baby.

If only Luc had said more, she thought wretchedly, getting into bed for the third time, but he had just gone on looking at the photograph of Marcus without moving a muscle, as though mesmerised by the sight of the thin, aristocratic face. Something in his stance told Emily very clearly that he was consumed by rage. Whether it was directed at herself personally she found difficult to tell. She had stood there, hardly daring to breathe, expecting him to turn on her with a torrent of accusation, demanding explanations, but Luc remained silent, eventually wishing her goodnight, thanking her for the meal, ignoring the incident upstairs as though it had never happened. She had followed his lead, behaving like the conventional hostess, and they had taken leave of each other like two polite strangers. Emily's hand had been on the door, ready to close it behind Luc's tall, elegant figure, her whole body beginning to relax with relief, when he had turned almost casually and smiled, a mere muscular movement of his mouth that left his eyes cold.

'I shall be back in the morning, Emily. Early. I would like to make the acquaintance of—our son.'

Emily had stood at the open doorway long after Luc's car had accelerated down the gravelled drive, until the realisation that she was shaking with cold and reaction had galvanised her into life again, and she had locked the house and cleared away the dinner things in a frenzy of haste, desperate to get to bed and try to come to terms with a situation she had never imagined would exist.

Instead of being Latin and emotional Luc had shown all the animation of a block of granite. The sight of the baby seemed to have rendered him speechless and icy. What did she expect?

thought Emily, burrowing into her hot pillows. A great dramatic scene, with cries of 'My son, my son!' and 'Why did you not tell me?' would have been embarrassing in the extreme. Of course, it was her own fault; sheer stupidity not to have hired a babysitter and met Luc outside somewhere. The very next day after Marcus was buried? enquired a polite inner voice; a marvellous story for the village that would have been! If only Jamie hadn't been sick, poor baby, then Luc need never have laid eyes on him. He could have said his say and gone on to Cornwall, or wherever, to transact whatever business had brought him to this country, and that would have been that. Finis. Nothing would convince Emily that he had come all this way solely to see her. And now what? Luc was coming back in the morning with what purpose in mind? she wondered. Would he demand that she hand over his son? But he could hardly do that, when, as far as the world was concerned, Jamie was Marcus Lacey's son. If anyone suspected any different from the sheer genetic impossibility of two fair, blue-eyed people producing an olive-skinned, black-eyed baby, no one had ever mentioned it to Emily's face.

None of her thoughts gave Emily any comfort, and it was a pale, wan mother with dark shadows under her eyes who got wearily out of bed next morning in response to the urgent cries of hunger from her son's room.

All through dressing Jamie and giving him his breakfast, Emily was tense and worried, anxious in case she communicated her state of mind to the little boy. But he sat happily in his high chair while his mother disposed of the laundry and cleared away the breakfast things, banging on the tray in front of him with a spoon, and drinking the milk Emily gave him without a murmur.

Giving thanks that this was not one of Mrs Giles's mornings, Emily defiantly set up the playpen in the drawing room. Luc might as well make Jamie's acquaintance first as last, and the baby sat gurgling happily amongst building blocks and various furry animals while Emily lit the fire, and whisked round the room with a duster in a fever of impatience to be ready and waiting when Luc arrived. God only knew what Luc meant by 'in the morning'. She should have asked him to be more specific, but it couldn't be helped. By nine Emily was doggedly pushing the electric polisher over the parquet floor in the hall, one eye through the open door of the drawing room on Jamie, when the doorbell rang. She took a despairing look down at herself, pushed her hair out of her eyes and yanked the door open on a blandly smiling Luc, who stood there affably, in a heavy cable-patterned white sweater and black cords over the leather boots of the previous evening. His comprehensive survey of her own dishevelled appearance did nothing to improve Emily's disposition, and conscious of her faded denims and much washed, rather tight pink jumper, her 'Good morning' was scarcely brimming over with warmth.

'You were not expecting me so early?' he enquired as Emily shut the door with a rather unnecessary bang.

'You said "morning", not the crack of dawn,' she answered irritably, and directed him into the drawing room. 'Well, here's the person you've come to see, I presume, so let me introduce you to—my son, James. Only I call him Jamie.'

Luc stood with hands on hips smiling down at the little boy, who, not in the least shy, shuffled nearer on his bottom and offered Luc his woolly rabbit, displaying his milky teeth in his usual irresistible smile. Luc squatted down on his heels and accepted the toy solemnly, stretching out a hand to touch the dark mop of curls gently, his dark eyes tender.

'He is beautiful, Emily,' he said huskily, not turning his head.

'Yes.' Emily's irritation evaporated. 'He's so happy and cheerful, I'm amazed at my good fortune sometimes. The only roaring I get is when his lunch is overdue, or just a bit when he's teething, and of course for something like last night. Though he's never been sick like that before.'

Luc detached his fingers reluctantly from Jamie's and stood up, his handsome face cold as he looked squarely down at Emily.

'Perhaps we may regard Jamie's sickness as an act of God, Emily, for I have the distinct impression that otherwise I might never have made his acquaintance. Am I right?'

She nodded dumbly, the colour flooding her cheeks, her eyes dropping before the accusation burning in his.

'Why, Emily? *Deus*, tell me why!'

'Until two days ago I didn't know you were even alive!' She flung it at him like a gauntlet. 'Lydia did. You made her keep silent. But all the time you knew everything that happened to me. Why could I not have known that you were at least alive——'

'But you were married to another man,' he cut in, nostrils flaring. 'So how could it have made any difference?'

'How can you be so obtuse!' Emily flung away to one of the long windows looking out into the winter chill of the garden, and with a swift glance at Jamie, who appeared quite unaffected by the emotions seething in the room, Luc followed her and stood close behind her, his voice low in her ear.

'When Lydia told me that you were married to Marcus Lacey, I presumed that you were merely carrying on with an arrangement understood before you met me. I knew he allowed you to live rent-free in the cottage; I suspected then that he took more than the remote interest in you that you insisted was all he felt.'

Emily took a deep breath and turned on him, her eyes cold and bright, like acquamarines in the pinched pallor of her face.

'When I didn't hear from you, through the agony of those hours and days after you left, I felt I had experienced the ultimate in unhappiness. I was wrong. In my sheer ignorance and grief I ignored certain messages that my body was trying to transmit. It wasn't until one afternoon up at the Manor after the visitors had gone that all became hideously clear. Colonel Hammond, the custodian, was in America on a lecture tour, and Marcus had taken over pro tem. He found me in the solar, desperately trying to get downstairs to the garden door before I was sick or fainted. Happily the latter overtook me first, which saved messing up National Trust property, and Marcus brought me here to the Dower House to recover.' She broke off to return to the fire to warm herself before the blaze, absently picking up a teddy bear Jamie had pitched out of his pen. She handed the toy to her son, smiling at him reassuringly before looking at Luc.

'Come and sit down, Luc, and I'll try to finish my little tale in a more reasonable manner.' Emily sat down on one of the sofas, waving Luc to the one opposite, but he sat beside her and took one of her hands.

'Go on, Emily,' he said quietly, and after a moment she took up her narrative, her face averted from him.

'That little incident took place about two months after you were here. In the face of Marcus's kindness I poured out my tale of woe, and he was obliged to point out that it was just possible I might be pregnant, even though he was a bachelor, and not really fitted to pass judgement on such things.' Emily turned a wry smile on Luc. 'Talk about stupid! After a little hasty basic arithmetic I realised how right he was, and felt as though the sky had fallen in. Up to now it had been tragedy as far as I was concerned, but the new development spelled disaster plus. Marcus was a tower of strength. He took me home and told me to sleep on it while he thought things over. Needless to say, I didn't sleep very well, but somehow having someone else involved in my problem made things marginally easier to bear.'

Luc shifted restlessly.

'*Deus*—if only I had known!' He shook his head as if to clear something from his vision. 'Go on, Emily.'

'Marcus came next day and suggested two courses of action he thought open to me. The first was that he try to trace you. I couldn't even remember the name of the town where you lived,' let alone what area it was in, and besides——' Emily paused.

'And besides?' he prompted, squeezing her hand gently.

'Put yourself in my place. I didn't know if you were alive or dead. There was every possibility that your father, poor man, *had* died. Even if we were able to make contact with your grandmother, how could I possibly burden her with a sorry tale from an unknown girl who claimed to be expecting her grandson's child?'

'But I was not dead.'

'No.' Emily's head lifted proudly. 'But the silence from you hardly encouraged me to acquaint you with my little problem. If you were alive I thought you'd just forgotten me.'

'Which I had, Emily. I had forgotten everything, or nothing in the world would have kept me from returning to you,' he said passionately.

Emily withdrew perceptibly.

'Possibly. But at the time begging had no appeal for me, even in my rather desperate circumstances. So Marcus suggested I marry him then and there. He told me about the leukaemia and how his life expectancy was not great. He had dreaded spending his remaining time alone, and somehow managed to convince me that I would be doing him as great a service as he was doing for me. I might add that his quiet way of describing his death sentence brought everything into proportion with an almighty click. My problem seemed suddenly minimal when compared to his.'

Luc moved to restore Jamie to a sitting position after the baby had fallen over on his back like a stranded duckling. He paused to look at Marcus's photograph before returning to sit by Emily.

'I would have been honoured to know him,' he said quietly. 'I apologise for my previous attitude.'

Emily shrugged.

'You weren't to know. We went off to London the very next day, and returned to Compton Lacey after two weeks with our marriage a fait accompli. It was the usual village nine-day wonder, of course.'

'But how——' Luc hesitated. 'Forgive me, but Jamie's arrival in the world was a little early by conventional standards.'

'Normally it would have been. Lydia and the family doctor knew the truth, of course. Up to then I had said nothing about my pregnancy to Lydia; after all, idiot that I was, I hadn't realised myself until my system gave me a nudge. I had the baby right here at the Dower House, with only the doctor and Lydia in attendance after a miserable waiting period when I felt nauseated the whole time. Poor Marcus swore that he had no time to get on with his leukaemia because he was so busy trying to keep me in one piece.' Emily's eyes filled with sudden tears and Luc's hand tightened on hers while he fished in his pocket and produced a folded white handkerchief.

Emily blew in it prosaically, mopping herself before going on.

'Jamie only weighed four and a half pounds, so it was very easy for Lydia to give the merest hint to Mrs Giles, the daily woman, that he was premature. He was so small that no one questioned it—I almost believed it myself, except for those black eyes of his that left me in no doubt. His appearance was the one thing neither Marcus nor I could do anything about. But with Marcus suddenly progressing to the terminal stage of his illness I haven't really taken Jamie out and about much except for walks in the grounds, and possibly Mrs Giles isn't too heavily into genetics to question any doubt about Jamie's parentage.'

Luc looked over at Jamie, who was absorbed in trying to balance one block on another. He smiled with a gleam of pure possession in his eyes.

'It is good that I am not known locally. Jamie looks exactly like me.'

Emily nodded in agreement.

'Carbon copy. It's been a bit painful lately as he's begun to grow out of the indeterminate baby stage and started to develop more strongly marked features. I've seen you looking at me out of his eyes.'

'And that was unwelcome to you?'

'Can you blame me?'

'No, Emily,' he said heavily, 'I cannot blame you. I know very well it does not lessen your love for him. Last night you stood like a tigress at bay when I came upstairs. I thought for a moment you would refuse to give Jamie to me.'

'I didn't want to,' said Emily honestly. 'But something about you commanded instant obedience.' She stood up as a wail came from the playpen and went to scoop the little boy up in her arms.

'What is the matter?' Luc's voice was alarmed as he stood close behind her. 'Is he ill?'

'Don't you know anything about babies?' Emily grinned at the worried frown on his face. 'Jamie has a little internal alarm clock which goes off mid-morning. It means his nappy needs changing and it's time for milk for him and coffee for us.'

Luc's face altered dramatically at the word 'us' and he reached for her, baby and all. But Emily dodged out of reach, Jamie in front of her like a shield.

'No, Luc,' she said softly. 'Nothing's altered.'

His mouth tightened and he stood back, his arms folded across his chest, glowering down at her.

'I do not understand,' he said, with a sulky look so like his son's that Emily had to restrain a smile.

'You've been extraordinarily good over all this,' she said reasonably. 'I appreciate what a remarkable restraint you placed on yourself last night when you were obviously thunderstruck by seeing Jamie.'

'Thunderstruck?'

'Well, astonished—shocked,' amended Emily hastily. 'Now I'm going to make my son smell a little less anti-social and when I come back down I'll make us some coffee. Would you like the morning paper?'

Luc shook his head emphatically.

'I will come with you and watch.'

'It's not exactly enthralling watching me change a dirty nappy!'

'For me it is. You forget, I have missed nine months of my son's life already. I have much to make up.' Luc relieved her deftly of his unprotesting son, striding swiftly from the room with a protesting Emily in his wake.

'Be careful of your sweater, Luc. Jamie, stop it!'

The latter had a handful of his father's thick black hair, and was pulling it gleefully, giving way to ecstatic giggles at the shouts of mock anguish issuing from this large new playmate.

'*O bichinho feio,*' panted Luc as they reached Jamie's bedroom. 'I shall be bald! Where do I put him?'

He laid the wriggling little body on the wide padded surface of the chest of drawers as instructed, and anchored him there with one long hand while Emily produced nappy, cream and a clean pair of dungarees.

'He is a handful for you, Emily, and will get more so as time goes on. No wonder you are so—skinny, I think you say.'

'That's right. How kind,' said Emily composedly, quickly undressing and cleaning up her son. 'But he won't always be in nappies—I should have potted him this morning, but I was so wrapped up in my woes I forgot. Now, up you come, you rascal!' She buried her face in the little boy's neck, blowing against the silky soft skin. 'Come on then, Jamie, I'll go and make coffee and you can go to——' She stopped, while her eyes met and clashed with Luc's above Jamie's unsuspecting head.

Luc took the child from her and held him in the crook of one arm while his other hand held Emily's wrist as he marched her from the room. The trio descended the stairs in silence, pausing at the drawing-room door.

'Your mother will go and make coffee,' said Luc, addressing his son, who gazed back at him attentively as though he understood every word, 'while you come in here and talk to—your daddy.'

Emily's wrist was released and she was left, feeling oddly forlorn for a moment before she went into the kitchen and put coffee to percolate. She glanced down at herself with distaste and ran back upstairs, hurriedly stripping off her jeans and sweater and pulling on a cream silk double-breasted shirt and soft charcoal flannel trousers which she tucked into calf-length grey suede wrinkly boots. She brushed her streaky fair hair and caught it away from her face on one side with a mother-of-pearl barrette, sprayed on some 'Chloe', added a touch of beige-pink lipstick and ran back down to the kitchen just as the thermostat light on the percolator went out.

Breathless, she set a tray with coffee cups, warmed some milk for Jamie, poured it into his lidded, spouted mug, and took the lot in to the drawing room to join the men. Luc was standing by the window with Jamie in his arms, pointing out the distant cows grazing in the parkland and various other objects of interest, including his hired car, which was parked just outside. He swivelled as Emily came in with the tray, his eyebrows shooting up into his hair at her transformation.

'Look, Jamie, *que Mamae bonita*,' he said softly in the baby's ear, and as though he was quite conversant with Portuguese the little boy promptly held out his arms with his usual 'Mum—mum.'

Emily's cheeks were pink as she put the tray on the fireside table and took Jamie from Luc.

'He goes back into his pen now for his drink,' she said hurriedly, giving Jamie a smacking kiss as she sat him down in the playpen and handed him his mug.

She seated herself sedately behind the coffee tray and poured a cup for Luc, telling him to help himself to sugar.

'I was hoping for something sweeter,' he said gravely as he accepted the cup. 'You gave Jamie a kiss with his.'

To Emily's annoyance she went scarlet, her poise shattered momentarily.

'Please, Luc,' she said repressively, 'let's keep things impersonal. It will be much easier that way.' She drank her coffee rapidly, heedless of whether it scorched her throat on the way down.

'For whom, Emily?' he mocked her silently across the long table. 'Not for me. I remember a different Emily, one who allowed me to become very personal indeed.'

'That's a very underhand sort of crack to make.' Emily kept her voice level by sheer will-power. 'That's all in the past. Things are different now.'

Luc leaned forward, his attitude implicit with menace.

'It is *not* in the past, Emily. We have a living reminder sitting there looking at us right now. *Deus*, can you imagine how I feel, when I have a son who is my image, and yet he bears another man's name?' He flung himself back into a corner of the settee, one booted ankle flung across his knee, his face black with anger.

'That's not exactly my fault,' retorted Emily, stung by the injustice of his words.

'I know,' he said more reasonably. 'It is no one's *fault*. But just to look at Jamie gives me such a surge of feeling—I had no idea how much I craved fatherhood until I saw him clutched in your arms last night. I was not trying to take him away from you, Emily, but the urge to hold him in my arms was irresistible.' He thrust an impatient hand through his hair, looking at her in entreaty. 'Do you understand?'

'Oh yes, I understand.' Emily sighed, then glanced at her watch. 'Look, do you want to stay to lunch? I must give Jamie his shortly, then he has a nap. Or do you have to get back to the hotel?'

'May I spend the day here with you—and Jamie?' Luc leaned forward, his hands clasped between his knees. 'Today is Tuesday; I must go back at the weekend. There is not much time.'

'When do you go to Cornwall?'

'Cornwall?' Luc looked blank. 'I am not going to Cornwall. Why do you ask?'

'I thought you must be on a business trip like last time.'

'Emily, I thought I had made myself clear. I came to England solely to see you.' Luc's voice was passionate in its sincerity and Emily moved restlessly, discomfited.

'I find it difficult to take in,' she said tonelessly. 'You knew me for such a brief while. Why should it have had such an effect on you?'

He closed his eyes for a moment, jaw clenched, as though hanging on to the last shred of patience.

'Nossa Senhora!' he said violently, then opened his eyes, glaring at her so fiercely Emily instinctively shrank back into her corner of the settee. 'I was almost thirty when I met you—not exactly a boy. I had known other women, of course, even considered one or two as prospective brides, but never with sufficient enthusiasm to do anything about it. My father and my grandmother kept dropping broad—hints?—about marrying and producing sons to carry on the name, but always they hoped I would find someone to love. I did.' Luc jerked his head violently towards the window. 'Across the park, in that old house, I found a girl daydreaming one afternoon, and instantly I knew why no other woman had ever appealed to me for long. You were what I wanted. God knows why—you are not stunningly beautiful.'

Emily was well aware of this, but it hurt to hear him put it into words so baldly. Luc smiled derisively.

'You do not have a voluptuous figure, even now after giving birth to a child. But one look from those dreaming blue eyes and I was lost. Now are you beginning to understand?'

Emily refused to comment, her eyes falling to her tightly clasped hands.

'When I knew you'd married someone else,' he continued bleakly, 'I did my utmost to forget you. But I could not. When Mrs Crawford wrote to me to say you had borne a child last August——'

'It was June, actually,' murmured Emily.

Luc's expression softened a little.

'Yes, of course—it must have been. But I did not know that then. For a while I tried to put you out of my mind, worked an eighteen-hour day and drove everyone mad, but eventually I gave in and started writing to Mrs Crawford again. It was like some sickness that was incurable.'

'Hardly.' Emily's voice was cold.

'No,' he agreed soberly. 'I am sorry, that was a gauche thing to say. But I am trying to make clear how I felt—how I still feel. And yet you say that is all in the past. How can you expect me to agree? Is that really how *you* feel?'

'It's not as clear-cut as that.' Emily collected the coffee cups and rose to take Jamie's mug from the corner of the playpen. The baby automatically held up his hands.

'Mum—mum?' he said hopefully.

'In a minute, darling.' Emily smiled at him lovingly.

'May I pick him up, Emily?' Luc was beside her, an unexpected humility in his request.

She looked at him consideringly, then smiled faintly.

'Yes. You don't need to ask permission.'

'I would not like to upset any routine you and Jamie have, Emily.'

She laughed outright.

'We don't have any. I don't know whether Jamie's a good baby because of the way I've looked after him or in spite of it. He seemed to sense that I had to devote a lot of time to Marcus in the end, somehow. It was odd, now I come to think of it, how I never felt torn between the two.'

Luc picked up the eager little boy, rubbing his nose against the child's, which was a miniature version of his own. Emily watched indulgently while the tall man tossed the laughing child into the air, then carried the tray to the kitchen, stopping short as she laid the tray down on the big deal table. Guilt flooded her abruptly as she suddenly remembered how short a time had elapsed since the day Marcus died, but in the wake of the guilt came a feeling of serene certainty. Her heart lifted. Marcus would want her to be happy in any way she could. Emily frowned anxiously. The problem was that for the time being she had no idea which way that was.

When Luc appeared with Jamie Emily surprised him by asking what he had had for breakfast.

'Er—coffee, that's all,' he answered. 'Why, what did you have?'

'The same, I'm afraid. I was merely sounding out what to do about lunch. What do you say to some of last night's soup followed by good old bacon and eggs?'

'I'd say *"otimo, senhora"*—perfect, splendid, whatever translation you like.' Luc's sobriety of a moment ago was replaced by a gaiety that Emily found infectious.

'Right. How about having a go at feeding Jamie?' She took a ladle of vegetable soup from the pan at the back of the stove and poured it into a small bowl, directed Luc in strapping in the eager baby and tying on his bib, then handed Luc a spoon and provided him with a tea-towel to put in front of him.

'He'll try to grab the spoon,' she warned, 'but I'm not letting him feed himself just yet. Not until he's a bit more co-ordinated.'

It was hard to decide who enjoyed lunchtime more, Jamie or Luc, though by the end of it there was a great deal of soup on the floor, joined by some of the scrambled eggs that followed.

'Piglet!' scolded Emily as she mopped the tray and the rosy face above the bib. 'Though, to be fair, you're not entirely to blame!'

'I could play with him all day,' said Luc ingenuously, grinning at her with an expression so like Jamie's that Emily failed to hang on to her reproving frown.

'Would you like to have a shot at putting him to bed while I cook lunch—or will the nappy defeat you?'

Luc looked startled for a moment, but he bore Jamie off obediently after a few basic instructions.

'If I get nervous at a vital stage I shall yell for help,' he said over his shoulder.

'Don't worry, Luc, I'll come running,' said Emily reassuringly.

He stopped short in the doorway, his face suddenly serious. 'Always, Emily?'

'Don't push your luck,' she said shortly, and turned away. It seemed a very long time before the expected cri de coeur came from upstairs, and Emily sprinted up to find a very smug Luc holding a drowsy baby dressed in pyjama top and a fairly adequately fastened nappy.

'Will that do?' The anxious look on Luc's face made Emily giggle as she handed him plastic pants and pyjama trousers.

'Fantastic!'

They ate lunch at the kitchen table and tacitly avoided any personal matters. They discussed the problem of dinner, and Emily apologised that there was very little in the house she considered suitable for a hungry man without doing some shopping.

'I don't think I should go out myself so soon after the funeral,' she said diffidently, 'but otherwise I shall have to call on Lydia to help me out by fetching some groceries.'

Luc jumped to his feet instantly.

'No problem. Just tell me what you want and where I should go to buy it, and I'll come back and even cook for you as well, if you would like.'

Emily looked at him doubtfully.

'Are you sure? I can hardly believe that you're used to shopping, somehow. Besides, English food's probably a lot different from Brazilian.'

'You will write a list. I will take it to the shop and pay for what I receive. What could be simpler? Where is the nearest town?'

After thinking of the easiest way for Luc to tangle with the intricacies of British shopping Emily sent him into Knowle, a pleasant little town not too far away. Provided with the necessary list and scornfully turning aside Emily's attempt to hand over some money, Luc set off in the Daimler Sovereign he had hired, and she was left in the sudden tomb-like quiet of the empty house. Hurriedly she cleared away and went to have a bath while Jamie was asleep. She had just finished drying her hair when the doorbell rang, and checking to see that Jamie was still out for the count she ran downstairs to admit a Luc laden with plastic carriers.

'That looks like a great deal more than I asked for,' said Emily suspiciously when all the bags and packages were lined up on the table. Luc threw his black leather jacket carelessly on a chair, grinning at her with such a sheepish, guilty look she hadn't the heart to protest as, in quick succession, he produced with the air of a magician taking rabbits from a hat, a potted azalea, a large box of chocolates, a glossy magazine and a bottle of Guerlain's 'Mitsouko'.

'Luc! You were very naughty really—I had no idea you'd go raving mad!'

'There was no insanity involved,' he returned with dignity, his eyes sparkling with pleasure at the expression on her face as she opened the perfume. 'You look like a little girl on Christmas morning.'

'That's more or less the way I feel,' she confessed, then leaned over to kiss his cheek. 'Thank you very much, Luc.'

He tensed beneath her touch, and Emily drew back instantly.

'Do not worry,' he said quizzically. 'I will not step over the barrier you have placed between us.'

'Thank you,' said Emily quietly, then turned to the other bags cluttering the table. 'I must put these things away.'

'Where is Jamie?' asked Luc, springing to his feet.

'Still sleeping—good heavens, it's half past three, he'll never go down again tonight!' Emily groaned.

'I'll get him up.' Luc made for the door.

'No, Luc, wait—he might be nervous if a strange man is there when he wakes up.' Emily hastily caught him by the arm.

He shrugged her restraining hand away.

'Nonsense, Emily, I am his father, after all. He must get used to me.'

A very thoughtful Emily was left in the kitchen to begin preparations for dinner. There was something the matter with her, she decided. Any normal female would be over the moon at the way things had turned out, but it all seemed too easy, too pat. Luc had not stated any intentions to the letter, but it seemed pretty obvious that he thought they could just take up where they had left off. Her eyes troubled, Emily considered this with care, and found that it was not a prospect that pleased. Not that Luc was vile, of course, as the hymn went on to say, but neither he nor she were the same people who had come together for such a brief time eighteen months before.

As she removed the newspaper wrapping from some celery, Emily's eye was caught by the picture above an article on a sheet from the week-old *Daily Clarion*. She smoothed out the newspaper, frowning. The journalese in the tabloid-style paper was very expressive; quite different from the sober broadsheet delivered to the Dower House. Perhaps she should change her order to the newsagent. She folded the paper automatically and put it in a drawer.

By unspoken consent for the rest of the day both of them avoided any descent into the personal and contented themselves with playing with Jamie and seeing to his simple, easily provided needs. It was dark very early and Luc fetched in a large supply of logs from the woodshed to make a substantial blaze which gave the drawing room an air of warmth and comfort when the rose-shaded lamps were switched on and the curtains drawn against the chilly March day that was more like midwinter than the forerunner of spring. After his prolonged nap earlier on Jamie was less inclined for bed than usual, and Luc gave him his bath while Emily prepared the supper. When she went upstairs to put an end to the noisy, prolonged hi-jinks going on in the bathroom she found Luc stripped to the waist endeavouring to wrap a wriggling, excited little boy in a bath towel, both faces flushed with their exertions.

'I can only hope he'll settle down to sleep after all this disturbance,' said Emily, casting a cold eye on them both. 'Come along, young man, let's get you into your sleeping suit and ready for supper.'

Luc surrendered his burden and put his sweater back on.

'He's an energetic little bundle,' he said breathlessly, 'though I repeat, Emily, he must be quite a handful for you to cope with on your own.'

'I manage,' she said shortly, as he followed her from the room. 'Some people have a lot more than one to cope with, after all.'

Some time later, when Jamie was fast asleep and both of them were seated at the dining table, Luc poured out the wine purchased that afternoon, and said seriously,

'It's time we had a talk, Emily.'

'Not over dinner,' she said instantly. 'I've taken great pains with this pork fillet, not to mention the apricot and chili sauce, so I don't want any tension spoiling my appetite.'

'It was not my intention to upset you in any way,' he said stiffly, his brows drawn together in a black bar across his forehead. 'I merely wished to clarify the situation in which we find ourselves.'

'Later,' she insisted, and began to discuss the history of Compton Lacey, giving him details of the old house's occupants down the years. He listened with polite attention, but from his rather tense attitude Emily was well aware that his mind was only half on her words.

Eventually the moment of truth could no longer be postponed. They were settled opposite each other in the drawing room, drinking coffee, before Luc launched into the discussion he had been waiting to start for some time. He looked at Emily, curled up quietly in the corner of the settee, her face washed a pale gold by the leaping flames, and said the last thing she expected to hear.

'I do not like your dress,' he said harshly.

Emily looked down at herself defensively.

'It's not unusual for someone in my position to wear black,' she said distantly. Some perverse instinct had prompted her to wear the dress bought for the funeral.

'I do not need to be reminded that you are another man's widow,' he went on, then broke off abruptly. 'May I have a brandy?'

'Of course. Help yourself.'

The truce was suddenly over. Hostility crackled between them as she refused a liqueur, and Luc sat down again, asking her permission to light a cheroot.

'I want my son, Emily.'

'Quite possibly.' Her breathing quickened, but her voice was calm and cold. 'However, he is *my* son first and foremost. Your part in his existence was minimal.'

Luc's eyes narrowed through the smoke curling up in front of him.

'Nevertheless, I want Jamie. The obvious course is for you to marry me and come back to Campo d'Ouro as soon as possible. After all, there is nothing to keep you here in Compton Lacey any more. Very soon, presumably, you will not even have this house.'

Emily's head lifted proudly.

'I don't intend to live in Compton Lacey. I'm going to buy a house somewhere else, possibly further north, and bring

Jamie up away from this area.'

Luc sprang to his feet, his eyes glittering like jet in his fury.

'What are you saying? What is to keep you from marrying me? And why should you want to move away from here? *Deus*—if you are not to stay here then what is to prevent you coming to Brazil?'

'The simple reason that I don't want to!' Emily glared back at him.

He sank down on the sofa, staring at her in disbelief.

'Emily,' he said, slowly and distinctly, his accent more pronounced in his agitation, 'I am offering you a life in a beautiful house, where the climate is very good, where Jamie can have everything he wishes, and where he will be my heir.'

'Very tempting. But no, thanks.'

'*Deus me livre!* Why not? What is your objection?'

Emily raised her chin.

'What precisely is to be my part in all this?'

He closed his eyes as though summoning the last of his patience.

'I thought I had made myself clear,' he said wearily. 'I want you for my wife. I can give you security, even wealth to a moderate degree. You will want for nothing. Now I have seen you again I realise how very suitable you will be. You are poised and adult now, attractive, a very good mother—what more could a man wish?'

'I'm afraid I'm not concerned with how I fit into your specifications,' said Emily, looking him squarely in the eye. 'I don't want to leave this country.'

'But, woman, you know I cannot leave Campo d'Ouro—my livelihood is there——'

'I'm not asking you to,' she interrupted. 'I don't think joining our lives together now is a good idea.'

Luc stared at her in blank incomprehension.

'Why, Emily, why?'

She hesitated, then sighed.

'I don't love you, Luc.'

CHAPTER SEVEN

FOR several minutes the only sounds in the room were the spurt and crackle of the flames and the ticking of the grandmother clock in the corner. Eventually Luc got up and helped himself to another cognac, gazing down into it morosely for some time before he put the glass to his lips and drank the contents in one swallow.

He returned to the sofa, legs stretched before him, his eyes on her face in brooding fixation, which made Emily inwardly restive, though outwardly she remained composed, sitting quietly with one sheer black-clad ankle crossed over the other, her small hands folded in her lap, her head turned to gaze into the fire.

'Do you mean that, Emily?' he said quietly after an unbearably long interval.

'Yes. I'm sorry if it's hurtful, but on an important issue like this I think one can only deal in the truth.'

'But you loved me once?'

She nodded.

'But you were the knight in shining armour who came and swept me off my feet. How could I not imagine myself in love with you?' Emily's eyes were candid as she tried to explain logically. 'But all the other emotion I felt afterwards, the bleak disappointment, the hurt, the panic when I knew I was pregnant, the gratitude I felt for Marcus, then the grief, and of course my love for Jamie. Such a long list, Luc, that I think it used up everything I'd felt for you.'

He flinched and raked his hand through his hair until it was a wild, curling tangle above his colourless face.

'Very well,' he said curtly, 'I accept that. But why must you take Jamie away from here? Is it that you wish to conceal him from me?'

'Oh no!' Emily leaned forward urgently. 'I shan't stop you visiting him, Luc, if that's what you want.' She stopped for a moment, then went on resolutely, 'I told you that when

Marcus and I returned to Compton Lacey after a fortnight in London we announced that we'd been married there. This was sheer falsehood. Marcus was set on marrying me, but I felt it was neither fitting nor possible.'

Luc jerked bolt upright, staring at her.

'You mean . . .?

'Yes,' said Emily levelly. 'To all intents and purposes Marcus made everyone believe I was his wife. The only person who knows I'm not is the family solicitor. I had enough knowledge about the family to know that if I presented Marcus with an heir the complications would have been endless. As it is, everyone believes that the bequest to the National Trust was irreversible and I'm more or less obliged to seek a new home. And I'm going to live somewhere else where I'm going to be Mrs Harper and her son James. It's on his birth certificate. James Marcus Harper.'

Luc sat like a statue, his face blank and cold. Emily waited a moment then rose to her feet.

'I'll make more coffee, Luc. Do have another cognac—you look as though you need it.'

Out in the kitchen as she waited for the percolator, Emily's heartbeat began to slow down to normal. Underneath her outward calm she had been terrified of the effect on him of her disclosure. Poor man! He had obviously taken a body blow, but she was very certain of one thing. No way was she willing to trail meekly off to Brazil just because Luc wanted his son. Unreasonable, childish, Emily admitted it all to herself as she carried the coffee tray back to the drawing room, nevertheless a quiet little cottage near a good school somewhere was infinitely more tempting than some mountain fastness in the wilds of Brazil.

Luc was on his feet to relieve her of the tray, and she examined his face in trepidation, but he seemed to have recovered somewhat, and sat opposite her with a reasonably civil expression on his dark face while she filled their cups.

'If you were not married to Marcus Lacey,' he began, 'why will you not come with me? Surely you cannot wish Jamie to grow up with the stigma of illegitimacy. God!' Suddenly he banged one fist into the other, his anger at flashpoint again. 'My son a bastard! You felt it was neither "fitting" nor "possible" to let Marcus Lacey father my son; I agree. But neither is it "fitting" nor "possible" for you to bring him up alone.'

'Don't be so old-fashioned, Luc. There are plenty of one-parent families these days.'

'But those families don't have any choice!' he almost shouted. 'I am offering you my name, my home, a proper background for our son.'

'And that's what it boils down to, Luc. Tell me the truth.' Emily stood up to face him, hands on hips. 'You haven't really come all this way to see me. I think you suspected all along that this child just might have been yours, ever since you knew of his birth. While Marcus was alive there was nothing you could do about it, but once he was dead it was different.'

'I admit that it all seemed a little suspect to me—the hasty marriage, the premature birth. It all fitted in with what might be possible.' Luc ground his teeth impotently. 'I *wanted* it to be true; prayed that it was. When I followed you upstairs last night I cannot find words to describe how I felt at my first sight of Jamie. He is the living image of a photograph Thurza has of me at the same age.'

'Thurza?'

'My grandmother. I have always called her by her name,' he said impatiently. He poured himself a generous tot of brandy. 'Please sit down so that I may also do so.'

My God, thought Emily, with a wild desire to laugh, never mind the fact that we're in the middle of a blazing row, we must preserve our tribal rules and customs to the last letter.

'I think I'll change my mind,' she said. 'Perhaps you would please pour me a glass of Grand Marnier.'

'*Pois é.*' Watching his tall, graceful figure as he measured out a far larger quantity of liqueur than she normally permitted herself, Emily braced herself for further skirmishes, the warmth of the fire making her a little flushed above the uncompromising black of the high-necked wool crêpe dress. Luc strolled back slowly and handed her the glass, and with a faint feeling of alarm Emily realised his hand was the slightest bit unsteady as she took the drink from him.

'I am amazed,' he said, scowling at her. 'What can I say to make you change your mind?'

'The truth?' suggested Emily.

'What do you mean!' His eyes narrowed.

'Wait a moment.' She rose and went out of the room, returning almost immediately with a piece of crumpled newspaper. Luc took it from her gingerly, his face growing grim as he read it.

The photograph above the piece was a little blurred, but the headline below it left no room for doubt. 'Attractive young gold magnate arrives to address Anglo-Brazilian Society at banquet'. The date of the paper was two days before Marcus's death.

'So you came especially to see me,' said Emily quietly.

His eyes dropped before her limpid blue look, and he moved restlessly.

'Very well, I embroidered things a little. Would it help to know that I contacted Mrs Crawford as soon as I arrived in this country?'

'Not really. However, I now see how you knew about Marcus so quickly.' She drank her liqueur in one draught recklessly and set the glass down with a click on the silver gallery tray. 'Do you know why I feel so—unenthusiastic?'

He shook his head bleakly.

'I loathe the feeling that I've been watched, that you were receiving information about me as though I were some sort of criminal. Can't you see, Luc? If I'd known you were alive it would all have been so different. Yes, yes, I would have been upset, but at the same time I would have known that you cared. Even if we had had no direct communication I could have been rid of that awful uncertainty about you that hung over me until you appeared two days ago. It would have altered nothing as far as poor Marcus was concerned, but at least I would have felt a little less like a cheap, casual push-over who'd been taken for a night and immediately forgotten.'

'*Deus*, Emily!' Luc sprang to his feet, glowering at her, his eyes like two coals glowing in his livid face. 'How could I communicate with another man's wife?'

'The same way you did all along,' spat Emily, 'but Lydia could have been allowed to tell me—oh, what's the use!' She flung away, her head on her hands, and tried in vain to hold back the tears.

Luc's face convulsed with pain and he knelt beside her, touching her shoulder gently.

'Do not cry, Emily!'

Emily shrugged his hand away violently, ignoring the torrent streaming down her cheeks.

'I'm not crying!' she said fiercely, then looked up sharply in dismay as a familiar sound came from upstairs. 'Oh God, Jamie, and I'm crying! Have you a handkerchief—he's never seen me cry—I mustn't upset him——'

'Stay here,' said Luc gently. 'I shall go to him. If it is something I cannot manage I will call you.'

Emily sat tense, rubbing her face fiercely with Luc's handkerchief, listening for his call, but none came. Wearily she went to the dining room and cleared the table, an intermittent sob still shaking her and her head aching from emotion and wine as she began to wash up. Suddenly too lacklustre even to worry whether Luc was coping with Jamie, she doggedly washed and dried plates, careless of the delicate dinner service that was now National Trust property. She was storing them away in the sideboard when Luc came downstairs to find her.

'What was the matter?' she asked dully.

'I changed his nappy and gave him some orange juice. Was that correct?' Luc looked at her face with concern. 'I think he really wanted to play, but I resisted that smile and settled him down. Are you all right, Emily?'

'Just tired,' she said wearily. 'I've had very little sleep for some time now.'

'Come into the other room for a nightcap,' he said persuasively, 'then I must go. It is late.'

Emily complied docilely, accepting another glass of Grand Marnier, too listless to raise any objection when Luc sat beside her, glass of cognac in one hand, her own cold hand in the other. She stared mutely into the dying fire, a random sob still catching her occasionally. They sat in a not uncompanionable silence, each one lost in thought as the fire died away, and the levels in both bottles of spirit grew decidedly lower.

'Must go to bed,' muttered Emily eventually, realising with vague surprise that her head was on Luc's shoulder, and sitting up muzzily.

He made no answer, getting slowly to his feet. Emily was in no fit state to register the unnerving fact that Luc was not entirely steady on his feet, not even to protest when he picked her up in his arms, turned out the lights and slowly mounted the stairs. Luc looked round him as he reached the landing, then made for the open door nearest Jamie's, and laid his somnolent burden on the bed without troubling to switch on the light.

Almost asleep, Emily was hardly aware of hands that slowly undressed her and slid her between the sheets. She flinched a little as her bare skin came into contact with cold linen, then she gave a little sigh and relaxed into deep, sweet oblivion.

At some time during the night she came near enough to consciousness to be aware of a long, hard bare body pressed close to hers. She opened her mouth to protest, but was silenced by the mouth that covered it instantly, any rebellion her body might have attempted instantly quelled by hands that restrained, then caressed, then moved over it in gentle, ceaseless, cumulative pleasure that moulded the lifeless clay of her body into a warm, willing vessel fashioned to receive the rushing, molten, surging tribute of the body that engulfed and encompassed her own. Gasping, fulfilled, she subsided helplessly back into blessed sleep once more, locked in the warmth of arms that refused to loose their hold.

'Emily, is there anything wrong—Oh, my God!'

The door closed with a thud, and Emily sat bolt upright in bed, blinking like an owl. She looked down at her nudity aghast, then at the brown back of the man who lay fast asleep beside her, his face buried in the pillow.

She tore out of bed, making little moaning noises of horror, threw on her dressing gown, vainly smoothing back the tangled mess of her hair.

Jamie! Emily closed the bedroom door firmly behind her and flew into her son's room to find him still fast asleep in his cot, neatly tucked up beneath the coverlet. She ran down the stairs and into the kitchen to find Lydia filling a kettle.

'Lydia!'

The other woman spun round, her face a picture of mingled remorse, laughter and embarrassment.

'What can I say, Emily! I do apologise. I called round before work to see what I could do for you, and the back door was unlocked, no Jamie in evidence—I thought perhaps you were ill.' She screwed up her eyes in repentance. 'I'm so used to barging into people's bedrooms unannounced I just didn't think.'

'Why should you?' Emily groaned and collapsed into a chair at the kitchen table, head in hands. 'You'd hardly expect to find anyone in mine, after all. Oh, my head!'

Lydia made a large pot of tea, then stirred the embers in the stove and set the fire to draw.

'I came along the back lane, otherwise I would have seen his car, I presume, and avoided embarrassing you like that,' she said ruefully.

'It really doesn't matter, Lydia,' said Emily apathetically.

'You seem to have settled your differences fairly quickly, anyway!' Lydia's eyes twinkled naughtily.

'But we haven't—I didn't—oh, God, how can I explain——' Emily wailed.

'You don't have to explain anything to me, pet. It's your business entirely.' Lydia poured out two mugs of fragrant tea and sat down opposite.

Emily opened one eye.

'Come off it, Lydia, you and Luc have been pen-pals all along, so you can hardly start playing the disinterested bystander! Mmm, what heavenly tea; my head is splitting.'

'At the risk of appearing nosy, what on earth did you get up to last night? And how come Jamie is still fast asleep at eight in the morning?'

'He had such excitement yesterday he didn't settle down properly last night. Luc and I had rather a rich dinner—he went shopping—with a large bottle of wine, followed by a flaming row and a great deal too much Grand Marnier on my part—ugh!—and cognac on Luc's. As for the rest of the night's events, I can only plead diminished responsibility, m'lud. I don't know why I'm joking—I feel ghastly!'

Lydia stifled her amusement with difficulty.

'I take it Luc has seen Jamie, then?'

'Oh yes; mutual love at first sight. They're besotted with each other.' Emily turned a mutinous look on Lydia. 'He tried to make out he came to England just to see me.'

'Can't blame him, love!'

'No. But I feel very bitter about what I can only consider as an infringement on my personal privacy. Don't be upset—I'm not blaming you, only Luc. And I deeply resent the fact that he thought he could just walk in and commandeer us both as if we were items on a supermarket shelf! Besides, you know what I'd planned, Lydia.' Emily looked at the older woman in appeal.

'Hardly much of a comparison for Jamie, though, is it?' said Lydia unanswerably. She searched in her bag and produced a couple of tablets. 'Here, take these. You'll feel better. Luc *is* offering marriage, I presume?'

'Oh yes.' Emily swallowed the pills obediently. 'One look at his son and you could see the covetous light in his eye, and unwelcome though the idea is to me, he feels he has to take me along with the package deal.'

'Oh, Em, come on!'

'I object to being played along like a fish. Anyway, I found out he was already in London, socialising, when Marcus died. You telephoned him at his hotel, I presume?'

Lydia nodded guiltily.

'Why couldn't you have told me, Lydia?' asked Emily sadly. 'It would have made life so much more acceptable for me.'

'Oh, darling, I'm deeply sorry, but I agreed with Luc that it would be infinitely harder for you. We just didn't understand.' Lydia coughed delicately. 'If—er—if things weren't very cordial last night how did—well, I mean——'

'How did we end up in the hay?' said Emily baldly.

'Emily!'

'I had too much to drink and fell asleep on his shoulder after we'd simmered down a bit. He must have taken me to bed and undressed me. I was out for the count, anyway. I half woke up in the night and he was in bed with me, and—well, I don't have to draw pictures, do I?' Emily stopped dead, her eyes on Lydia's in horror. 'Oh, Lydia—oh no! It was only once last time and that was it! Jamie. What if—Oh God, not twice!' She buried her head in her hands in despair.

'Have some more tea. I'll put the kettle on again.'

Both women swung round as a deep voice spoke from the doorway.

'What a good idea. We are both very hungry.'

Luc stood watching them, a slight smile on his face, wearing only his black cords, his beaming son in his arms in all the glory of white sweater and red velveteen dungarees.

'You've dressed him!' Emily stood up unsteadily, trying to smile at Jamie, while Lydia looked from father to son and whistled softly as she sat down abruptly.

'Oh dear, oh dear,' she said slowly. 'I don't think you should let anyone see those two together if you want to keep your affairs private, Emily. Talk about a chip off the old block!'

'Good morning, Mrs Crawford,' said Luc, surrendering his son to Emily. 'A "chip off the old block"—what is that?'

'It means Jamie looks just like you,' said Emily impatiently, inserting the baby in his highchair.

'What about Mrs Giles?' asked Lydia. 'Doesn't she come in today?'

Emily groaned and rounded on Luc.

'You must get out of here. She'll be here in an hour. And if she sees you we might just as well put an announcement in the paper.'

'And what is wrong with my being here——' Luc began stormily, but Lydia interrupted soothingly.

'Why don't I call in at her place now on my way to the clinic, and tell her you don't need her for a day or two? You can ring her when you want her.'

'That would be a great help, Lydia, thank you.' Emily smiled, wincing as it aggravated the throbbing in her head. 'I'd rather be on my own for a bit. All right, young man, I shan't be long.'

Lydia made her farewells, leaving a strained silence behind her.

'Right,' said Emily purposefully. 'Porridge and a poached egg for Jamie. How about you?' She studiously avoided Luc's eye, busying herself at the stove.

'What are you having?' He sat at the corner of the table,

one leg swinging, his eyes on what he could see of her averted face.

'Just coffee.'

'That's not enough. I shall make us some omelettes.' Luc sprang to his feet, caressing Jamie's cheek as he passed.

Emily closed her eyes and swallowed, nauseated at the mere thought.

'No, thank you,' she said hurriedly. 'I'll have a—a piece of toast. Perhaps you'd care to feed Jamie his oatmeal while I do his poached egg.'

'Of course.' Luc accepted the small bowl from her and began to spoon porridge into the eager mouth impatient to receive it. 'Not so fast, *filinho*, one mouthful at a time. Is he always as hungry as this?'

'Mostly. He's late this morning. He overslept.'

'We all did.' Luc grinned unrepentantly at the wave of colour that washed over Emily's face.

She resisted the impulse to throw something at him and carefully cut fingers of bread and butter to accompany Jamie's egg, handing Luc the plate and retrieving the porridge bowl.

'If you'd cope with this I'll just dash upstairs and brush my hair while the coffee perks.' Emily looked at his bare chest with dislike as she passed. 'Shall I bring down your sweater?'

He smiled in obvious enjoyment of her disapproval.

'Does the sight of my bare chest offend you?'

'Now that you mention it, yes!' Emily flounced out of the room and retired upstairs to the bathroom for a sketchy wash and a vigorous brushing of teeth, noting with affront that Luc had obviously borrowed her toothbrush earlier.

And why not, she thought bitterly, he's had the use of practically everything else!

When she returned to the kitchen a few minutes later, neat in caramel cord jeans and matching sleeveless sweater over a black wool shirt, Luc had washed up his son's breakfast things and Jamie was contentedly pushing a solid little wooden engine round the tray of his highchair.

'Where did he get that?' Emily pointedly handed Luc his sweater.

'I bought it yesterday.' He pulled the sweater over his head, his face emerging dark and smiling at her pained expression. 'What's the matter, *carinha*?'

'Don't call me that!' she snapped viciously, then put a hand to her head. 'I'm sorry, but I think I must be experiencing my first hangover. I feel terrible!'

He pushed her gently into a chair.

'Sit down and I'll make breakfast. What should I do with Jamie?'

'Leave him where he is for the moment.'

Emily sat, her head throbbing, while Luc made toast and laid the table with the yellow pottery mugs and plates Emily used in the kitchen. She knew she ought to be feeling outraged and indignant, but it seemed like too much effort. The new engine clattered to the floor and Jamie pointed to it imperiously.

'Mum—mum!'

'Let your mother sit quietly,' Luc told him firmly, retrieving the engine himself. Jamie beamed happily at him, Emily noted with resentment. She looked glumly at the slice of toast on her plate.

'You will feel better if you eat,' said Luc, in much the same tone of voice that he'd used to Jamie.

Emily sighed, but it was less effort to munch the toast than to argue, and after the first cup of coffee went down she actually did feel better.

Luc sat opposite her and they both ate in silence while Jamie patiently pushed his engine from one side of his tray to the other.

'Better now?' Luc asked softly.

'Yes, thank you.'

'You are angry?'

'Angry?'

'You must surely remember last night? If only because I was in your bed when you woke up!'

A quick rush of colour burned in Emily's cheeks and she bent her head, a great lump rising in her throat. She dropped her piece of toast on her plate and stumbled blindly from the room, running upstairs to cast herself down on the rumpled bed, which still seemed warm from the heat of their bodies.

How could she have allowed such a witless thing to

happen? You were a tiny bit smashed, said a hateful inner voice. Even so. It was disgusting to give in without a murmur, even allowing for the fact that she was half asleep. Her instincts ought to have reared up and made her fight tooth and nail, but they must have been drowned in a sea of Grand Marnier. A great shudder ran through her, and she sobbed harder than ever until she was hauled up to rest against a wool-covered shoulder, while Luc stroked her and whispered unintelligible comfort into her ear.

'*Coitadinha, faz isso não!*' He rocked her gently until her sobs began to lessen.

'Where's Jamie?' she asked, sniffing.

'I put his pen up in the kitchen. He's still playing with his train.' Luc tilted her face up to his. 'Was it so terrible an experience?'

'That's not the point.' Emily pulled away from him. 'It's not the point at all. Why on earth did you do it?'

Luc cast his eyes heavenwards.

'You need to ask such a question? I am a man.'

'I had noticed.'

'Than you must make allowances for the baser side of my nature.' He gave an exasperated sigh. 'I did not mean to sleep with you, but after drinking too much of that excellent but potent cognac, I was not fit to drive. When I put you to bed suddenly I could keep my eyes open no longer and I just slid in beside you, then pssst, I knew no more until I became conscious of a delectable little body wriggling against mine somewhere in the small hours. I could no more have resisted what followed than tried to stop breathing.'

Emily got up decisively.

'This doesn't alter anything, you know.' She looked at him militantly. 'I shan't alter my plans.'

'Very well.' He got up unhurriedly and went from the room, leaving Emily to trail behind feeling decidedly deflated.

Luc collected his leather jacket and went to the kitchen to plant a kiss on Jamie's cheek.

'Bye-bye, Jamie.' He turned formally to Emily, raised her hand and kissed it. 'Goodbye, Emily.'

'Goodbye,' she said faintly, then saw him to the door, watching the long car out of sight.

Closing the door with an irritable bang, she returned to the kitchen, flopped down in the carver chair at the head of the table and sat looking at her son blankly.

'Mum-mum,' he said, beaming at her as usual.

For once the smile failed to strike its usual chord.

'I'll have to teach you a new word,' she said huskily.

The little boy shuffled on his bottom to the side of the playpen, looked at the bars, then, frowning furiously, he pulled himself upright, grinning at her in triumph as he stood unsteadily upright for the first time.

'Oh, my lovely boy,' said Emily, a catch in her voice. 'What a cleversticks!'

Jamie wavered on his feet, looking towards the open doorway.

'Da—da?' he said questioningly, then sat down abruptly, a look of such comic surprise on his face Emily had to laugh in spite of the lump in her throat.

'Well, my lad, you're learning quickly all of a sudden,' she said ruefully. 'Da—da, indeed!'

CHAPTER EIGHT

SUCH a feeling of anti-climax swamped Emily for the rest of the day that she was hard put to it to keep even moderately cheerful for Jamie's benefit. She took him out in his pushchair later in the morning, but the park was enveloped in chill damp mist after only a short walk, and she was glad to get indoors and light the fire in the drawing room. While Jamie was having his nap Emily doggedly worked her way through a pile of ironing, trying to map out her next course of action. She was a little stymied by Luc's sudden volte-face. The last thing she had expected was Luc's abrupt departure like that, without any further persuasion. Her face flamed. Perhaps he had changed his mind after sleeping with her—possibly she had been tried and found wanting. She tossed her head angrily. It hardly mattered, after all, as there was no likelihood of the incident recurring. She didn't *want* to marry Luc, and the thought of uprooting herself to go to Brazil filled her with antipathy. Suddenly she sat down, thoroughly depressed. The thought of uprooting herself to move anywhere else at all was giving her nightmares. Oh, Marcus, she thought despairingly, what ought I to do?

She jumped up as the phone rang, annoyed with her own disappointment when the caller proved to be Lydia.

'Everything all right, Emily? Just thought I'd check.'

'Oh yes, just fine.' She gave a forced little laugh. 'I told Luc he was wasting his time, so he just went.'

'Oh, Emily—and here was I thinking it was happy-ever-after time!' Lydia was obviously distressed. 'Look, love, shall I pop in for an hour this evening? I don't like to think of you alone up there.'

'No, it's all right, thanks. I thought I'd get an early night. I'll see you tomorrow perhaps.'

The afternoon seemed interminable, and for once Jamie was fretful and disinclined to amuse himself. Twice the phone rang, and each time it was someone offering condolences. Emily was thoroughly out of sorts by the time Jamie had eaten his evening meal and the bathtime ritual had been observed. All the attention given him the day before had had a considerable effect, and it was much later than usual before he finally consented to sleep. Emily decided to get into her dressing gown and have her supper on a tray by the fire with a book. There had been precious little time for reading lately, so she would enjoy what was an unaccustomed luxury. She made herself concentrate on a novel set in the time of Henry II, or Fitzempress, as the book called him, ate the cheese sandwich and drank her coffee absentmindedly, her mind switched off from her personal problems for the first time in days.

The doorbell cut through her absorption and she jumped nervously to her feet, looking at the ormolu clock on the mantelshelf. Nine-thirty was a bit late for Lydia. The bell rang again as Emily crossed the hall, then she heard Luc's voice faintly through the door.

'It is I, Emily.'

She drew back the heavy bolts and opened the door to let him in, though with some reluctance. He brushed past her into the hall, taking off his trenchcoat and shaking it, his hair glistening with rain.

'It's a little late for calling,' said Emily coldly. 'You might have rung first to ask if it were convenient.'

'You would have refused to see me, I think.'

Emily bit her lip. All day, ever since his departure, she had hoped he would come back. Now he was here all she could feel was animosity. What was the matter with her? she thought irritably.

'You'd better come in by the fire,' she said ungraciously, tightening the wide satin girdle of her dressing gown. 'I'm afraid I'm not dressed for receiving visitors.'

She led the way to the drawing room and sat down, pulling the folds of the pale blue robe securely over her knees. Luc smiled and seated himself opposite.

'You look charming. The colour is just a little lighter than your eyes.' He looked at the open book beside her and the tray on the table with the remains of her supper. 'Is that all you had for dinner?'

'It was what I wanted.'

'You do not eat enough.'

'Fascinating though the subject may be,' said Emily sarcastically, 'I am sure you didn't come here to discuss my eating habits.'

'No, you are right, I did not.' Luc leaned back and fumbled in his pocket for a cheroot. 'With your permission?'

Emily nodded impatiently.

'How is Jamie?' Luc lit the cheroot, inhaling deeply as he settled himself more comfortably.

'He's been thoroughly disagreeable. All the attention and fuss he enjoyed yesterday must have gone to his head. I was expected to dance to his bidding all day. For once I was heartily glad to get him finally settled down!'

Luc laughed. 'I apologise for disturbing him.'

Emily shrugged indifferently. 'He'll be back to normal tomorrow.'

'Emily, I have left you to yourself today to give you time to think. Have you done so?'

She laughed shortly.

'What do you imagine? My mind has been somewhat agitated, as you might expect, but it isn't changed in any way, if that's what you mean.'

Luc sighed. 'I had hoped you would have become more reconciled to my proposal.'

'Sorry.' Emily was immovable. 'I don't want to be your wife, and I don't want to go to Brazil. I just want to find somewhere quiet where no one knows me and where Jamie and I can live in peace.'

Luc leaned forward, his brows in the familiar black frown.

'For "peace" don't you mean isolation, Emily, and might not "quiet" turn out to be loneliness?'

Emily drew her breath in sharply.

'I will just have to take that chance,' she said stubbornly. 'I must go away from here—indeed it's better that I leave. This place is full of painful memories now.'

'Then marry me and come home with me,' he said promptly.

'No, I won't! I don't want to marry you. I don't want to marry anyone!' Emily's voice cracked. 'I just want to live in peace with my son.'

'*Our* son, Emily,' he said inexorably, his eyes glittering. 'I will take you to court for him if necessary.'

Emily froze, her heart hammering.

'You couldn't do that,' she whispered, her eyes enormous on his implacable face.

'You think not?' Luc sat back and crossed his legs, smiling faintly.

'But no court would give you custody. As far as the world is concerned I'm Mrs Marcus Lacey. Jamie is Marcus's son.' Emily felt sick.

'But he is not. You told me yourself that the birth certificate gives his name as Harper; the family solicitor could be called as witness—no possibility of perjury or collusion there. Then there is the undeniable likeness of Jamie to myself.' Luc's face was hatefully smug.

Emily sprang to her feet and stood over him.

'You'd never win,' she said passionately. 'No court in the country would let you take Jamie away from me. I'm his mother.'

'And I am his father. I am offering you marriage and Jamie the security of my name, a home and an eventual inheritance of some magnitude.' He sat looking up at her, all quiet reason. 'I might not win, Emily, but think of the publicity such an emotional case would attract. Imagine newspaper pictures of Jamie and me together. I might lose the case, granted. But the possibility of your quiet life in some rustic Utopia would have dramatically diminished, I think.'

'You bastard,' said Emily quietly.

'That is what you insist on making my son, Emily. My own birth was above reproach.'

Wounded beyond reason by this last sally, Emily was unable to stay in the room with Luc a moment longer. She seized the tray and stormed out to the kitchen. In the grip of an anger so great she shook from head to foot she set up the percolator with trembling fingers. So this was why he had left her so meekly this morning! This had been his intention ever since last night, when her idiotic confession had handed him all the trump cards in the pack. And after all that he had slept with her, made love to her, and for all she knew made her pregnant again. What kind of defence would she have if any court knew about that? Emily shuddered. The tabloids would have a field day!

When she was calmer she went back to the drawing room with the coffee tray, which Luc sprang to take from her. He looked at her warily as he set it down. Emily refused to meet his eye and began to pour coffee, as composed outwardly as though this were one of the charity coffee mornings in aid of the church.

'Very well,' she said conversationally, holding out a cup. 'You win. I could never cope with the type of distasteful notoriety such a court case would give. It would be beyond me to subject an innocent child to such a traumatic experience. Victory is yours, Senhor Fonseca.'

Luc's eyes narrowed.

'Do you mean that, Emily?'

'It's hardly a subject for levity,' she said distastefully.

'Then you will marry me?'

'Yes.'

'And you are reconciled to coming with me to Brazil?' Now that Emily had capitulated Luc's implacability had gone, and he looked at her with concern.

'No,' said Emily flatly, 'I am *not* reconciled to it. I dislike the thought of a strange house in a foreign country, where presumably my company will consist of a husband I don't want, and your grandmother, who will no doubt be somewhat suspicious of your wife when she's in possession of a son already nine months old. You expect me to relish the prospect? However, you've made any other course impossible for me.' She rose to her feet with dignity. 'I think you should leave now. You may return some time tomorrow to make whatever arrangements are necessary.'

Luc got up instantly, looking down into the pale, proud little face with something like admiration in his eyes.

'Of course; you must be tired. I will return in the morning.'

'Not too early, if you don't mind,' said Emily, unsmiling. 'I would like to make one or two things clear. You've made your position quite plain, so perhaps you will bear with me if I make one or two trivial conditions?'

'What are they?' he demanded, instantly suspicious.

'I will marry you, as you wish, and come and live with you in Brazil, thus allowing you to attain your goal—Jamie. However, the only capacity in which I'm prepared to function is as Jamie's mother. For anything else, Luc Fonseca, you'll just have to whistle—though I don't suppose you know what that means?'

'I think I understand the general meaning, Emily.' He smiled frostily. 'Jamie's mother, but not my wife.'

'Oh, I didn't say that,' said Emily ingenuously.

Luc raised an eyebrow.

'What, then?'

'I'll play hostess, housekeeper—even cook, if you wish. But I won't sleep with you.'

'In that case,' he said coolly, 'you are more or less superfluous. My grandmother has been hostess at Casa d'Ouro for many years, I have several servants, including an excellent cook. But as I realise I cannot have Jamie without having you too, I shall just have to make the best of things. Goodnight, Emily.'

CHAPTER NINE

IN a shorter time than Emily would have thought possible the dreaded day had arrived and she sat in the Pan-Am V.I.P. lounge of Heathrow Terminal Three, waiting for the flight to be called for Rio de Janeiro. For the moment she sat alone, an untasted cup of coffee on the small table at her side, unopened glossy magazines in her lap, her eyes fixed unseeingly on her new Kurt Geiger sandals that matched so perfectly the beige knitted silk coat thrown down on the seat beside her. Luc was roaming around with Jamie in his arms, keeping him amused until the time came to board the plane. Emily wished it never would. She was ill at ease at all the discreet attention shown her, and had refused various offers of refreshments and drinks, wanting only to sit alone in her misery.

Perhaps if she closed her eyes for a while all this would disappear and she would wake up in the Dower House, plain Emily Harper again. She knew very well, really, that nothing could alter the fact that a special licence had made it possible to transform her into Emily Fonseca in an amazingly short time. The Dower House had been vacated, painful farewells made to Lydia; Emily's whole life turned upside down. The past three days had been spent in London, where Luc had insisted on looking after Jamie while Emily bought some clothes. Brushing aside her objections that she had enough, he had given precise instructions as to what would be suitable and ignored her protests that Marcus had provided her with sufficient clothes already. Submitting, after several clashes of will, she had followed his instructions with a reckless extravagance intended to dent his bank balance. Her eyes followed his tall figure, elegant in brown and black striped jacket and brown trousers, worn with a cream shirt and fawn silk tie. Emily looked at him dispassionately. Very, very attractive, no doubt; and he was her husband, unbelievably, though this fact had failed to sink in yet. The antique keeper Marcus had given her had been replaced by a plain wide gold ring which looked oddly stark on her slim finger. It weighed heavy, like a fetter. She sighed, and craned her neck to see Jamie, in the crook of his father's arm, attracting not a little attention from a group of cooing, elegant ladies. Dressed in a smart yellow cotton jumpsuit, he looked particularly adorable. It was to be hoped he would be good on the plane. Oh lord, the plane! thought Emily, her eyes down on her shoes again, her heart right down there with them. It was immature to be so uptight. She was quite normal, heaps of people were afraid of flying, she was by no means the only one. But did everyone else feel as if all the blood was draining from their bodies, the ice in the stomach and the teeth that would have chattered like castanets but for the fact that her jaw was too tightly clenched together with tension to give them the chance.

'Surely you are not asleep, Emily?'

Her eyes opened guiltily, to see her husband and son in front of her.

'No, of course not; just relaxing for a moment.'

'Relaxing! You look as though every part of you is tied up in little knots.'

Luc's smile was teasing, then his voice changed as he saw how white she was.

'Are you not well, Emily? No, Jamie, you may not go to your mother just now. Stay with me.'

Jamie looked crestfallen and laid his head on his father's shoulder, his thumb in his mouth.

Emily smiled with stiff lips.

'Jamie must be a bit confused with all this upheaval.'

'He will be fine. You are the one who's giving concern. What is it, Emily? Do you feel ill?'

'Luc, I'm terrified!' It burst from her.

'Terrified? How is that?'

'Of flying,' she said desperately. 'I've never flown before.'

'Ah, I see.' He shifted Jamie a little and took her cold hand in his warm one. 'There is nothing to fear, I promise—try to relax. It will be just like sitting in a comfortable armchair, and much less dangerous than trying to cross a busy street. Look at Jamie, he's not a bit worried.'

'Blissful ignorance,' said Emily ruefully, then started violently as a flood of Portuguese came through the tannoy, followed by a cool English voice calling Varig passengers for the Rio flight. Glad in one way that the waiting was over, Emily picked up handbag and coat, smoothed down the skirt of her brown linen dress and received Jamie in her arms, leaving Luc to follow with the hand luggage. Once on the plane the first-class section surprised her with the luxury and space of its accommodation, and some of her panic at take-off was lessened by her interest in the surroundings, and all the attentive care given by the air hostesses, who, without exception, were dark, glamorous and looked like entrants for the Miss World contest.

It was only when the plane was actually airborne, and Emily began to believe that possibly it actually might not plummet straight down again, that she was able to relax just a little. Jamie was fast asleep on her shoulder, and despite Luc's desire to detach him from her, something in the warmth of the small body against hers gave her comfort. Fear shortly gave way to boredom, and she was glad when Jamie woke up with his usual 'Mum—mum' and seraphic smile for her. As she shifted him to her knee he saw Luc and held out his arms.

'Da—da,' he said quite distinctly, and Emily could see a pulse throb at the corner of Luc's mouth as he heaved the little boy over into his lap, where the intricacies of the seat-belt kept him occupied for a while.

Luc's eyes met hers.

'He learns quickly,' he said softly, his hand stroking the black curls.

Emily nodded silently, feeling oddly forlorn.

The plane landed at Lisbon for an hour for refuelling, and when it took off again Emily was slightly less petrified this time. There was a tempting dinner and a film she had always wanted to see, but the hours passed slowly, despite all the attention given to her, the stewardesses so charmed with her son—and possibly her husband—that one was always discreetly on hand to take over for Emily to eat the delicious food served to her, or visit the washroom. In answer to her shy request they brought her tea instead of coffee in an effort to woo sleep, but Emily found this impossible, and was glad when the interminable journey was over and it was time to land.

Her impressions of Rio were confused. After the first breathtaking glimpses of the Corcovado, the great mountain-top figure of Christ, and the Pañ de Açucar, the conical mountain with cable cars for access to its summit, the plane came in low over the island-studded blue waters of Guanabara Bay in the early morning sunlight. They had arrived. They were through the hassle of Customs and baggage in a remarkably short time, its brevity due in part to Jamie, who was a tremendous asset, the Brazilian nation en masse seeming to idolise babies.

'I will show you Rio properly another time,' Luc promised when they were in a taxi en route for the city. Emily craned her neck this way and that in an effort to see as much as possible. It was very hot. Her linen dress soon felt as heavy as wool, and she was very glad she had taken Luc's advice and changed Jamie into brief cotton rompers on the plane.

'You're not obliged to treat me as a visitor, Luc,' she said coolly. 'I don't intend to be any trouble.'

'Do you not, Emily?' Luc eyed her sceptically until she turned back to what glimpses of the beautiful city the short drive afforded.

It was necessary for Luc to visit his Rio office before finally flying to Boa Vista, and Emily spent what seemed like several exhausting hours on the nineteenth floor of a multi-story office block, trying to amuse Jamie while Luc consulted with his Rio agent. Breakfast was sent in, but this only resulted in Emily's dress being splashed with milk and coffee, despite willing help from two pretty secretaries, as Jamie began to get more and more fractious.

After an eternity of courteous farewells another taxi was called, their luggage loaded up and they headed for Santos Dumont, the internal airport, where they caught the plane for Boa Vista by the skin of their teeth, Emily speechless with fright at their spectacular take-off from a runway which seemed to head straight into the sea. She endured a short but terrifying flight through an electric storm over mountainous country, where the peaks were illumined by constant flashes of lightning and the plane bumped constantly owing to turbulence, making her sick with fright. After they had landed Emily was almost numb when Luc told her they still had a journey of some sixty kilometres by car.

They were met by a smiling, dark-skinned chauffeur who stowed the luggage in the capacious boot of a large Mercedes, and drove them along a road that wound through bare, high mountains, at times with sheer drops on either side of it down to ravines many feet below. The assault on Emily's nerves of so many ordeals in quick succession finally took their toll, and she fell asleep against Luc's shoulder.

Oblivious to the beauty of the palm-shaded house at the end of a long, curving drive through a lush tropical garden, she made her first entrance into Casa d'Ouro carried over the threshold by her husband in traditional manner, but fast asleep. Her son was

borne along behind her, also slumbering deeply, in the arms of
the woman who had taken him from his father, her face tender
as she cradled her great-grandson to her breast.

Emily began to surface slowly, aware she was in a blessedly
still bed, but her eyelids felt too heavy to open and let her
look at her surroundings. Vaguely she was aware of a
whispered conversation near at hand, but the voices died
away again. After a long interval while she just lay enjoying
the comfort of the bed, she opened her eyes cautiously to find
herself in an enormous, cool, high-ceilinged bedroom with
white filmy curtains moving gently at two large casement
windows screened by wire mosquito netting. Emily pushed
herself up gingerly, propping the pillows behind her, admiring
the beautiful white embroidery on the sheets. She was lying in
a wide bed, almost the size of a British double bed, but this
one had its twin a short distance away with a small table
between the two on which stood a beautifully carved wooden
lamp with an amber silk shade.

The furniture in the room was massive, made of some black
wood with great wrought-iron hinges on the two huge
wardrobes, and intricate carving on the high headboards of the
beds. A dressing table with a swivel mirror stood diagonally
across one corner near the windows, and a large chest was
placed between them. The floor was a gleaming expanse of
wooden boards polished to a glass-like finish, punctuated here
and there by fluffy rugs the same dead white as the walls and
ceiling and the thick fringed cotton of the bedcovers.

Emily was unwillingly enchanted. Unwilling because she
had intended to hate anything Brazilian. Enchanted because
the room, despite its absence of colour, was quite the most
attractive bedroom she had ever seen. She looked down at
herself. She was wearing one of her own cotton lawn
nightgowns, but there was no sign of any of her belongings,
except her handbag on the table beside her. She knew she
should get out of bed and go in search of Jamie, but she was
consumed by a nervousness that held her in the safe cocoon of
the bed, unwilling to venture into whatever—and whoever—
awaited her in the unfamiliar world beyond the closed door.
She glanced at the other bed. Had Luc slept there last night?
If he had there was no outward sign of his occupancy

anywhere. She put that thought, and all its attendant problems, firmly from her. She would cope with one thing at a time in this new life fate had thrust upon her. This sensible decision was unable to stop her sitting bolt upright, heart thumping, as the door opened to admit the tall figure of her husband, looking subtly different in white cotton narrow trousers and a collarless white cotton-knit shirt.

Luc closed the door quietly and came over to the bed, looking down at her with a faint smile at her first words.

'Jamie? Where is he?'

'In very good hands, Emily, I assure you. Do you feel rested?'

'Yes, I feel fine. What time is it? Are my clothes here? Have I held you up for breakfast——'

'*Calma, calma,* Emily! It is nearly noon. Breakfast is long over, your luggage is outside, the maids will unpack while you have a bath, then I shall come back and take you to lunch. My grandmother is waiting to meet you.'

Emily had been afraid of that. She stirred restlessly beneath the sheets.

'If you'll leave, then, Luc, I'll get out of bed.' She flushed, her eyes falling before the amusement in his.

'Are you afraid that the sight of you in that prim little nightgown will drive me to bestial deeds in the full light of day?' The jeering note in his voice rubbed Emily raw. 'After all, who do you imagine undressed you and put you to bed last night?'

She looked at him in horror.

'Couldn't—someone else have done it?'

'Who would you suggest as more appropriate?' Luc sauntered nonchalantly to the door. 'You forget, I am your husband. Besides, I must confess I have rather a preference for undressing a woman when she is fully aware of what I am doing.'

This was too much for Emily. She threw back the bedclothes and slid to her feet from the rather high bed, her chin lifted, ignoring the unkempt tangle of her hair and the brevity of the lawn nightgown.

'If you would please send someone with my clothes I'll do my best to keep you waiting as little as possible. I am anxious to see my son,' she said with dignity.

Luc's black eyes flared momentarily.

'*Our* son!' He opened the door and called loudly. 'Maria, Dirce, *vem ca, faz favor.*'

Two dark-skinned girls wearing print dresses and white aprons came into the room carrying Emily's suitcases. They smiled shyly as Luc introduced them by pointing to each one in turn and saying their names, and busied themselves with unpacking Emily's clothes. She took out a dressing gown, one of her new purchases, café-au-lait heavy satin cut like a kimono, and wrapped it around herself, tying the girdle tight with a yank, and pushing her feet into matching mules.

'If you'll show me where the bathroom is?'

Luc took her outside into a cool corridor, floored in the same gleaming wood, which caught the sun from regularly spaced windows which appeared to give on to a verandah. He opened the door next to theirs.

'I'm afraid the house was built long before bathrooms en suite. You have to share this one with Jamie and me. Thurza sleeps in the other wing, and has a bathroom to herself. I'll return in, shall we say, twenty minutes?'

He left her with a formal little bow, and Emily flew into the bathroom, hardly with time to take in its marble floor and old-fashioned white suite with gleaming brass taps. She made for the huge separate shower stall, protecting her hair with one of the snowy white towels piled on a bamboo chair. In desperate haste she returned to the bedroom to find one of the maids quietly waiting, all Emily's clothes put away except for a change of fresh underwear laid out on the bed. Emily smiled tentatively at the girl.

'Maria?'

'*Não, senhora;* Dirce.' The girl giggled in confusion, opening the door of one of the wardrobes to indicate Emily's clothes hanging in an orderly row, obviously asking which of the dresses was required.

Emily shed her robe and pulled on briefs and bra, any embarrassment at Dirce's presence eclipsed by the thought of what Luc's grandmother would consider suitable. She wanted very much to make a good impression, but had no idea what would help most towards it. After a few moments' hesitation she pointed to her choice, and Dirce helped her into it, fastening it at the back and helping her tie the sash. The dress was off-white, cut like a gymslip, sleeveless and pleated, hanging straight except for a wide aquamarine silk scarf slotted round the hips and tied loosely. Emily hastily put on the sandals worn to travel in, brushed her hair furiously and coiled it in an uncompromising knot on top of her head. A touch of lipstick was all she had time for before the door opened to admit Luc, carrying Jamie.

Forgetting her appearance, Emily held out her arms to her son and hugged him fiercely, to the accompaniment of ecstatic gurgles and incoherent noises, interspersed with 'Mum—mum' and, quite definitely, 'Da—da'.

'You diplomat,' she muttered into his neck, yielding him up reluctantly to his father under the wide, adoring eyes of the maid, who was unable to restrain an outburst of Portuguese which Luc translated to Emily as being a mere outpouring of baby adulation.

'This young man has disrupted the whole household this morning,' he said severely, scowling fiercely at Jamie, who merely chuckled and tried to grab his watch.

'Has he been naughty?' asked Emily anxiously.

'Not in the least, but everyone wishes to play with him instead of whatever they should be doing. Now let us go and have lunch.'

Luc led the way across the corridor on to a wide verandah which ran round three sides of a patio filled with flowering plants. The verandah obviously served the house behind it as a great, three-sided extra room, and had a view through the patio on to a garden which gave the impression of such lush profusion that Emily exclaimed in wonder.

There were palm trees everywhere, giving shade to the house without in any way dominating it, so that Emily received the impression that the building and the trees were interdependent. From what she could see of the garden beyond, roses and azaleas predominated, interspersed with beds of multicoloured coleus, before a glossy green hedge, alight with scarlet blossom, cut off the rest of the garden from view. Suddenly Emily jumped at the raucous noise from one end of the patio, where macaws with brightly-coloured plumage shrieked a strident welcome from a gilded metal aviary which glinted in the noon sunlight.

The middle section of the verandah was obviously used as an extra sitting room, with bamboo furniture padded with cushions covered in cool green and white batik, and a glass-topped bamboo table set for lunch, Luc waved Emily to the settee, plumping Jamie alongside her, and turned to a trolley laden with bottles and glasses.

'What may I give you, Emily? You should have had some coffee, but you seemed in a hurry to dress.'

'I won't have anything just yet, thank you,' she said politely. 'Don't let me stop you, of course.'

Luc poured himself a long gin and tonic, added ice and lemon and sat down on the other side of Jamie, his glass out of reach of his son's inquisitive investigation.

'No, you don't, *bichinho*. He's had his lunch, by the way.'

Emily was startled.

'What did he have? How did you know what to give him?'

'He just had what any child in this country might eat—we manage to raise quite a few children successfully here, you know.'

She felt foolish.

'Of course. I was just interested in his menu, that's all.'

'He had *canja*—chicken soup with rice—then vegetables and minced beef, followed by a fresh fruit salad.' Luc looked at her in enquiry. 'Satisfactory, I trust?'

'Sounds delicious.' Emily was aware that her own stomach was in need of food also, despite her nerves. 'This house is beautiful, Luc. I had no idea it would be so large.'

'You showed very little interest in your future home before you left England.' Luc stared down into his drink. 'I would have described it to you—but perhaps it was better to view at first hand. The wings of the house which form the three sides of the square at one time each had a separate function. Where you slept was all bedrooms, the main wing behind us was the reception area, and over to the right, kitchen, dining room and servants' quarters. Now my grandmother has her rooms in the main wing, and we are alone in our wing—except for Jamie.'

Something about the way he said the last words chilled Emily, though she was saved from comment by the need to hang on to Jamie as Luc jumped to his feet to greet the small figure of his grandmother, who was walking towards them along the polished wooden boards, her erect, graceful carriage giving the lie to her seventy plus years.

Emily picked up Jamie and rose to her feet, wishing suddenly that she were anywhere in the world but where she was at this precise moment.

Thurza Treharne Fonseca, the daughter of a Cornish landowner, had been swept off to Brazil by Luc's grandfather, Jaime Fonseca, at the tender age of seventeen, where she had taken to her elevated position in this exotic, beautiful country like a duck to water. After more than fifty years she was the complete autocrat, and to her servants her word was law. The only person who treated her with any degree of normality was her grandson, who held a unique and unassailable place in her affections, and the only one, since the death of her husband, who ever called her Thurza.

To Emily's surprise Thurza Fonseca was barely the same height as herself, her body slim and erect, grey hair expertly, if a little rigidly, coiffured above a discreetly made-up face with piercing dark eyes that examined her grandson's wife with detached interest. Her grey and white dress was severely tailored but made of finest silk, her only jewellery a string of perfectly matched pearls and the huge diamond on her left hand above her wedding ring.

'Thurza, this is my wife, Emily.' The slight emphasis on the word 'wife' was lost by neither woman, and Thurza gave her grandson a swift amused look before touching her cool, powdered cheek to Emily's pale, smooth one.

'How do you do, my dear, please sit down again. Has Luc not given you anything to drink?' She seated herself gracefully in the chair nearest to Emily and stretched out her arms imperiously to Jamie. 'Come to Vo-vo, then, my darling.'

To his mother's surprise Jamie happily accepted the invitation and was instantly enthralled by his great-grandmother's pearls, to Emily's trepidation.

'How do you do, Mrs Fonseca. Are you sure Jamie won't be a nuisance—he's not very civilized about grabbing whatever he fancies.'

'Men are like that,' Luc murmured softly as he turned to the drinks trolley.

'What was that, Luc?' Thurza looked sharply at him, but he merely turned a bland smile on her and asked what she wanted to drink.

'Just a small dry sherry as usual. I'm sure Emily will enjoy the same.'

Emily meekly accepted the unwanted drink and sipped a little, trying not to wince at the astringent assault on her uneducated palate, aware that Luc was watching her with amusement.

'I trust you slept well,' said Thurza Fonseca, settling Jamie more comfortably. 'When you were still asleep at eleven I was becoming anxious, but Luc wouldn't allow anyone to disturb you.'

'I'm sorry if I inconvenienced you——' began Emily defensively.

'Of course not, my dear,' interrupted Thurza smoothly, 'but we are early risers here, so naturally I was a little concerned. However, it gave me an admirable opportunity to make friends with this captivating young man—no, little one, not Vo-vo's pearls.'

'Emily has been under a great deal of strain recently,' said Luc evenly. 'Coupled with our rather daunting journey I think things rather caught up with her. She is feeling some reaction.'

'Yes, of course,' said Thurza guardedly. 'Luc has been telling me. To have been widowed and then married again in such rapid succession would tax the strongest of constitutions.'

Emily's head came up with a proud lift. She drained her glass and handed it casually to Luc, then rose to her feet.

'How kind of you to be so understanding,' she said sweetly. 'Now I think I should put Jamie down for his afternoon nap, if you'll excuse me for a short while, Mrs Fonseca. I trust I haven't held up lunch too long.'

Thurza waved a hand gracefully, a look of reluctant admiration in her eyes for a fleeting instant.

'Lunch will wait on your return, my dear. Go to Mamae, then Jamie. *Dorme bem.*'

Emily bore her son off with dignity, her back very straight, Luc following in her wake.

'I think the score was about even, don't you think?' he

grinned as they turned in to the wing where Emily had slept the night before. 'You haven't asked where Jamie's room is.'

'You said it was in the same wing as us, so I presumed he would be next door, or at least near at hand.' Emily ignored the sally about scoring, still ruffled by Thurza Fonseca's remark.

Luc opened the door beyond Emily's room and disclosed another bedroom of slightly smaller dimensions, furnished with beautiful, modern nursery furniture, complete with toybox, playpen and a single bed ready for when Jamie outstripped his cot. Emily was surprised.

'This is all new!'

'I telephoned Thurza as soon as you—agreed to come back with me. This is all her doing.'

'How very kind.' Emily handed Jamie to Luc. 'Hold on to him a minute, please, while I investigate.'

The chest of drawers was filled with her son's clothes, neatly folded, some new toys lay in the playpen, and, best of all, when Emily turned down the cot sheet, there was the old woolly rabbit, ready to accompany Jamie for his nap.

'I'll cope now,' she firmly said to Luc. 'You go back to your grandmother and I'll come as soon as I've undressed him.'

'You can find your way back?' Luc laid Jamie on the single bed and straightened, his eyes searching Emily's face. 'Do not worry about anything. You will soon settle down here once you're used to us.'

'And once everyone's used to me!' Emily waved him away and set about preparing her son for bed.

When she returned to the others, her high heels clicking on the hard wood floor, Luc sprang to his feet.

'Did Jamie settle down fairly well? He seems quite happy in his new room.'

'How could he not be?' Emily fumed inwardly at the unnecessary jog to her manners. 'You've been to a great deal of trouble, Mrs Fonseca, Jamie's room is charming. Thank you very much.'

Thurza Fonseca got to her feet with surprising agility.

'I had a great deal of pleasure in choosing it, Emily. Luc had to put up with his father's things, but I thought it was time to get something new. The only piece we kept was Luc's highchair, but it was hand-carved specially for him and it seemed a shame to discard it. Now, let us begin. They brought in the first course while you were away.'

They sat down to chilled avocado halves stuffed with huge prawns in a pepper sauce, and went on to succulent slices of filet mignon served on pâté-spread rounds of crisp-fried bread, eaten with a puree of potatoes and a green salad. They finished with some of the fresh fruit previously enjoyed by Jamie, or in Luc's case, cheese; finally lingering over coffee.

'This is Emily's very first taste of Brazilian coffee, Thurza.' Luc lit a cheroot and watched his wife lazily through the smoke as she took her first experimental sip.

'Good gracious, child, didn't Luc send for any when you woke up?' Thurza frowned at him in exasperation.

'She was too concerned with getting dressed,' Luc smiled at Emily. 'What do you think of the coffee, *carinha*?'

Emily finished the diminutive demi-tasse almost in one swallow.

'It's different from what I expected,' she admitted, 'but delicious. Yes, thank you, I'd love another cup.'

Thurza manipulated the heavy silver pot with dexterity, looking at Emily expectantly as she laid it down.

'And what do you think of Brazil, now that you have come to live here?'

Emily waved a hand around her.

'Apart from the road through those rather terrifying mountains I've seen only this, which is very beautiful. But the one thing I'm very aware of is the smell.'

Both faces turned to her in amused query.

'Smell, my dear? What do you mean?' Thurza seemed to thaw a little.

Emily thought carefully.

'I think it must be the earth that smells different here— nutty, is the nearest I can come to it. Possibly the vegetation contributes to that, and the smell from Luc's cheroot, and now I've sampled it, the coffee too, also a faint hint of perfume. It's all mingled in a general pervasive scent that's new and foreign, though very pleasant.'

'I think I know what you mean.' Thurza rang the little silver bell beside her. 'Though one becomes accustomed to it, especially after over fifty years. Shall we sit over there and let the maids clear away.'

Luc pushed a cushion behind Emily's back before seating himself beside her on the settee.

'What time can we expect Jamie to surface? When he wakes I thought we'd go for a drive and show you the town.'

'Perhaps I'd better check on him now,' began Emily, but Luc put a restraining hand on her knee.

'Stay there. I will go.'

Thurza Fonseca watched her grandson stroll along the verandah, then cast a watchful eye on the verandah table to see that the maids had fulfilled their duties satisfactorily before turning purposefully towards Emily.

'Well, my dear, and how do you think you will cope with making my grandson happy?' she asked, without preliminary.

Emily took her time before answering, wondering suddenly if Luc had told his grandmother anything of their artifical situation, or was she under the impression that theirs was an idyllic affair merely disrupted for a while by circumstances.

'I hadn't really considered it in the light of an occupation, Mrs Fonseca,' she said at last. 'I don't think one can "make" another person happy, but I believe that two people can work together as a team to make a good marriage and a good background for one's child.'

'H'm. Do you not intend to have more children?' The dark eyes were eagle-like on Emily's downcast face. 'I was blessed with only one—Antonio—and he had only Luc. Antonio refused to marry again when Helenita died giving birth. I would like to think that you and Luc might do better; though you don't look particularly strong to me.'

Neither had noticed Luc's return and his voice was coldly reproving to his grandmother.

'Emily has been through a great deal lately, Thurza, enough to make anyone look a little fragile. There is time enough before thinking of any further additions. We have only just met Jamie, after all.'

'Through no fault of ours——' began Thurza sharply.

'Nor of Emily's,' said Luc with finality. 'Now, let us plan what we shall do this afternoon. Jamie was showing faint signs of stirring, *carinha*, so let us get him ready and then I shall show you Campo d'Ouro—everything you missed by falling asleep yesterday. Will you accompany us, Thurza?'

The older woman refused.

'Show her the sights alone while I have my rest, then you may bring my great-grandson back for me to play with later.' She paused, then looked at Emily with something approaching kindness. 'You have done well with him, my dear. He is a delightful child.'

CHAPTER TEN

WITH Jamie enthroned in the back of the large Mercedes, in the car seat thoughtfully included by Thurza in the rest of his new belongings, Luc took Emily for a tour round the steep little town of Campo d'Ouro, with its two churches, a cinema, several shops and many streets of houses all built to house employees of the mine. Nearer the mine he showed her the aqueducts that were such a physical feature of the town, passing right over the narrow main street. She saw the hospital on a quiet hillside, where treatment was given for all ailments from the common cold to major surgery. The general effect of red-roofed white-painted houses clinging to the steep hills of the town among lush greenery and the rich, red earth of the region was very picturesque, the postcard effect mitigated by the mountain rising above the town, surmounted by a great cross which was illuminated at night.

Emily looked about her with intense interest. Everything was so foreign and different from the quiet Warwickshire village of her upbringing that she felt Campo d'Ouro might disappear like Brigadoon if she as much as blinked. As they returned towards the big house, Luc told her to close her eyes for a moment as they reached the main gates, which stood permanently open in welcome.

'Now look,' he instructed, as he drove slowly through the gateway.

At first the house was hidden, as the driveway curved through the green lawns and clustering palms, a blaze of colour here and there from scarlet poinsettias and the tumbling pink and purple of bougainvillaea, until a final bend brought it into view, beautiful and complete, at one with the tropical beauty of its surroundings. Only the reception wing was visible from this part of the garden, and Emily realised it had a verandah on the outward side as well as the inner one looking over the patio.

Luc brought the car to a halt at the foot of the flight of steps leading up to the verandah and through a main hall out to the section where they had had lunch.

'I'm sorry you had to carry me all that way,' she remarked apologetically. 'You should have woken me up.'

Luc leaned over and undid her seatbelt.

'I enjoyed it. After all, if you will not allow me the normal pleasures enjoyed by a husband you must expect me to gather up what crumbs of comfort I can whenever possible.'

Emily opened the door with a jerk and got out, leaving Luc to extricate a clamouring Jamie from his seat, while she marched into the house, nose in the air.

Thurza laid down a book and removed gold-rimmed spectacles as she greeted them from one of the bamboo chairs on the verandah, her smile warm as Luc brought Jamie to her. A tray with a jug of lemonade floating with ice-cubes and fruit was on the table beside her and she waved Emily towards it while she held up her arms to Jamie.

'You do the honours, my dear, I expect you're thirsty after your drive, though you look very cool in that clever little dress.'

'Thank you.' Emily smiled politely, filling Jamie's mug and two tall glasses, then looking at Luc in enquiry.

'Thank you, no, *querida*. I'll get myself a beer.' Luc kissed her cheek casually as he passed on his way through to the kitchen, leaving Emily in no doubt as to how their relationship was to seem as far as the rest of the world was concerned.

'I hope he won't tire you out, Mrs Fonseca,' she said doubtfully as she sat down, watching with concern the way the little boy was bouncing up and down energetically on the old lady's lap.

'He's a lively boy,' said Thurza indulgently, though somewhat breathlessly, 'but a little of this won't do me any harm.'

Emily looked over her shoulder as Luc reappeared.

'Darling,' she said demurely, noting gleefully how his face went suddenly still at the unexpected endearment, 'perhaps it might be a good idea if you brought that smart new playpen out here until Jamie's suppertime, then he can be part of the fun without wearing out your grandmother.'

'Good idea, *carinha*,' he answered instantly, smiling down at her so fondly Emily was almost ready to believe he was as besotted with her as he obviously meant Thurza to believe.

His grandmother watched him go with such an intense look of love on her face that Emily looked away with a feeling of intrusion.

'The Fonseca men have the knack of reproducing themselves with great exactitude,' said Thurza. 'Luc is the image of his father and grandfather. I have often wondered what my other children would have been like if they had survived.'

'You had others?' asked Emily gently.

'Two miscarriages before Antonio, and a girl born after him who only lived a day.' Thurza laid her cheek on Jamie's curly head. 'Childbearing was not my forte, to my great disappointment. I wanted very much to give Jaime a large family, but my size was against me.' She looked across at Emily, a look of delicate enquiry on her face. 'You had a difficult time with Jamie?'

Emily tried not to feel antagonism at the thinly-veiled feeler as to her prospects as a brood mare.

'All my troubles were in the months leading up to his arrival,' she said lightly, 'the actual birth was surprisingly straightforward. Of course he was rather small, which helped.'

Luc arrived at that moment, laden with the playpen and an armful of toys. Emily jumped up to help him.

'You never told me how it was when Jamie was born,' he said shortly, frowning as he put the pen together.

'No. Men aren't usually interested in the boring details.' Emily took Jamie away from Thurza. 'Come on, you bruiser, leave your poor——' She shot a look at the other woman. 'What was the word you used?'

'*Vo-vo*. Grandma, roughly, in Portuguese,' explained Thurza, smiling in approval. 'And what are *you* going to call me, Emily? Mrs Fonseca sounds rather a contradiction in terms.'

Emily was a little flustered, avoiding Luc's eye.

'I hadn't thought——'

'You will call her Thurza, as I do,' said Luc firmly, and sat down on the settee beside her, taking her hand in his. 'That will be acceptable, Thurza? I presume you do not require Emily to say Dona Teresa, like the maids?'

'Of course not.' Thurza was unruffled. 'Of course in England one is not generally on first name terms with one's grandmother, but that hardly concerns us, I feel. I shall be very pleased to have Emily use my name—oh, by the way, my dear, the maids will probably convert your name into something easy for them, so I expect you will become Dona Emilia.'

Emily smiled.

'That sounds very pretty.' She turned to her husband. 'What do they call you, Luc?'

'When my father died I inherited his title.' He grinned at her mockingly. 'I am referred to as *"O Patrão".*'

'Which means Lord and Master, I presume,' said Emily sweetly.

Very deliberately Luc raised the hand he was holding to his lips, kissing it with a flourish, gazing at her with an expression in his glinting black eyes that brought the colour to her cheeks.

'Exactly,' he agreed solemnly.

Emily was aware of Thurza following the little exchange with interest, and turned to her with determination.

'I enjoyed the trip round the village,' she said brightly, 'though I gather it's referred to as a town.'

'I rarely venture down there these days,' said Thurza regretfully. 'The local hairdresser comes to the house once a week, and now and then I'm driven into Boa Vista for a little frivolous shopping, but generally speaking my life is spent within the confines of the house and garden. I quite enjoy a little gardening, though José, the gardener, strongly disapproves. You haven't shown Emily the garden yet, Luc. Leave Jamie here while you take a stroll.'

As Luc raised Emily to her feet, Jamie's face crumpled a little and his attention wavered from the toys in the pen. Laboriously he hauled himself to his feet, with such an imploring look on his face Emily's heart was wrung.

'Couldn't we——?' she began tentatively, but Luc shook his head.

'Leave him with Thurza for now. You'll see why in a moment.'

With misgivings Emily left her objecting son to be soothed by his 'Vo-vo', while she accompanied Luc down in to the patio with its plants; ferns and rubber plants and many more that were strange to her. The gaudy macaws shrieked at them as they passed the aviary and emerged into the garden proper with its beautifully tended lawns and beds of roses, some of them taller than Emily, but all of them scentless. A great expanse of coleus of all colours edged the brilliantly green grass, and Emily smiled in amazement.

'One of those in a pot costs quite a lot of money at home,' she said pensively. 'They had a big brass pot full of them on the staircase at Compton Lacey—I used to look after the houseplants.'

Luc's hand closed over hers and he turned her to face him.

'This is your home now, Emily. Do not dwell in the past.'

She looked up at him squarely.

'You want me to forget that I lived in another man's home and existed for eighteen months without knowing what had happened to you?'

'Yes, I do,' he grated, bruising her fingers, his eyes cold and implacable. 'You are now Emily Guimarães Fonseca, Dona da Casa d'Ouro, mother of my son and my wife. Do not forget it.'

Emily's head lifted with hauteur.

'I am hardly likely to, am I? But I refuse to put my past life, especially Marcus, out of my mind. They are a part of me every bit as much as this place is part of you. I have a heritage too, Luc Fonseca, so don't browbeat me.'

He grinned suddenly, disarming her completely.

'I am beginning to realise that "browbeating" you, as you put it, is not as easy as one might think. You may look gentle as a gazelle, but behind that façade beats the heart of a tigress!'

They walked on slowly, the sudden flare of animosity dissipated a little.

'Nevertheless, Luc,' said Emily thoughtfully, 'how will you explain a new wife with a ready-made son who is pretty obviously yours?'

They had reached a white-painted garden seat, and Luc motioned Emily to sit down. He sat close and slid an arm along the back of her shoulders, which stiffened at his touch.

'Just think what a picture of felicity we present to Thurza,' he murmured in her ear. 'She can just see us at this point.'

'And is it so important that she believes our marriage is all sweetness and light?' Emily felt resentful at this nerve-racking game of charades she seemed to be playing with Luc.

'Oh yes, indeed, Emily. If she believed for one moment that you were anything but a normal, loving wife to me she would make your life a misery. She can be a tyrant as far as her family is concerned; or indeed about anything that does not fall in with her way of thinking.'

'I *had* suspected as much,' said Emily dryly. 'You haven't answered my question about your somewhat precipitate rise to fatherhood status.'

'Everyone knew of my amnesia,' said Luc bleakly. 'Failing to get here for my father's funeral, and the reasons for it, were naturally highly publicised. What no one knows, except Thurza, is how completely my memory returned. I was very cagey—is that right?—about claiming full recall, as frankly I felt that if I had forgotten about you, God knew what else had been erased from my mind. So the general message to those that matter is that we had a lightning romance and wedding the first time, cut short by the tragedy of my father, and that I only remembered about you just before I went to England this last time.'

'What was I supposed to be doing in the meantime?' demanded Emily.

'You thought I'd been killed, and had too much pride to apply to my family for support, which is not too different from the truth.'

'And people are going to believe that?' Emily was sceptical.

'I care little whether they do or not,' said Luc indifferently. 'I am answerable to no one but God and my family.' He squeezed her shoulders hard. 'Do not worry. Whatever anyone thinks privately, to you they will behave with the utmost circumspection, or they answer to me.'

The menace in his deep, quiet voice made Emily shiver, and she got up quickly.

'The sun's going down. Show me the rest of the garden, then it's time to give Jamie his bath. What lies beyond this spectacular hedge, Luc? What lovely blossoms!'

'Hibiscus. We go through this narrow opening at the end and—*o piscina*.'

Luc ushered Emily through the gap in the hedge with the air of a conjuror, and laughed at her gasp of pleasure at the sight of a large swimming pool paved with turquoise tiles, complete with a high-diving board, garden chairs scattered along the grass beside it.

'Oh, Luc, how fantastic! I haven't swum since I was in school——' her glowing smile faded. 'Oh, but——'

'Exactly,' he agreed. 'Our son will soon be walking, so I must arrange for a high gate in the opening back there so that he can never accidentally get through to the pool.'

Emily shuddered, white to the lips at the thought.

'But how did you manage when you were small?'

'It's only seven years old,' he explained. 'It was made for me when I came home for good after college. Now you see why I don't want Jamie to see it before I can get this part of the garden closed off. I shall teach him to swim as soon as possible.'

'But he can't walk yet!'

'No matter, Emily. He can learn both at once.' He grinned at her doubtful face. 'Come, let us go back, *carinha*, Jamie will be growing impatient.'

'I'm *"carinha"* in private again as well as in front of your grandmother?' Emily looked up at her husband's handsome jutting profile mischievously.

'Not if you dislike it, Emily.'

For some reason Luc's quiet answer made Emily feel deflated again, an annoying little habit of his, she thought irritably as they went back to the house.

Bathtime was its usual lively but exhausting pastime, with Thurza a delighted spectator a little distance from the inevitable splashes hurled around by the exuberant Jamie. He had been provided with a new boat which his father helped him sail while Thurza conducted Emily to the kitchen to discuss the little boy's supper. Emily inspected the large square room with pleasure. A window in two of the walls gave maximum light, and the same marble floor as the bathroom gave a coolness she assumed would be very welcome in the middle of the day. The double cooker, refrigerator and freezer were obviously up to date, as were various gadgets like blenders and food mixers, but the rest of the kitchen looked unchanged, its cupboards and large table very much in keeping with the rest of the house.

'You probably find such a kitchen somewhat antiquated,' said Thurza.

'No indeed,' Emily laughed. 'The Dower House kitchen was more or less in its original condition of three hundred years earlier, except for the basic modern appliances, cooker, etc. But it was a bit dark and dismal. And my kitchen in the cottage was minute.' Her face clouded. 'Luc wants me to forget all that, though, and just live in the present.'

Thurza laid a hand on her arm, her face softening.

'Try to bear with him, Emily. He has been brought up as a Brazilian, despite his cosmopolitan education, and the thought of the woman he loves, and his son, both belonging to someone else is abhorrent to him. I had great reservations myself, I admit freely, until you arrived, but I am sure we will all learn to live together in harmony if we each of us do our best.'

Inwardly Emily had grave doubts, but she smiled at Thurza, nodding, and both of them turned to thoughts of supper.

Jamie settled down very well in his new bedroom, and, not for the first time, Emily gave thanks for his equable disposition.

'It's surprising how easily he adapts himself,' she said to the other two when they were eating the cold meal prepared earlier by Dica, the cook, and left ready for them to serve themselves.

'I wouldn't describe Luc as the most placid man in the

world,' said his grandmother dryly, 'so Jamie must have inherited your nature, Emily.'

'Don't make the mistake of thinking her meek and mild,' warned Luc, smiling evilly at Emily. 'She has claws that scratch when she's roused.'

'Then stop trying to provoke me,' said Emily calmly. 'I think Jamie learnt very quickly that roaring his head off was no use, as often I was—well, unable to come running just when he wanted. And during the time before he was born, of course . . .' She trailed away, embarrassed, and took one of the crisp nut cookies Thurza offered with the coffee.

'What were you going to say?' asked Luc gently.

'Well, I merely meant that I wasn't too happy myself, so one would think it might have affected him adversely, instead of which he's always been a happy little soul.' Emily looked away, unable to meet his look.

'A fortunate compensation for you, my dear,' put in Thurza smoothly. 'Now shall we repair to the morning room and discuss plans for a little reception I intend to give next Saturday.'

Luc scowled.

'Reception?'

'Of course, dear.' Thurza smiled at him blandly. 'We must introduce Emily to our friends, and some of the mine officials. It will be expected. Come along.'

Emily gave Luc an agonised look as they followed the small, regal figure to a pretty room, with chintz-covered furniture, a pastel Chinese rug on the floor and several watercolours on the walls. There was a large fireplace, to Emily's surprise, and a wall devoted to shelves holding books and records and hi-fi equipment.

'This is the morning room,' said Thurza.

'*Your* room, you mean, Thurza,' said Luc. 'Sit down, Emily, and I'll fetch us a drink. What would you like? Grand Marnier?'

Emily refused to rise to his bait, wishing his memory were less efficient.

'A soft drink, please.'

'I thought about thirty people,' went on Thurza inexorably. 'A buffet, of course, and we'll have drinks down in the patio first. For some reason people adore those noisy macaws; then we'll serve supper on the side verandah and repair to the drawing room afterwards.'

Luc sighed, handing her a small Benedictine, then giving Emily a glass of chilled orange juice. He sat on the floor beside Emily's chair, leaning against her knee with a familiarity she resented fiercely, but took care to hide. He drank some whisky, regarding his grandmother with resignation.

'I suppose it is really necessary?'

'You know it is,' she answered firmly. 'A Fonseca bride is not an event that happens often. As there was no wedding reception to attend everyone will be agog to meet her, therefore we shall present Emily in style. I believe—and you will forgive me for being outspoken, I know—that the best way to deal with any possible rumours or gossip is to behave as though they don't exist.'

'If I hear anyone make so much as a reference to my wife or son in any derogatory way——' began Luc harshly, the sudden tension in his body communicating itself to Emily where it touched her thigh.

'You will ignore it!' Thurza's arrogance faded as she looked at Emily's white face. 'What is it, my dear? Does the prospect of a little party frighten you?'

Emily smiled valiantly, her eyes glittering in her pale face.

'No, of course not, it's just that suddenly I feel a little tired. It's very embarrassing. I've done nothing at all today, and yet I'm sleepy again. I promise to be more lively tomorrow.'

'Drink your orange juice, then bed,' said Luc, turning his face up towards hers. 'I must turn in, anyway, back to normal tomorrow.'

Emily felt a little pang.

'Are you starting back already?'

'He spent an hour or so down at the office this morning, while you were sleeping,' said Thurza tartly. 'He has a lot to make up after spending the additional time in England with you, after all.'

Luc rose to his feet in one lithe movement and held out his

hand for his grandmother's glass, looking down at her unsmiling.

'I think perhaps it would be a good thing for you to retire also, Thurza. Tomorrow you may introduce Emily to the rest of the servants and familiarise her properly with the house.' He paused significantly. 'I am sure that you will do your best to see that Emily settles in comfortably. I shall not be home for lunch, I have to visit Congonhas dam, so take care of my wife—not to mention my son.'

Obviously a message was received and noted between the two, thought Emily with interest, as a very slight flush mounted Thurza's well-modelled cheekbones.

'Goodnight, Emily,' she said with dignity. 'Sleep well. Goodnight, Luc.'

She presented her cheek to Luc, but merely nodded to Emily as she passed through the door held open by Luc.

'Oh dear,' said Emily faintly, downing the rest of her orange juice with a gulp. 'I think she was put out. She was beginning to thaw towards me, too.'

Luc stood leaning against the carved wood mantelpiece, kicking a suede-booted foot irritably against the curb.

'She will ride roughshod over anyone if they don't stand up to her. She likes to aim those little barbs just when one is lulled into thinking what a sweet old lady she is. It doesn't work with me, nor did it with my father, but I have been told she made my mother's short life none too happy on occasion.'

'Did she not approve of your mother?'

'Oh, very much so. She more or less arranged the match. Helenita de Carvalho was a great matrimonial prize. The family is old Portuguese colonial, owns vast areas of land in Minas, and my mother was beautiful and sweet in to the bargain. But she had been brought up in true, high-class traditional Brazilian style, obedient, ornamental, waited on hand and foot and protected from everything. My father never saw her alone before their wedding day.' Luc's wide mobile mouth twisted at the look of horror that Emily turned on him.

'But that's barbaric! I mean, it isn't human to expect people to—to——'

'Sleep together when they have never even held hands?'

'Well, yes, it takes time to get used to someone in that way——' Emily stopped dead, but it was too late.

'You mean that they should have waited at least five days first.' His voice was silken and cruel. 'It took you all of that, Emily, if I remember accurately.'

Emily sat still and silent, cursing herself for a fool. She had led with her chin, so had only herself to blame for the inevitable coup de grâce. Utterly drained and exhausted by this strange, quiet yet wearing day, she rose to her feet and handed Luc her empty glass, silently turning towards the door.

'Would you like some more orange-juice, Emily?'

Did she detect a faint note of contrition?

'No, thank you. Perhaps the oranges are different here, but I thought there was a strange aftertaste,' she said politely.

'I put some vodka in it,' he confessed, face straight. 'If I remember correctly, alcohol—er—relaxes you.'

Emily suddenly and completely reached the end of the very frail tether she'd been hanging on to. Taking Luc off guard, she gave him a vicious swipe on his cheek with the flat of her hand, all the conflicting emotions of the day compressed in to one great wallop, which gave her enormous satisfaction.

'Goodnight,' she said flatly, and left the room unhurriedly.

Luc caught up with her immediately, his hand reaching out to catch her elbow in a painful grip as they went to Jamie's room in a pulsating, tangible silence that was loud with things unsaid. Emily straightened out the crumpled heap at the foot of the cot into a tidily disposed little boy, tucked the satin-edged cellular blanket round him and left him peacefully sucking his thumb, blissfully unaware of the dark, violent currents that eddied back and forth between his parents as they silently left the room.

Luc followed her in to their bedroom and closed the door with an ominous thud. Emily rounded on him, eyes like chips of blue ice in the glow from the bedside lamp.

'You can't sleep here!'

'Indeed I can, *minha esposa*, this is *my* room, you are merely sharing it.'

He stood with arms folded across his chest, such

malevolence on his dark face that Emily suddenly knew fear, and drew in her breath sharply.

'Then tell me where *I* may sleep,' she said desperately. 'How can you expect me to get any rest in these circumstances?'

'You managed very well last night!'

'That was different. I knew nothing of where I was, or indeed anything else.'

'Nevertheless, this is our room, and this is where you, and I, will sleep. Nothing goes on in a Brazilian household that is ever concealed from the servants.'

'And you care for servants' gossip!' Emily bit the words out, shaking with rage.

'Not particularly. But my family is one subject that I do not care to be discussed intimately all over Campo d'Ouro. There is enough subject matter for speculation already. I do not intend that there will be one iota more.' Luc spoke quietly, yet with a deadly emphasis that chilled Emily to the bone.

She took a deep breath and flung her head back defiantly.

'I said in England that I would act as your wife in public—and I use the word "act" intentionally—but I will not sleep with you.' Her breathing was ragged as she got the last words out, and she recoiled instinctively as Luc moved.

But it was only to sit on the far side of the other bed, however, where he leisurely removed his boots, then his clothes, getting up casually to open his wardrobe and take out a white towelling dressing gown. Emily watched him, hardly breathing, paralysed by nerves and apprehension. He strolled indolently towards the door, turning to look at her before he opened it.

'Perhaps you should wait until you are asked,' he said cruelly, then sauntered out, closing the door softly behind him.

CHAPTER ELEVEN

To say Emily spent a miserable night was an understatement. Her rage and frustration at Luc's Parthian shot made her shake so violently her fingers were all thumbs as she got out of her clothes and into the fresh nightgown laid out for her. She feverishly wrapped the satin robe round her tense body and brushed out her hair vigorously, trying to calm down before Luc returned.

If he *is* returning, she thought viciously. Tears came to her eyes as she pulled the bristles through a particularly tight knot. But of course he was returning. The servants might gossip if not. The reputation of *o patrão* must be upheld at all costs, especially if there were any danger of his machismo being in question. There were doubtless numbers of well brought up Brazilian maidens who would give their solid gold pedigrees to be in her place right now. Emily forced back a choked little sob. None of them had her supreme advantage, however, one ready-made firstborn son, created in the exact image of his sire, with not one feature of his mother to mar the effect. She started as the door opened. Luc came in quietly, his hair wet from the shower, and with complete disregard for Emily's sensibilities, stripped off his dressing gown, stretched, and slid into bed.

'*Boa noite,*' he said with a yawn, and rolled over on his side, with his back to her.

Emily's temper boiled up again and it took every last ounce of self-control she possessed to get herself quietly into the bathroom and make her preparations for the night. Conflicting emotions were poor bedfellows, and hours of tossing and turning passed before Emily finally slept, hours made all the more unbearable by the quiet, even breathing of the deeply sleeping man in the bed next to hers.

It was almost seven when she cast a bleary eye at her watch next morning. She rolled over quickly, but the other bed was empty. Yawning and heavy-eyed, she tiptoed next door to

look at Jamie, but he was still asleep. A quick shower revived
her a little, and she dressed rapidly in a denim skirt and
sleeveless shirt, brushing her hair to hang loose to her
shoulders. Emily arrived at her son's cot in time to see him
dragging himself upright by the cot-rail, unusually dis-
gruntled.

'Mum-mum,' he said predictably, a scowl on his face
laughably like Luc's.

'What's the matter with you, grumpy?' As Emily lifted him
out it became all too evident. Jamie was in crying need of a
bath and change of apparel.

'Bom dia.'

A shy voice behind her made Emily turn round, as the maid
who had helped her the day before stood there, her white
teeth displayed in a wide smile.

'Dirce?' said Emily tentatively, and the girl nodded
vigorously. 'Good morning, Dirce.'

With gestures and smiles the girl indicated that she wanted
to help, and Emily soon found it a great deal quicker to bathe
and change a little boy when there was someone at hand to
dispose of soiled linen, pass towels or hold a wriggling little
body still while it was dressed. Jamie palpably enjoyed having
this admiring addition to his handmaidens, and gurgled as she
clapped her hands in compliment to the picture he made
finally dressed in smart pale blue towelling shorts with
matching blue and white striped tee-shirt. He immediately
tried to imitate her, flapping his hands and laughing
uproariously. No language barrier here, concluded Emily,
with the guilty thought that it was really very pleasant to walk
away with Jamie on her shoulder, leaving Dirce to dispose of
all the unpleasant bits.

It was a beautiful morning, already quite warm, and as she
wandered slowly along the verandah to the kitchen she
breathed in the air deeply, remembering that last night there
had been a definite perfume in the air that was missing this
morning. But last night had hardly been very opportune for
asking about trivia like that in the midst of their quiet, furious
little altercation. Emily dismissed this from her mind as she
entered the kitchen to a chorus of *'Bom dias'* from Maria, the
housemaid, Dica, the large black cook, whom she greeted for

the first time, also a thin, wiry little man who was introduced
a little unintelligibly as José. Ah, the gardener, thought Emily,
surrendering Jamie willy-nilly to the arms of Dica, who
poured floods of baby worship over him while Maria
presented her new mistress with a large cup of milky coffee.
Ambrosia, thought Emily, watching her son's installation into
his father's ornate rosewood highchair. Everyone suddenly
sprang to attention as Thurza Fonseca came into the room,
immaculate to the last hair, dressed in crisp pale green linen.

'Good morning, Emily.' A cool kiss was bestowed on
Emily's surprised cheek, then Thurza greeted her staff, finally
bestowing her attention on her grandson, who smiled cheerily
at this other member of his court. Spoiled rotten, thought
Emily with resignation; what else could one expect? Still, Luc
had obviously survived the same treatment. Yes, and look
what it had done for him—used to having his own way in
everything, she thought acidly.

Thurza suggested Emily leave her son to breakfast with
Maria in attendance while the two of them took theirs on the
verandah.

Emily was reluctant, looking at her son with misgivings.

'I really don't feel I should leave him yet just like that.'

'He managed perfectly well yesterday morning,' said Thurza
tartly. 'You'll probably find he eats more with the girls than
with you. Come along.'

Powerless against Thurza's bracing personality, Emily
allowed herself to be shepherded out on the verandah, with an
anguished look over her shoulder at Jamie, who ignored her
completely, entirely wrapped up in his new adoring entourage.
Maria was spooning porridge into his mouth while Dica
prepared scrambled eggs for his next course.

Emily sat down at the breakfast table opposite Thurza
feeling forlorn and superfluous. The other woman smiled at
her not unkindly as she raised the delicate china teapot and
poured tea into matching Spode cups.

'No guilt is necessary about leaving him to the maids for a
little while now and then, Emily. Motherhood need not be
quite as draining an occupation now that you're living here at
Casa d'Ouro. Not that I approve of children being left to the
care of servants too much. On the contrary. But delegating

nappy-washing and the occasional meal to Maria or Dirce will do Jamie very little harm, and you a great deal of good. You're much too thin and there are shadows under your eyes. You obviously need feeding up.' She passed Emily's cup to her briskly. 'There, enough lecturing, I think. Now while you try some of this *mamão*—perhaps you know it better as papaya?—you shall tell me something of this historic house where Luc found you.'

Emily tasted her melon-like slice of fruit with interest, enjoying the smooth, peach texture very much, deciding it had a flavour all its own.

'I rather thought Luc meant me to put all that behind me,' she said, 'and concentrate on my life here.'

'Men are not always reasonable. I think it would be a great mistake to forget your heritage. I never lose sight of the fact that I was once a Treharne, a family every bit as good as the Fonsecas in their own way, and I never allowed my Jaime to forget it. Strange that you should give his great-grandson the same name.'

'My father's,' explained Emily, 'a happy coincidence, as it turned out.'

'He has a second name?'

'Marcus.' Emily looked levelly at the other woman.

'Your—former husband, I presume,' said Thurza, touching her lips delicately with her hand-embroidered napkin. Emily nodded and changed the subject swiftly.

'I didn't even hear Luc get up. Does he start very early?'

'Six-thirty. He likes to be down at the mine before the others, just like his father,' said Thurza proudly. 'He comes home for lunch at noon, though he's away today, and his hours rather vary after that. I'm never sure when to expect him home in the evening—any time between five and eight.'

Emily stared at Thurza in surprise.

'That's a very long working day!'

'Luc is a very hard-working man. But now he has a wife and son to attract him home perhaps he will come home earlier.'

Maybe to see his son, thought Emily, but certainly not his wife.

After breakfast the two women strolled in the garden, with

Jamie in his pushchair, Thurza taking pleasure in pointing out
many plants strange to Emily, in particular a small flowering
tree with mauve and white blossoms.

'I expect you've noticed its perfume once darkness falls. Its
name is *dama de noite*—lady of the night; scentless by day, but
heavenly once the sun goes down.'

There were also some gnarled trees with damson-like dark
fruit growing directly out of the greyish bark. These were
apparently called *jaboticabas*, and the fruit made excellent
jam, some of which Emily had enjoyed on her toast for
breakfast. She could have wandered around the fascinating
garden indefinitely, but before long the heat of the sun drove
them back to the shade of the verandah and a pause for coffee
while the little boy was installed in his playpen. For once he
was not too happy about being left to his own devices, and
clung to the bars shouting 'Mum-mum' in a very imperious
tone indeed.

'I think His Highness is letting all this new attention go to
his head,' said Emily ruefully, and turned her back on him
until he gave up and sat down with his toys.

'Well done, my dear.' Thurza smiled in approval. 'He must
realise that you're not always at his beck and call.'

'It's understandable. After all, I have been until just recently.'

'You must both find it strange.' Thurza was surprisingly
understanding. 'But I hope you will both settle down quickly.
Now let's make plans for my little reception.'

Emily listened with growing disquiet as plans for Thurza's
'little reception' revealed that it was to be quite a large, formal
affair.

'People have so few reasons to dress formally these days it's
pleasant to give them an excuse for doing so.' Thurza looked
up at Emily over the top of her spectacles. 'You have a
suitable dress?'

Emily nodded, almost wishing she could truthfully say no,
but then it would have made little difference as without doubt
she would have been packed off to the nearest town to buy
one if Thurza thought it necessary.

'I did a little shopping in London before I left,' she said. 'I
can only hope that what I have will be in keeping with Campo
d'Ouro standards.'

'Don't be meek, Emily. If *you* think it suitable that should be all that matters.'

Emily laughed.

'I presume that's the rule you live by!'

'Yes, indeed. It has served me in very good stead.' Thurza smiled and returned to her list. 'There, I think that will do. Not much point in confusing you with a string of names, but generally speaking it's a handful of mine officials, and the rest are local people with the odd relation or two mixed in. And some of Luc's Carvalho relations really *are* quite odd, in an aristocratic kind of way. What Fonsecas are left live in Sao Paulo, so we'll just have to leave them out.'

Emily was intrigued, and would have liked to hear more, but Thurza was bent on showing her round the house properly, so with Jamie settled on one hip Emily followed the older woman through a succession of large, high-ceilinged rooms filled with beautiful furniture, the two largest of which were connected by wide double doors and would be used for the party. Some rooms were kept closed now that the family had dwindled in size, but Thurza intimated that this would all be changed if Emily would kindly turn her thoughts to producing several more little Fonsecas. One long room was lined with portraits and photographs, more like a small museum than a private room. Rock samples were displayed on shelves, with various mounted animal heads on the walls between family portraits, the men all possessed of thick dark curling hair, heavy black eyebrows and dominant noses, quite irrespective of the characteristics of the relevant spouses hung alongside. Emily stopped before the photograph of one girl, and stood looking at it for some time, shifting Jamie to her other hip. Thurza Treharne Fonseca looked out at her, a proud smile on her lovely face beneath a misty cloud of dark hair, slender as a reed in a white, bias-cut satin evening dress with a great white rose on one shoulder, one hand touching the long rope of pearls that hung to her waist.

'How lovely,' said Emily involuntarily.

'Thank you, my dear. That was taken in 1930, soon after my marriage.'

'And this is your husband?'

Thurza looked fondly at the photograph.

'Yes, of course, though it might equally be Antonio, or Luc. As you see, it's only the clothes that change. The men are more or less identical. The Fonseca genes must be very powerful, they overcome all others with unfailing inflexibility; although I believe some Treharne blood contributed to Luc's height. My brothers were quite tall for Cornishmen.'

Emily moved to the next portrait, a mere head and shoulders of a girl with flawless white skin, huge dark eyes and an other-worldly look of purity and innocence more in keeping with a nun's habit.

'Luc's mother, Helenita.' Thurza sighed. 'Antonio worshipped her, but sadly she proved very delicate and the rigours of childbearing were too much for her. Like me, she had miscarriages, then finally gave birth to Luc only at the expense of her own life. Ridiculous, isn't it, when down in the village women regularly produce a baby once a year with no fuss at all. Come along, then.' She chucked Jamie under the chin as the little boy grew restive, bouncing up and down on Emily's hip. 'Leave your poor *mamae* alone and come and have your lunch.'

Emily was made to rest on her bed after a light meal, and to her surprise slept soundly for two hours. She woke up with a start to find it was nearly four o'clock. I'm lotus-eating, she thought, hurriedly putting on her blouse and skirt. This life of sloth will become all too addictive if I don't watch it—I must find something to do with myself. Jamie's room was empty and she hurried along the verandah to find Thurza enthroned behind the tea-tray and Jamie being pushed around the garden by both Dirce and Maria, each taking turns to pick up his woolly rabbit as he hurled it at them with shrieks of delight. The macaws set up a great sqwawking which the little boy tried to imitate to the laughter of the two maids and Emily smiled. How different Jamie's life had become in such a short time!

'You look much better.' Thurza examined Emily's face critically. 'You obviously need rest. Now have some tea and some of Dica's delicious coconut biscuits.'

After tea both women applied themselves to the invitations embossed in gold on thick white cards. Thurza kept a supply

which merely needed filling in with the correct date and name,
ready to be delivered by hand next day.

'Isn't it rather short notice for Saturday?' asked Emily.

'Not for an invitation to Casa d'Ouro,' said Thurza grandly.

Insisting on giving Jamie his bath and supper herself, Emily
passed the time until Luc arrived home by keeping herself as
occupied as possible, scarcely admitting to herself how ill at
ease she felt after the rather less than cordial interchange of
the night before. When Maria called her to the telephone as
Jamie was finishing his supper Emily felt a start of surprise,
not even remembering where the telephone was. She followed
the girl to the morning room, where Thurza was speaking into
an elegant onyx and gilt instrument which stood on the small
rosewood escritoire. She handed over the telephone to Emily
and tactfully left the room.

'Hello,' said Emily cautiously.

'Hello, *carinha*,' said the startlingly caressing voice of her
husband, 'I've just arrived from Congonhas and I shall be
home in about half an hour. Will you please keep Jamie up
until then?'

'Yes. I'm sure he'll be delighted,' said Emily blankly.

'How has your day been, darling?'

'Er—fine; very pleasant. And yours?' She looked at the
instrument with suspicion.

'A little hectic. I greatly look forward to a relaxing evening
with my wife.' In the background Emily could make out the
sound of other voices, and she raised a sardonic eyebrow.

'Keeping up appearances—"darling"?'

'Of course, my love. *Até logo.*'

The telephone looked too ornamental and costly to treat
with any disrespect, so Emily laid the receiver carefully on its
cradle, scowling at it with irritation. Hypocrite! She turned,
arranging a smile on her face as Thurza came back into the
room to say Jamie was in the playpen under Maria's watchful
eye and Emily had just nice time to bathe and change before
Luc arrived home.

Complying mutinously, Emily felt thoroughly put out.
Everything must revolve around the wishes of the *patrão*—no
matter if Jamie was tired or not. The incontrovertible fact that
Jamie was as bright as a button made it even more annoying.

Emily had to admit that she looked a lot better this evening than she had for some time. Her eyes shone as she applied a little silvery blue shadow to them, and her face was definitely less drawn. Her aquamarine cotton dress, cut low and square like a sundress, with wide straps, had a matching loose jacket in the same colour, checked in citrus and white, and there were new backless white kid sandals with four-inch heels to go with it. She was hurrying to play with Jamie just as Luc arrived home. They met head-on in the middle of the verandah, and to her annoyance he held her close for a moment and kissed her hard. She opened her mouth to protest, then saw Thurza smiling indulgently at them both.

'You look better, *carinha*,' said Luc, examining her in some detail. 'Good evening, Thurza.' He bent to kiss his grandmother's delicately rouged cheek and gave a stifled yawn. 'Forgive me, it's been a long day. Did you keep Jamie up?'

'Of course,' said Emily meekly. 'You told me to.'

He shot her a glinting look.

'What a compliant little wife! Then let me see him before you put him to bed.'

'He's in the kitchen in his playpen,' said Thurza, following him and leaving Emily to bring up the rear.

The scene in the kitchen as Luc entered was comic enough to dispel Emily's ill humour. The maids fluttered like doves in a cot and Jamie hauled himself up to his feet with a huge smile, saying 'Da-da' quite clearly before subsiding with a thump when he released the bars to reach up to his father.

Luc instantly bent to scoop him up, disregarding the dust on his khaki shirt, holding the small pyjamaed figure close, his face buried in his son's curls.

Emily turned away from the unashamed tears in Thurza's eyes and the worshipful expressions on the faces of the maids, prey to a mixture of emotions herself.

'Come and sit on the verandah with your Da-da while he has a drink,' Luc said to his son, 'and perhaps Mama and Vo-vo will come too while Dica gets on with the dinner.'

Both women followed in his train to sit on the verandah, where candles in glass-shaded copper holders shed a soft glow to augment the light of a new moon in the warm, still evening sky. As Luc was preoccupied with Jamie Emily felt obliged to pour the drinks in deference to Thurza's seniority. She gave the older woman her habitual sparing quantity of dry sherry, mixed a double gin with a large tonic and placed it in Luc's reach on the table, then had a swift look at the rest of the drinks for something she herself fancied.

'Try a Cuba Libre, Emily. You will enjoy that.' Luc took his attention away from Jamie for a moment. 'A small quantity of white rum, plenty of ice, the juice of a fresh lime and as much cola as you like.'

After carrying out his instructions Emily was pleased with the resulting concoction and sat down on the settee next to Luc in response to his imperious gesture.

'You look very charming tonight,' he said gravely. 'I like your dress.'

'Thank you.' Emily felt embarrassed and put out a finger to tickle her son's ribs.

'Mum-mum,' said Jamie immediately, and held out his arms, but Luc laughed and restrained him, turning his son's attention to his watch, holding it to the small ear for Jamie to hear the tick.

'I have been showing Emily the family portraits,' said Thurza, watching the little family tableau with bright eyes.

'A little repetitive on the male side, don't you think?' Luc grinned.

'*You* aren't there yet,' remarked Emily, enjoying the flavour of her drink.

'I thought I would create a precedent. You and I shall have our portrait taken together in a few weeks' time, when you are completely rested, and your new life has restored the bloom to your cheeks.'

Emily flushed, oddly put out.

'I'm not photogenic,' she muttered.

'Have you had a photograph taken recently?'

'Well, no, not since I was at school——'

'I thought not. This will be different.'

Privately Emily considered this last an understatement, every instinct in rebellion at the thought of her own unremarkable features cheek by jowl with the beauties already on the wall in the gallery.

'Perhaps you should be thinking of changing for dinner, Luc,' suggested Thurza quietly. 'I think one small gentleman has finally fallen asleep.'

Luc looked down tenderly at the small drooping head and rose carefully to his feet, Emily going on before him to Jamie's room to turn down the cot sheet and make sure Rabbit was waiting. Luc laid his son down with care, watching in silence as Emily tucked the cover round him, then following her out quietly as they left the room.

'I'll be as swift as I can,' he said softly, some of the tenderness still in his face.

Emily shrugged.

'No rush,' she said casually, and walked unhurriedly away, aware that two coal-dark eyes were boring into her back.

Dinner was a leisurely meal in the long, cool dining room, Thurza's presence ensuring that an atmosphere of reasonable cordiality prevailed. Emily found Dirce's cooking very much to her taste and enjoyed the minute steaks fried in crisp batter with their accompaniment of green beans and crisp salad, also the compote of chilled fresh figs with delicious creamy coconut ice-cream that followed.

'Dirce's speciality,' said Thurza. 'Very good, isn't it?'

'M'm, superb.' Emily licked her spoon childishly, then flushed as she looked up to catch the amusement in her husband's eyes.

'You look like Jamie when you do that,' he said, grinning.

'A little difficult, wouldn't you say, when he's the image of you?'

'A fact that gives me great pride and pleasure, I assure you, *carinha*.'

'Let's hope that when you have a daughter she will resemble Emily a little more,' said Thurza genially. 'That nose of yours could be a handicap to a girl.'

There was a little silence, while Emily busied herself with meticulously folding her napkin, relieved when Maria brought in the coffee tray.

Thurza told the girl to take it outside on the verandah so that they could enjoy the starry evening as long as possible. Emily was grateful for the more muted light of the candles, though felt ill at ease when Luc led her to the bamboo settee and settled himself alongside her, capturing her hand. Thurza smiled indulgently as she handed them their coffee cups.

'You will need two hands, Luc, release her for just a moment.' She looked at Emily quizzically. 'I believe you've missed him today, haven't you, dear?' Luckily she went on without waiting for an answer. 'But Emily feels you don't care for her to speak of her life in Warwickshire, Luc. You can hardly expect her to erase the past twenty years like chalk from a blackboard, you know. Besides, I'm very keen to hear all about the old manor house where she lived, and what must be a fascinating historical background.'

Luc lit a cheroot and leaned back, his long, black-clad legs stretched out before him, his white shirt glimmering in the dim light. He recaptured one of Emily's unwilling hands and held it fast.

'Emily lived in the Dower House, not the Manor House, and it is her life there that I particularly desire forgotten. She may regale you with as much historic data of Compton Lacey as you wish.'

Emily was stung by the autocratic finality of his words.

'That particular period incorporates the first nine months of Jamie's life—*darling*,' she said, her tone patently saccharine. 'Am I to proceed as though he sprang into being at almost a year old?'

'I would prefer that Jamie is not informed of that time, yes,' said Luc heavily.

'Even though without Marcus Lacey we would both have been in a very unenviable situation!' Emily made no attempt to stem the bitterness in her voice, careless of any impression given to Thurza, who came unexpectedly to her support.

'Emily is right, Luc. It is only just that full credit is given to this man who married her for her protection.' Thurza sat, straight-backed, regarding her grandson with unwonted disapproval. 'After all, from what little I know, it sounds as though he was able to trace his lineage back a great deal further than the Fonsecas.'

Luc's mouth was rigid, his body tense, and he was obviously exerting considerable control over himself.

'A typical comment, Thurza,' he drawled finally, 'but totally irrelevant. My little wife has a stronger personality

than you imagine. She refused to *marry* Marcus Lacey, even
though she was fully aware that the poor devil had only a
limited time to live. Apparently that would have created
complications with the laws of inheritance, etc. She would
have let Jamie grow up with the slur of bastardy—did you
know?'

Emily felt stunned, cold with shock, unable to marshal any
defences, and was taken aback when the old lady spoke
sharply to Luc.

'That is naturally a surprise to me. I do not approve or
condone such a decision. But in the light of the alternative
readily available as Mr Lacey's wife, it took courage, I think.'
She looked searchingly at Emily. 'You have no other family?'

'Two old aunts in Scotland,' said Emily tonelessly. 'I felt it
hardly fair to confront them with my predicament. It was my
fault; my problem, after all. I had no idea what had happened
to Luc. If he were dead it was no use. If he were alive—well, I
had no taste for begging, even if I'd known where to contact
him. Besides, eventually the short time we had spent together
seemed ephemeral, unreal.'

'If it were so easily put aside,' said Luc harshly, 'it must
have been a great inconvenience to bear a son who looked so
much like me.'

'It didn't help,' agreed Emily bitterly.

'So this impression of connubial bliss you have been trying
to make on me has been a charade.' Thurza's shrewd old eyes
turned from one to the other. 'You must both have found it a
strain.'

'Emily has. I find it remarkably easy, and necessary. We
shall go on doing so,' said Luc with a warning note in his
voice. 'We have servants, remember, Thurza. Whatever we
feel in private our public attitude is one of newly wedded
harmony.' Emily moved away from him instinctively, but his
hard, immovable arm brought her back. 'I am tired and I
would like to go to bed. You will do so too, Emily. You may
read if you wish, the light will not disturb me. Goodnight,
Thurza.'

Luc rose and bent to kiss his obviously thoughtful
grandmother. Emily stood awkwardly.

'Goodnight, Mrs Fonseca.'

The latter regarded her wryly.

'You have avoided addressing me as anything in particular all day, my girl. I thought we'd agreed on "Thurza". Bend down and kiss me.'

Emily obliged, surprised.

'Goodnight—Thurza,' she said quietly.

'Goodnight, my dear. There are some paperbacks in the drawer of your bedside table.'

Luc stood with impatience, waiting for the little interchange to end, then took hold of Emily's elbow and bore her off in the direction of their bedroom. Any fears of his behaviour once there were soon dispelled, as he did exactly the same as the night before, apart from the shower. Emily averted her eyes while he stripped off his clothes, then she gathered up her nightgown and robe in silence and took herself off to the bathroom to undress before taking a final look at Jamie. When she got back to the bedroom, Luc was lying with his back towards her and was apparently fast asleep. Emily shrugged, quietly opened the drawer in the bedside table, and after a quick look through the handful of books it contained, decided to re-read *A Town Like Alice*.

CHAPTER TWELVE

IN some strange way the revelation of their true relationship to Thurza made life easier for Emily. There was no longer the need to pretend, something which had gone against the grain. Hypocrisy was one of Emily's least favourite human failings, and to have Thurza know the truth made dealings with her straightforward without having to watch every word she uttered.

The situation was by no means to Thurza's taste. She made no bones about the fact that Emily should try to effect a reconciliation with Luc.

'Whatever you say, my girl,' she said in her usual astringent manner, 'the fact remains that Luc was nearly demented when his memory finally returned, and you with it. He burned up the telephone lines to your friend—Mrs Crawford, if I remember correctly?'

Emily nodded. They were taking their after-breakfast stroll with Jamie in the pushchair, and had just passed out of earshot of the noisy macaws.

'Better than dogs as regards intruders, but ear-splitting at times,' said Thurza. 'Let's sit on the garden seat and put Jamie to crawl around on his blanket for a while. Did you speak to Luc this morning?'

Emily shook her head, dumping her son on the grass with a selection of toys, perching a floppy white sunhat on his head.

'I woke when he did, but decided to play dumb and pretend I was asleep. I'm a coward.'

'No, I wouldn't agree there. A coward would hardly take on a dying man to cope with during a pregnancy.'

'But Marcus wasn't a "dying man", as you put it, until well after Jamie's birth. He was the one who looked after me until then. I was sick all the time and constantly tired, not really the sort of burden to wish on a man with a death sentence.'

'No doubt it took his mind off it very effectively.' Thurza bent to retrieve a rattle. 'And now the poor man is dead and you and Luc are very much alive. Are you going to remain at loggerheads indefinitely? I'll be very honest and say that I would very much like to see a brother or sister or two for Jamie before I die.'

Emily laughed ruefully.

'You don't mince words, Thurza! Anyway, you look pretty fit to me; better than I do, so I don't think you can pull that one for a while.'

'Then tell me, Emily, why do you feel enmity towards Luc, when I know very well that his feelings for you never altered?' Thurza's voice lost its usual cadence of authority in her anxiety to clarify the situation.

'I was anguished when I heard nothing from Luc.' Emily looked down at her hands, flushing. 'He was the first—the only man to—to——'

'Yes, I understand. Go on.'

'I thought he was Lancelot and Galahad and the Black Prince all rolled into one. I suppose the hours I spent in that ancient old house made the past more real to me than the humdrum present I lived outside it, and Luc was everything I had ever dreamed of. We spent as much time together during those five days as we could. My life was transformed. What happened between us was entirely mutual; utterly natural and inevitable. So that when he had to leave so suddenly I felt as though half of me had gone with him. Then came the agony of that awful silence. Every day was an endurance test of time to be lived through somehow until the post arrived again. But nothing came, ever. And then I realised I was pregnant. There are no words to illustrate how I felt—I was utterly desperate. You know the rest.' She turned impulsively to the other woman. 'If only I could have been told what had happened to Luc, somehow, in some way, my life would have been easier. It was the not knowing that nearly destroyed me. And in some way half of me never recovered, and I just don't feel the same. Luc should have let Lydia tell me, even if he made no direct communication with me himself.'

Thurza was thoughtful and silent as she watched Emily replace the hat on Jamie's unwilling head.

'Luc was stunned when he learned you had apparently married so quickly,' she said slowly, her brow furrowed. 'Then the day he learned of Jamie's birth he shut himself up in his study for a day with a whisky bottle and refused to emerge. After that he went back to the mine and began to work an eighteen-hour day, driving himself mercilessly. Eventually he learned to live with himself—and me—again and I thought that would be the end of it, until your Mrs Crawford rang here to speak to Luc. By the greatest of ironies he had left for England only a day earlier to attend a conference and give some lectures.'

Both women were quiet for some time, watching the child as he made fruitless efforts to catch a brilliant blue butterfly.

'You're not what I wanted for Luc,' said Thurza, characteristically frank. 'I had my heart set on a Brazilian girl brought up to cope with a house like Casa d'Ouro.'

'I'm in full agreement. I had no wish to leave England,' said Emily sadly. 'But Luc made it utterly impossible for me to do anything else, so I shall just have to make the best of it. Although,' she slid a sly little look at Thurza, 'Luc's grandfather married an English girl a lot younger than me, and *she* seems to have coped remarkably well.'

Thurza laughed and patted Emily's hand.

'Well said, my dear! We'll just have to try to rub along together, won't we?'

Any further soul-searchings were cut short by a roar of frustration as Jamie fell on his back and both of them rushed to comfort him, pushing him back to the house for their *merenda*, the mid-morning snack.

Life fell into a fairly civilised pattern, helped greatly by preparations for the party. Luc came home to lunch each day, returned each evening in good time to play with Jamie for an hour, but refused adamantly to associate himself in any way with the approaching festivities. Emily and Luc occupied a sort of no-man's-land where each treated the other with civility and a wary, tense neutrality, while Thurza played a role very similar to that of a U.N. peace-keeping force, ready to step in whenever the truce looked likely to break down. Each night Emily and Luc retired to their bedroom together, for all the world like any normal married couple, except that behind the bedroom door not a word was exchanged beyond the obligatory 'goodnight'.

Despite this artificial situation Emily found herself beginning to unwind, her appetite better, her pallor changing to a faintly sunkissed glow by her strictly rationed sessions in the garden each day. After-dinner conversation became a pleasure rather than an ordeal, and Luc even told Emily a little about his working day, which interested her enormously and gave her a greater insight into what made this complex husband of hers tick.

'By the way, Thurza,' he said one evening, 'I haven't seen Chico since we arrived.'

'Chico?' asked Emily.

'Chico is a toucan,' said Thurza. 'At least that's his official description. To me he's a constant headache.'

'Doesn't he live in the aviary?'

Thurza looked at Luc significantly.

'No indeed. He has a perch out near the maids' room, and is supposed never to come inside the house.'

Luc grinned.

'Whereas in fact he enjoys tea and toast with me every morning before the rest of the household is up.'

'I thought you never drank tea!' Emily was highly amused.

'He doesn't,' said Thurza acidly. 'Luc drinks his usual coffee and he makes a pot of tea especially for that wretched bird—you may well laugh, Emily, but every now and then he decides to go what I believe the dear Queen does these days— walkabout, isn't it?'

'Is it difficult to get him back?'

'I hope every time that he *won't* come back,' said Thurza bitterly, 'but he does, after pecking holes in every *mamao* and tomato he can find ripening on anyone's window ledge. Then I shall have to despatch the maids with grovelling notes of apology and various fruit to make up the deficiencies. So lowering!'

Emily was enchanted. She lay laughing helplessly, her head near Luc's shoulder on the back of the settee in the morning room. Luc put a hand over hers and her laughter died away instantly. He stiffened, removed the offending hand and stood up.

'I have a little work I must do in the study for a while,' he said wearily, the lines at the corners of his eyes suddenly pronounced. 'Do not wait for me, Emily. I am sure you are tired. I will say goodnight to you now, Thurza.'

There was a lengthy silence after Luc had closed the door quietly behind him.

'For a moment there I saw things as they could be,' Thurza sighed.

'I know,' said Emily defensively, 'but I need time. I realise things can't go on for ever like this, but I just—need more time.' She rubbed her eyes like a tired child. 'I think I will go to bed. I'm very tired, though I can't imagine why when all I do is a lot of nothing.'

'You look a great deal better on it,' Thurza assured her, 'so get as much rest in as you can. You'll need it for Saturday.'

'Oh yes—Saturday.' Emily felt no enthusiasm at the prospect. 'Will it be very grand, Thurza?'

'Brazilian ladies like to dress up; silk, satin, that sort of thing.' Thurza looked at her in enquiry. 'Are you worried about what to wear? If it's any help, my dress is grey and violet printed chiffon, suitably high in neck and sleeve, as becomes my age.'

'Your age! I shall be delighted if I look half as good as you if I reach seventy.'

'A very nice turn of phrase, Emily.'

'I meant it!'

'I know. That's what made it such pleasant hearing. Now go to bed.'

Emily took herself off to see Jamie and prepared for bed obediently. She had read several chapters of a rather dull historical novel before the door opened and Luc came in.

'I thought you would be asleep.' He stood at the foot of the bed, staring down at her moodily.

'I sleep in the afternoons, you know,' said Emily reasonably. 'I find it difficult to get to sleep at night without reading for a while.'

Luc came towards her, sitting on the edge of her bed.

'There are other ways of wooing sleep.' His eyes stared hypnotically into hers, and very slowly his hand moved to touch her hair. Motionless, Emily lay looking up at him as his head came slowly down towards her. His mouth hovered above her own for what seemed like minutes, then he lightly kissed the tip of her nose and got up. She watched him strip his clothes from the powerful body that gleamed like copper in the light from the lamp, held motionless by some strange paralysis as, just the same as each preceding night, he slid into bed with his back to her and settled down to sleep.

'Goodnight, Emily.' His voice was barely audible.

'Goodnight, Luc,' she answered, her lips dry, then returned to her novel, the words on the printed page suddenly as meaningless as though they were in a foreign language.

Next morning Emily made no pretence of sleep when Luc got up, and she lay unashamedly watching him dress in the fresh set of khaki trousers and shirt he wore every day. A lot of laundry, she thought drowsily. Luc realised he was being watched and came over to the bed, smiling faintly.

'I woke you—I am sorry.'

'I wake every morning.' She pushed a hand through her tousled hair, flushing a little as he touched a long finger to her cheek.

'Go back to sleep.' Then he was gone, only to return a few minutes later.

'Come with me,' he whispered, handing her her robe. 'I want to introduce you to someone.'

'What! I haven't washed . . .' Emily was dragged protesting through the door.

'He won't mind.'

They tiptoed along the verandah in the near chill of the early morning, taking care not to disturb anyone in the slumbering household, and entered the kitchen. There, perched on her son's highchair, was a glossy black toucan, his long yellow bill and bright blue eye turned on her with such a look of impudence that Emily giggled helplessly.

'The famous Chico, I presume. But Luc, he doesn't look real!'

'He's real enough,' said Luc, grinning. 'I expect he'll spare you a cup of tea from his pot if you would care for one.'

'Isn't that big of him! Yes, please.'

She sipped her tea, watching in fascination as the bird consumed a piece of toast, enjoyed a small bowl of tea, then hopped on Luc's arm for a lift to his perch outside. Emily stood up as Luc came back in.

'Now I'm here can I cook you bacon and eggs or something, Luc?'

'Thank you, but no. I had some coffee. Usually I have nothing else in the morning. However,' he looked down at her, his black eyes gleaming from beneath half-closed lids, 'this morning there *is* something else I would like.'

Swiftly he pulled her into his arms and kissed her mouth even as it opened to protest. For a moment she resisted, then yielded abruptly. After a long moment he thrust her away, and they both stood staring at each other, breathing raggedly. He started to speak, then changed his mind, shrugged and turned on his heel, leaving without a word.

Emily sat at the table limply, staring blankly, then she got up and wrung out one of Dica's snowy dishcloths in hot soapy water and wiped down the highchair. Something would have to be done with the irresistible Chico; one could hardly allow a toucan to share a chair with Jamie. She refused to think about Luc, then sat down again and thought exclusively of nothing else until the maids came in and caught her at it.

Jamie had to be content with more of Dirce's company that

morning than his mother's, as Emily became caught up in the preparations for the party. Thurza usually liked to serve several hot dishes as well as cold at her buffet suppers, and was anxious to provide something different to augment the usual repertoire at Dica's command. When Emily hesitantly tendered her mother's recipe for the beef casserole she had once made for Luc Thurza was delighted, and Maria was sent to take the necessary meat from the freezer after breakfast. Immediately it had thawed sufficiently there was a strange, three-cornered cooking session with Emily giving instructions in English to Thurza, from whom they were transmitted in Portuguese to Dica, who carried them out with a broad smile, cries of rapture coming from all sides as the tantalising odours of the mingled ingredients began to rise from the enormous pot.

Any constraint Emily anticipated when Luc came home to lunch was lost in the vociferous welcome given him by his son, who seemed indignant at Emily's desertion, coupled with Thurza's account of the new dish Emily had taught Dica.

'I believe I may have tasted it before,' he said, smiling at Emily over Jamie's head. 'But in the meantime have you anything to offer a hungry man for lunch? What I was allowed at breakfast was meagre in the extreme.'

Thurza watched in fascination as a flood of colour rose in Emily's cheeks, but made no comment, merely chivvying the maids to put on some speed with the meal.

'Of course, you *will* organise the drinks for the party, Luc?' she asked as the shrimp bisque was served. 'I always think that should be left to a man.'

'How many are coming?' he asked with resignation.

'About forty.'

'That many?' Luc groaned. 'Poor Emily will never remember names! I shall stay close by your side, never fear.'

Emily smiled nervously, then looked guilty as Luc asked Thurza if she knew that Chico was back.

'No, I didn't.' Thurza obviously had no pleasure in the information.

'Didn't you mention it, Emily?' Luc's eyes gleamed across the table.

'Er—no, it slipped my mind.' To Emily's distress the hateful tide of colour engulfed her again, and Thurza looked across at her sharply.

'I hope you're not coming down with a fever, Emily. The party is entirely for your sake, after all.'

'She would hardly be so inconsiderate as to fall ill at such a grossly inconvenient time, I'm sure,' said Luc silkily, and Thurza had the grace to look a little ashamed. She leaned across and patted Emily's hand apologetically.

'You know I didn't mean it like that, Emily. That bird affects my blood pressure.'

'Which is excessively normal for your age, so do not be dramatic!' Luc winked at Emily, who felt immediately better. 'What are you going to wear, Emily?' he asked idly.

'If something formal is necessary I have only two dresses suitable for hot weather, one red, one blue.'

'Blue,' said Luc, instantly.

'Why?'

He shrugged.

'I like you in blue.'

'Did you buy it in London?' asked Thurza with interest.

'Yes. It's quite plain, really, but I—I liked it.' Emily glanced mischievously at Luc. 'It was sinfully expensive.'

'I fully expect my wife to be appropriately gowned, Emily. Whatever the cost I am sure it is worth it.'

When Luc had returned to the mine Emily decided to forgo her nap in favour of the swim she had longed for ever since seeing the pool. A new gate of trelliswork now closed off the gap in the hibiscus hedge, and she unbolted it with anticipation. She threw off the huge brown bath sheet which served as a wrap, and in the plain white bikini she had owned since she was sixteen she let herself into the inviting blue depths, gasping momentarily at the cool water, then she struck out and swam six lengths quite slowly with her modest school-taught breast-stroke. Tiring rapidly towards the end of the last length, she hauled herself up the white-painted steps and collapsed in a heap on the bath sheet, gasping for breath. The sun was very hot and she got up wearily, still breathing heavily, decided the garden chairs were too heavy to move, and spread the towel far into the shade of the eucalyptus trees at the far end of the garden. She fell into a deep sleep, only to awaken grumpily moments later to the sounds of shouting and hard hands grasping and shaking her.

'Stop it,' grumbled Emily irritably, peering up at Luc in surprise. 'What are you doing home?'

'You may well ask,' he said hoarsely, wrapping her in the towel and picking her up.

'What on earth are you doing?' Emily was rapidly coming back to her senses and realised the garden was full of people; Thurza, Jamie crying his eyes out in Dirce's arms, Dica and Maria apparently in hysterics with their aprons over their heads—even José the gardener.

'What's happened?' she asked frantically, struggling to get down. 'What's the matter with Jamie?'

'Nothing,' said Luc tersely, striding swiftly towards the house past the ear-blasting macaws, with Thurza and the rest following only slightly less rapidly behind him.

'Luc——'

'Shut up,' he said through his teeth. Emily was too astonished to be angry, and it suddenly struck her how grey Luc's face looked, with great drops of sweat rolling down it.

'Are you sick?' she asked, as they reached the bedroom.

He dumped her unceremoniously down on the bed.

'Only with worry, you—idiot girl!'

To Emily's consternation she realised he was shaking.

Thurza came in, her face lined with worry.

'Is she all right, Luc?'

'Yes. Tell Maria to stop crying and run a hot bath. Dica can make some tea—Dirce can bring Jamie in here so he can see his mother. Oh, and tell José to make sure that gate's bolted.'

Thurza obeyed with unwonted docility and the next moment came back with a sodden crying little boy who hurled himself out of her arms to get to his mother. He clutched his arms round Emily's neck, hiccuping and repeating 'Mamae'.

'Whatever happened to "Mum-mum"?' asked Emily, holding him tight.

'Precisely. What *did* happen to you, Emily?' Luc was completely in command of himself once more, and he stood beside the bed, looking accusingly at her.

'We were very worried, Emily.' Thurza sat on the edge of the bed, and patted Emily's arm.

'I'm very sorry. But I haven't been long. I just fancied a swim instead of a nap as I was so hot after lunch, and I took my towel into the shade for a few minutes' rest. . . .' Something in their faces stopped her.

Luc held out an arm, his wrist with its gold Longines watch thrust before her eyes. It was five o'clock. Emily stared at it incredulously.

'It can't be!'

'I went back after lunch at a little past one. It possibly took you until say, one-thirty before you went in the pool. That is well over three hours ago. You will never use the pool alone again. Do you understand?' Luc's face was grim.

Emily smiled weakly.

'Why? Sharks?'

Her joke died a little death, as Luc bent over her menacingly.

'Jamie's crying brought Dirce running and she told my grandmother your bed hadn't been slept in. There was a frenzied search. This is a big house, and it took quite a long time. No one thought to look near the pool, as the gate was bolted on this side. So Thurza called me.'

'I'm sorry, Luc,' said Thurza, obviously distressed, 'but I was at my wits' end to know what to do.'

'Please don't apologise, *querida*,' Luc smiled gently at her, 'you did the right thing.'

'I still don't see——' began Emily, who was rapidly beginning to feel like a criminal.

'I unbolted the gate as a last resort,' went on Luc, interrupting her. 'Even then I didn't see you. On that brown towel, right under the trees, you were almost invisible. But then José, the gardener, returned from an errand and said *he* had bolted the gate during the afternoon, so I began to search.' He let out a deep breath. 'And there was Sleeping Beauty.'

'But I felt as though I'd only dozed for a moment or two,' said Emily dazedly, smoothing Jamie's hair, then looked down to see he had dropped off to sleep, worn out with emotion.

'Give him to me,' said Thurza. 'I'll just sit on the verandah and nurse him while you have a hot bath, otherwise you may get chilled.'

Emily handed over the sleeping child reluctantly and sat up quickly, only to fall back against the pillows again as the room swam round and great black dots danced before her eyes.

'Heavens,' she said faintly, then gasped as Luc swung her up in his arms and carried her next door to the bathroom.

'I'll manage now,' she said firmly.

He ignored her, unwrapping the towel and stripping off her bikini as impersonally as if she were Jamie. He deposited her in the bath, and deaf to her protests sponged her vigorously all over, quickly scooping her out again to put her on the cane chair while he dried her thoroughly. Wrapping her in a dry towel, he took her back to the bedroom and laid her down on his bed.

'Where are your nightgowns kept?' he asked.

'But I want to get dressed——' Emily stopped short at the look on Luc's face. 'In the top drawer of the chest.'

He took one out and came over to the bed, motioning her to sit up.

'I can do it, thank you.' The hateful, ever-ready flush rose immediately.

'Having gone this far, *linda flor*, I hardly think now is the time to turn prudish!'

Without more ado he sat her gently upright, unwrapped the towel and dropped the white broderie anglaise garment over her head, then fetched her satin wrap and enveloped her in it.

'Are you warm enough?'

She nodded, eyes downcast, then looked up at him pleadingly.

'I don't have to go to bed, do I? I seem to have slept far too much today already. Please let me come on the verandah with Jamie and Thurza.'

He looked at her expressionlessly.

'Will you promise to lie on the sofa?'

'Faithfully. I won't move.'

'Very well. I will bring something to cover you in case you get cold. That is not a warm dressing gown.'

Emily smiled shyly. 'It's pretty, though, don't you think?'

Luc's eyes softened and he smiled back genuinely for the first time since he'd found her.

'It is beautiful. Now I think you should brush your hair, it is standing up on end.'

This was enough to bring Emily to her feet instantly, only to sit down again, feeling decidedly weird.

'What is it?' Luc knelt beside her, frowning blackly.

'Nothing much—sort of giddyish, that's all. Perhaps you would fetch me the hairbrush.'

'Better still, I will brush it for you.'

Luc drew the brush through the fair strands, already showing lighter streaks of colour where the sun had caught them. Slowly and methodically he restored her hair to shining order, then he laid the brush down and picked her up.

'You'll get tired of doing this.' Emily felt uncomfortable at his proximity.

'I think the habit could become addictive,' he said gravely, and walked slowly back with her to where Thurza sat holding a still sleeping Jamie in her arms.

Luc laid Emily carefully down on the settee, watched critically by Thurza.

'You look better now—fetch the light rug from the foot of my bed, Luc, in case she feels cold, that robe isn't much protection.'

'But very decorative,' murmured Luc, smiling wickedly at Emily as he went off to do Thurza's bidding.

'I'm very sorry,' began Emily apologetically. 'I can't imagine what made me sleep like that. Sleeping sickness isn't prevalent in Brazil, is it? I swam a bit too much and honestly only meant to have a few minutes' rest in the shade as I was tired.'

'I shall ask the doctor to come down tomorrow. He can check you over to make sure.'

'Good idea.' Luc returned with the rug and tucked it over Emily's knees. 'Now lie still and keep out of mischief for five minutes while I have a bath.'

'I was thinking it might be better to cancel the party,' said Thurza thoughtfully, looking at Emily with a worried frown.

Emily shot up in alarm, ignoring the egg-beater apparently whirring inside her head.

'Please, don't do that. There's another day before the party. I promise to sit still, do nothing, eat everything I'm given.'

She looked up at Luc in appeal. 'People will think I'm afraid to meet them. Besides——' she smiled at them both ingenuously, 'I've never been to a party like this.'

'How can we resist such a plea?' Luc looked down at her militantly. 'But one false step, one attempt at insurrection, even——'

'Yes, yes, all right,' said Emily hastily. 'I *have* given my word.'

'If you're sure, Emily,' said Thurza doubtfully. 'Ah—I think my little love is waking up.'

Jamie stirred in her arms and blinked up at her drowsily, muttering indistinctly.

'What did you say, my precious?' asked his great-grandmother adoringly.

'Vo-vo,' repeated Jamie plainly, then came fully awake as he heard the delighted laughter of his parents.

'You have to admire his timing,' said his mother proudly.

CHAPTER THIRTEEN

EMILY obeyed her orders to the letter next day, lying meekly on the verandah settee with Jamie in the playpen beside her. Thurza came at intervals to sit with her, but the greater part of her time was spent in overseeing the frenzy of preparations for the party. José's wife came in to help as the maids turned out the two main connecting reception rooms and brought them to gleaming, burnished perfection. José ensured that the patio was tidied, swept, washed—even the aviary had a turn-out, to the annoyance of the protesting occupants, and its brass bars polished for the occasion.

Emily was frustrated by her enforced inactivity, but Jamie, obviously pleased to have his mother to himself, entertained her by demonstrating how easily he could pull himself to his feet and sidle along the side of the playpen, carefully holding on to the rail, with a look of such intense gratification on his face that his mother laughed outright. He was rapidly learning to say several words in both languages, and had no trouble at all in making his desires known to anyone who would listen.

Jamie soon tired of so much physical exertion and sat down to play with his favourite engine, 'chuff-chuffing' endlessly to himself as he pushed it to and fro. Emily watched him dreamily, marvelling at how quickly her life had changed. Just a short time ago she had been, to all intents and purposes, a grieving widow with a lonely future, and now she was in a different house in a different country half a world away, leading a life completely foreign to anything she had ever known before, as another man's wife. Well, more or less. With Jamie looked after by maids, no cooking or housework of any kind to do, in fact waited on hand and foot, Emily was beginning to feel decidedly useless. Unable to venture anywhere at the moment without someone anxiously querying her whereabouts, she felt as much penned up as the macaws in their great shining brass cage. In fact, from one point of view this whole house was just one great gilded cage where she was held prisoner by the ties of love; love for her child, of course. Whatever feelings she had for Luc could best be described as amorphous at present.

He had been very kind after his initial anger over yesterday's foolishness had cooled down. She was bound to admit that some inner chord had been stirred by his attitude towards her over the past day or two, almost erasing the memory of the hard, implacable man who had threatened to fight her in court for possession of his son. Emily's face hardened at the thought. What kind of man would threaten a woman with such treatment! She must never forget the basic granite of Luc's nature whenever the softer, kinder Luc took over to cozen her into thawing towards him.

'That's a strange expression on your face, Emily.' Thurza broke briskly into her reverie, instructing Dirce to put the coffee tray on the table beside her. 'I thought you were sleeping, until I saw the frown.'

'Mere guilt at lying here while all of you are so busy,' said Emily lightly. 'It's too bad to have to loll about when I could be contributing.'

'Nonsense! There are more than enough of us to see to everything.' Thurza poured a larger cup of coffee than usual and added plenty of hot milk. 'I think you ought to drink more milk, Emily.'

'Honestly, I'm fine; there's nothing at all the matter with me.'

'H'm, we'll see. Dr Ferreira is coming to have a look at you in half an hour or so. I had a word with him earlier.'

'But, Thurza, I feel such a fraud.' Emily frowned. 'Does he speak English?'

'Yes. Did most of his training in America, so no problems there.' Thurza turned to Jamie, who was clamouring for her attention. 'What is it, my lovely?'

'I rather think he's asking for his elevenses, too,' chuckled Emily.

Thurza threw up her hands in apology.

'Vo-vo's sorry, darling. Here, you can ring the little bell for Dirce.'

Jamie was so delighted to comply that eventually he had to be forcibly parted from the silver handbell before anyone could resume a conversation. In the heat of the disagreement that ensued between the little boy and Thurza, the slim, elegant man whom Maria had shown through the main door stood unnoticed, a smile on his long, intelligent face as he watched the family group.

'I trust I do not intrude,' he said finally, coming forward to greet Thurza, who smiled at him ruefully offering him her hand.

'Forgive me, Dr Ferreira, this young man has rather a forceful personality. We were indulging in a clash of wills.' She turned to Emily. 'May I present Dr Ferreira, my dear Doctor, this is Luc's wife, Emily—and this is their son, Jamie.'

The doctor took Emily's hand for a moment, murmuring *'Muito prazer'* before looking at the small boy who was now silenced by the simple means of a mug of orange juice hastily fetched by Dirce. He laughed.

'At least it is evident that this young man is not the patient.' He sat down beside Emily and took her hand. 'Senhora Fonseca tells me you were not feeling well yesterday.'

Emily flushed with embarrassment.

'I was stupid and overdid some swimming, then I went to sleep for a long time in the garden where no one could find me. I upset everyone very thoroughly, but I don't feel ill. In fact I feel very well today, Dr Ferreira.'

He held her wrist silently for a moment, looking at his watch, then apparently satisfied with her pulse he asked a few routine questions about her general health and smiled reassuringly.

'Nothing to worry about, I would say, young lady. Possibly you have overtaxed yourself lately.' He turned to Thurza. 'Will you bring her up to the hospital on Monday and we shall run a few tests? She could be a little anaemic, which could account for the dizziness. We shall see.'

Thurza was relieved.

'Do you think she's well enough for this little party I'm giving tomorrow, Doctor?'

'As long as she does not exert herself then I see no reason why she shouldn't enjoy the party every bit as much as I—and all the guests—will. Until then.'

Dr Ferriera bowed to them both and bent to look at Jamie before leaving.

'Another Fonseca in every detail!' His eyes twinkled as he made his adieus.

'Well,' Thurza relaxed in her chair, 'that's a relief! I was very worried about you yesterday. And worried was scarcely the word for Luc, poor boy. He was frantic!'

Emily stirred restlessly.

'I'm sorry to have caused so much trouble. I'll try not to do it again.'

'Well, never mind, let's forget about it and concentrate on tomorrow evening. Maria Braga is coming at five to do my hair—would you like her to do yours?'

Emily was doubtful.

'I'd thought just to knot it up on top of my head.'

'Then let her do it for you. She's really very good, and she might just as well do both of us while she's here.'

At seven-thirty the following evening Emily had to admit that her hair looked much better than if she had struggled with it herself. Still in her robe, she looked at herself in the mirror, turning this way and that to see her head from all sides. The glossy fair hair had been swept up puffily in a seemingly careless pompadour, secured in a swirling knot at the crown of her head, leaving soft curling fronds on her forehead, at her ears and at the nape of her neck. She looked up expectantly as Luc came in in his dressing gown, his hair still damp.

'What do you think of my hair?' Emily demanded.

Luc studied her gravely.

'Very, very lovely,' he said at last. 'When are you putting on your dress, so that I may see the finished effect?'

'I'll just go and tuck Jamie up and then I'll add the final touches.'

Luc smiled mockingly.

'Are you afraid to stay in the same room while I dress?'

'Hardly!' Emily made a face at him as she passed. 'After all, it's hardly a novelty by now.'

She tiptoed in to Jamie's bedroom and straightened him out as usual, covering him up, lingering over the process as long as she could. When she returned to the bedroom Luc was at his impressive best in white dinner jacket and narrow black trousers, with a loosely tied black bow at the neck of his white silk shirt.

'I hate ties of any sort,' he groaned, loosening the bow a little more. 'Do you think Thurza's idea of what is proper will be satisfied?'

'Oh, I think so,' Emily put her head on one side consideringly. 'Very elegant.'

'H'm.' He sounded disbelieving. 'I need a drink. Come down to the patio as soon as you are ready and I shall have something cool for you.'

As soon as he was gone Emily stripped off her robe and reached into the wardrobe for her dress. It was a little awkward to do up the long zip unaided, but she managed it eventually, and then stood examining herself in the mirror that lined one of the wardrobe doors.

The dress was plain and unornamented, a sheath of pale aquamarine silk, strapless, cut straight across her breasts to fall uninterrupted to just above her ankle bones, the shimmering fabric hugging her narrow hips lovingly, the skirt slit to just below the knee in the front to allow for movement. High-heeled sandals, mere strips of kid in the same colour, gave Emily height, a touch of nerves and excitement adding a glow to the face she made up with extra care, darkening her brows and lashes and using a slightly more vibrant shade of

lipstick than usual. When she was ready she added the final
touch, a long, long scarf of matching aquamarine silk was
thrown around her throat to hang down her back to the hem
of the skirt, its edges finished with ostrich feathers dyed to
match the dress.

Emily walked slowly along to the steps leading down to the
courtyard. Lights had been strung to glow effectively among
the palm fronds and gave an immediate air of festivity to the
patio. Luc looked up as the macaws warned him of her
arrival, standing very still as he gazed up at her in silence.
Emily made her way carefully down the steps in the new
sandals and he came to life, coming forward to meet her.

'This is my blue dress,' she said unnecessarily. 'I hope you
approve.'

'How could I not?' His voice was husky as he took her
hand. 'You look—breathtaking; very sophisticated and
beautiful.'

'I'm glad you like it,' she said in a matter-of-fact voice that
gave no inkling of the havoc he was causing by the
unwavering burn of the black eyes that strayed over her from
top to toe. 'It was a frightful price.'

'*Nao faz mal*—it is beautiful. Only one thing is lacking.'
Luc brought out three small jewel boxes from his pocket and
led Emily to the lights over the improvised bar. The first box
held a magnificent oval aquamarine pendant from a fine gold
chain, the second a ring, a matching aquamarine flanked by
four small diamonds on either side.

'Luc!' Emily was at a loss. 'They're exquisite!'

'Allow me.'

He slid the ring on the third finger of her right hand and
moved the silk stole a little to fasten the pendant round her
neck. Then he opened the third box and slid the ring inside on
her left hand to join her wedding ring. Emily looked silently at
the large baguette sapphire between two rose-cut diamonds
and stared up at Luc, overcome by the magnificence of the
jewels. She was spared the struggle to find further words by
the appearance of Thurza, magnificent in floor-length grey
chiffon printed with violets, a silk-lined stole of violet chiffon
around her shoulders, diamonds glittering in her ears to
match her ring.

'Let me see you, Emily,' she commanded. 'Turn round. Yes—perfect. Striking without being vulgar.' She bent forward to examine the pendant lying on Emily's breast. 'So the jewellery arrived, Luc.'

'Today, after a great deal of telephoning.' Luc's mouth lifted at the corners. 'I had to use all my powers of persuasion.'

Emily was fascinated by the play of light on the rings.

'Were they being altered?'

'Bless you, child,' said Thurza indulgently. 'They were being *made*, not altered. Luc had the stones made up into the pendant and ring especially for you, though I believe the sapphire ring just needed altering in size.'

Emily felt disorientated by her sudden acquisition of so much costly magnificence.

'There was no need . . . I mean, I never expected——'

'My wife would naturally be expected to wear jewels as beautiful as her clothes,' said Luc carelessly, then signalled to José, who, transformed into a waiter for the evening, had unobtrusively appeared to await their order. A little of Emily's glow dimmed, but she pulled herself together firmly and smiled brightly as she accepted her drink, going on to compliment Thurza on her dress.

'No one will be looking at *me* tonight, my dear,' said the older woman with a smile. 'Thank you just the same. All eyes will be turned on the new Senhora Fonseca—and some of the eyes are likely to be just a tiny bit green!'

Before Emily had time to ask what she meant the first of the guests had begun to arrive, and she took her place with Luc and Thurza to receive them.

A bewildering list of names was murmured which she despaired of ever attaching to the right faces, but she smiled radiantly and said what she hoped were the right things as Luc presented the Estate Manager, the Commercial Manager, the Chief Engineer, the Head Chemist, her mind reeling as her hand was kissed by a succession of men of varying ages, all of them dark, few of them tall, each one accompanied by a wife who, regardless of age or figure, was coiffured and gowned with an elegance that bordered on the elaborate on occasion, but was always superb down to the last detail.

All of them looked at Emily with a curiosity politely veiled in courtesy, and she was fiercely glad that her dress, her hair, and above all her jewels, were rivalled by no one.

It was pleasant to see an even faintly familiar face as Dr Ferreira arrived alone, followed by the Prefeito—the Mayor, murmured Thurza discreetly.

Then two elderly men of medium height arrived to greet Luc in English, to Emily's delight.

'Emily,' Luc slid his arm round her shoulders, 'I would like you to meet John Trelaur, the Mine Captain, and Tom Enys, the drill doctor, both crusty bachelors—their description, not mine—and both countrymen of yours.'

Emily smiled warmly as each man shook her hand in turn, welcoming her to Campo d'Ouro before greeting Thurza.

'Never thought this grandson of yours would take the plunge, Mrs Fonseca,' said John Trelaur, blue eyes twinkling.

'Nor have the good sense to pick an English girl,' put in Tom Enys.

'I was set such a good example by my grandfather,' said Luc suavely, 'what else could I do but follow suit?'

Thurza laughed appreciatively, tapping her grandson playfully on the arm, while his other arm tightened round his wife's slender bare shoulders, Emily glanced up automatically to meet black eyes gazing down into hers with every appearance of devotion. She flushed and dropped her eyes as a husky voice interrupted them, feeling Luc stiffen.

The two Cornishmen moved away to mingle with the crowd at the bar, and make way for the trio who stood waiting to be presented. A handsome, rather portly middle-aged Brazilian stood flanked by two young women, each of them strikingly beautiful in different ways.

Rose Red and Snow White, thought Emily with interest as Luc presented Ildefonso Machado, the company lawyer, and his daughters Analha and Teresinha. The latter was the lady in red; vermilion chiffon in handkerchief points with a neckline slashed to a depth that riveted all male eyes in the vicinity, a fact Teresinha acknowledged with a flash of great dark eyes and a flick of tumbling black satin hair. Analha, in white cotton lace, was equally dark and vivid, but her face was as sweet and charming as her sister's was unashamedly, sexily alluring.

'*Que coisa!* To bring a bride back from Inglaterra, Luc!'
Teresinha's heavily accented English came from pouting
vermilion lips as she cast an all-encompassing look at Emily
that took in every last detail and dismissed it as unworthy of
her attention. Her father frowned and hastily intervened.

'Who could blame him? You are to be congratulated, Luc.
Senhora, please accept our sincere wishes for your happiness.'

'Thank you, you're very kind.' Emily decided it was time to
take a hand in the procceedings. 'Please allow us to offer you
a drink.'

Even as she spoke, more guests arrived, who proved to be
Luc's Carvalho relations, and once more she was engulfed in
introductions, with much kissing of cheeks this time as they
claimed the privilege of family.

'Well done,' said Thurza approvingly, when it appeared
everyone was present, 'you bore all that well, my dear. How
do you feel?'

'Dazed, but fine otherwise. Do you think I was a
disappointment?'

'On the contrary, I can assure you. Now, Luc, is everyone
here?'

'Not quite.' Luc waved a hand towards a sandy-haired
young man of incredible height who was loping down the
steps, the lights glinting on his gold-rimmed glasses as he
came up to them breathless and smiling, his hand
outstretched.

'Mrs Fonseca, Luc—forgive me, I'm late.' He stopped dead,
blinking as he took Emily's hand. 'And you are Emily—I
suppose I should say Mrs Fonseca Jr.'

'Emily will do very well.' She smiled at the newcomer with
such warmth he was apparently rendered dumb.

'This is Bob McClure, Emily,' said Luc. 'We were in college
together——'

'So he took pity on me and gave me a job,' put in the
American, grinning.

'And you just happen to be the best geologist in the U.S. of
A.,' retorted Luc.

'And you must be the luckiest guy under the sun,'
answered the other with such sincerity in the gaze riveted on
Emily's face that even the dim lighting failed to conceal

Emily's brilliant blush. 'Holy Moses, I didn't think anyone could still *do* that!'

'And if you carry on like that she'll never *stop* doing it,' said Thurza with asperity. 'Now then, Mr McClure, get yourself a drink and then I must herd my guests to the supper table.'

She moved off with the American, leaving Emily and Luc alone for a moment, apart from the voices and laughter.

'You are quite sure you feel well, Emily?' Luc lifted her chin with a peremptory finger.

She nodded, smiling.

'I feel fine, really. Now perhaps we should help Thurza marshal her troops.'

'*I* shall be pleased to help you Luc, *querido*,' a husky voice interrupted, and Emily turned a thoughtful blue gaze on Teresinha Machado, who smiled lazily up at Luc, a slender red-tipped hand stretched out to touch his white sleeve. 'Perhaps Luc has told you; I am accustomed to aiding Dona Teresa on these occasions.'

'It must have slipped his mind.' Emily smiled meltingly at the girl with all the forbearance she could muster. 'It's *so* kind of you, Miss Machado. Nevertheless this time you'll be able to enjoy yourself so much more just as a guest, I'm sure, now that I am here to take over.' Still smiling, she ignored the amused admiration on her husband's face and mounted the steps to the verandah, the feather-tipped ends of her scarf floating behind her as she almost collided with Thurza at the top in her fury. The other woman looked over Emily's shoulder at the couple at the foot of the steps, Luc's arm still held fast by the beautiful Brazilian girl.

'Having a chat with Teresinha?'

'It was more a slight skirmish. I presume that, despite her colouring, she is the one with the green eyes you mentioned so cryptically?' Emily kept her tone light, but inwardly she was in a rage.

They went to inspect the array of food on the long buffet table set up on the far verandah, Thurza inwardly very much tickled by Emily's badly concealed militance.

'I must confess I always thought she would do well for Luc. Well educated, beautiful, accustomed to running a large household; her mother's dead and she rules Ildefonso

Machado's home with a rod of iron. Analha is artistic—paints landscapes, she's a different kettle of fish, but a very nice girl. I must say I really thought Luc was about to take the plunge with Teresinha at one stage.'

Emily pretended to be absorbed in checking on the various dishes keeping warm on the hotplate.

'What prevented him?' she asked casually.

'He took a trip to England, my dear, and everything changed. By the time he came back my poor Antonio was dead and Luc was preoccupied with all the duties of the *patrão*—also in trying to forget a certain young woman.' Thurza cast her a significant look.

Emily's chin lifted in the way that was rapidly becoming familiar to the other woman.

'Miss Machado offered to help you, Thurza. I told her that now I'm here her help would no longer be necessary.'

'Very right and proper. *You* are Luc's wife, Emily. It is your duty to fulfil that position in all ways to the best of your ability.' There was something in the shrewd old eyes that made Emily turn away hastily. 'Now then, my girl, ring the little bell and let us feed the troops.'

All through the demanding evening Emily circulated amongst the guests, Luc sometimes at her elbow, sometimes not, as the pressures of host took him away from her. Bob McClure appeared like magic whenever she looked in need of support, and Emily was grateful to the lanky, charming American, especially when language difficulties arose, as only a sprinkling of the Brazilian guests spoke enough English to make conversation a practical proposition. One of the most fluent was Mario de Carvalho, Luc's cousin, a slim young man whose flowing dark hair and the red rose in the lapel of his white suit gave him a studiedly romantic air, which he exploited to the full. He was lying in wait for Emily when she returned from a check-up on Jamie.

'Luc is very, very fortunate,' he said, cornering Emily at the end of the verandah. He stood too close for comfort, gazing soulfully down at her. She smiled at him uncertainly, wishing Luc would appear.

'How kind of you to say so, Senhor de Carvalho,' she said politely.

'So fair and cool, a creature of the moon,' he said extravagantly, capturing her hand. 'Is there fire beneath that calm, little cousin?'

Before Emily could reply a familiar husky voice interrupted.

'And you would like to be the one to ignite it, *amigo*?' Teresinha Machado brushed past them, smiling mockingly over her shoulder. 'Do not presume on your relationship *too* much, Mario—*caro*.'

Emily watched her go with an intense dislike she hoped was not too obvious, then smiled brightly at her companion.

'So nice to meet you, Senhor de Carvalho. . . .'

'Mario, *por favor*!' he said fervently, his eyes glowing.

'Ah, here comes Luc,' said Emily with relief at the sight of the tall figure approaching them with purpose.

'*Como vai*, Luc?' said the young man, suddenly full of propriety.

'*Bem, 'brigado,*' answered Luc briefly, something in his demeanour telling his cousin to depart with promptitude.

'What are you doing with Mario in this dark corner?' Luc's eyes were blazing, to Emily's indignation.

'Precisely nothing. He was impressing me with his romantic charm, I think—which I merely found embarrassing.'

'You should not have allowed it,' he said harshly, taking her wrist in a bone-cracking grip and forcing her to walk quickly at his side to rejoin the guests in the reception rooms. Emily was furious.

'What's the matter, Luc, lost your little playmate?'

He stopped dead, looking down at her with menace, his eyebrows in the black bar across his forehead that usually meant trouble. Emily stumbled against him and he held her captive with a hard arm.

'What does *that* mean? Tell me!'

Emily licked her lips, her mouth suddenly dry at the look of cold anger in the eyes glaring down at her.

'Teresinha—the lady in the vulgar red dress,' she snapped defiantly. 'You seemed happily occupied with her earlier on.'

The verandah was now deserted, and Luc jerked her face up to his to kiss her mouth so hard her lips ground against her teeth.

'There is an insolent phrase in Portuguese which you might learn,' he said tightly, his face raised a little from hers, 'just in case I am compelled to use it again. It is *"cala boca"*, or in English, shut up, little wife. Now come, some of our guests are ready to leave.'

It seemed a very long time before the last of the convivial crowd showed signs of departure, by which time Emily's smile began to feel pasted on her face.

'*Boa noite*, Senhora Fonseca such a pleasure to meet you.' Analha Machado smiled shyly and pressed Emily's hand. 'I hope you are very happy here in Campo d'Ouro. Perhaps one day I may come to visit you and meet your little son?'

Emily smiled warmly.

'Of course. Please. Whenever you wish.'

'*Eu tambem?* Does that include me also?' Teresinha's challenging glance stung Emily, as the girl stood close to Luc in a proprietorial attitude he was apparently doing nothing to discourage, merely smiling down at her indulgently.

'I shall be pleased to receive you at any time,' lied Emily.

'We are all very interested to meet your son,' said Teresinha. 'His existence was a great surprise; so romantic, the forgotten bride, *nao é*?'

Inwardly outraged, Emily kept her face in its polite social mask as Ildefonso Machado kissed her hand and shepherded his two daughters away. Only Bob McClure remained, and he soothed Emily's ruffled feelings by holding her hand in a mangling grasp and gazing down at her earnestly from behind his spectacles.

'It's a great pleasure to make your acquaintance, Emily. Perhaps you'll cheer up a lonely bachelor's existence and let Luc bring you to dinner at my place some time soon.'

'I'd be delighted,' said Emily warmly, glad to mean what she said this time.

'I'll look forward to that.' The tall American released her hand, said goodnight respectfully to Thurza, clapped Luc on the shoulder and left them finally alone.

'Well, I think that all functioned very successfully,' said Thurza cheerfully, looking triumphantly from Luc to Emily. 'Your wife made a very good impression on everyone, Luc.'

He raised an eyebrow at Emily.

'Greater on some than on others.'

She ignored him, moving to kiss Thurza goodnight.

'It was a wonderful party, Thurza, thank you.'

'Would you like something to drink before you go off to bed?' asked Thurza, well pleased. 'I noticed you drank and ate very little all evening.'

'I was too busy trying to remember names and make sure no one was neglected.' Emily yawned widely. 'What I'd love is a cup of tea.'

Luc turned her towards the door.

'You go to bed and I shall bring a tray to our room. May I do the same for you, Thurza?'

'No, dear, I'll see to it. I'd like some hot milk, I think, and I shall make Emily's tea at the same time. You can come with me to the kitchen. I sent the maids to bed once they'd cleared up.'

Luc waved Emily away.

'Off you go. I shall not be long.'

Emily wandered slowly into Jamie's room and inspected her sleeping son before reaching the haven of her own room. Suddenly she desperately wanted sleep, the hectic evening all at once catching up on her and making her stupid with fatigue. She trailed her feather scarf across the bed and drifted over to the dressing table, staring at her reflection dispassionately as her fingers fiddled behind her trying to find the hook at the top of the zip. Her eyes glittered in her flushed face, rivalling the brilliance of the aquamarine that hung between her breasts. Did Luc consider her fairness insipid beside the vivid, glowing beauty of Teresinha Machado? More than likely. In the straight blue sheath she no doubt appeared sexless in comparison with the Brazilian girl with her incredibly narrow waist and the lush curves both above and below it. The damned woman's probably even highly intelligent as well, she thought crossly. Funny no one had thought fit to mention her before. She'd been just a shade too obvious in her take-over bid, though, and Emily was fairly sure that she wouldn't try that little ploy again. Grinning at her own smug expression, she turned her attention again to her zip as Luc came in carrying a tea-tray.

'I thought you'd be in bed by now,' he said, frowning.

'I can't undo the hook on my dress.'

Luc put the tray down on the dressing table and turned her round, his fingers cool against her skin as he examined the fastening.

'It is caught in the silk. Hold still, or it will tear.'

He gave a final tug and the hook was free, her back suddenly chill as without warning the dress dropped to the floor before Emily could clutch at it. She dived instinctively to retrieve it, but Luc was too swift for her and jerked her up against him, her feet clear of the restraining folds, his arms crushing her ribs and his lips bruising hers in an onslaught whose very suddenness made Emily unable to resist. Helpless before the spate of passion all the more frightening for its sheer silent intensity, Emily submitted to an embrace whose only aim was subjugation. The temperate, considerate man of the past few days was gone, succeeded by a merciless, frightening stranger who ignored her feeble attempts to free herself, his hands and mouth overcoming her with an effortless strength that ignored any futile denials. His mouth holding hers, he pushed her flat on the bed, one hand indolently restraining her as he shrugged himself out of his clothes and removed the one remaining fragile scrap of covering left to her.

Their panting, ragged breath mingled together as he raised his head a little to look down at her flushed, mutinous face, his eyes gleaming like jet through half-closed lids as he laid a finger on her mouth to stop her furious protest.

'Say nothing.' A chill ran down her spine at his whisper. 'I will wait no longer.'

A great wave of indignation surged through Emily, and she made one last violent effort to free herself. Luc merely laughed softly, deep in his throat, and controlled her efforts with insulting ease, demonstrating his dominance with his mouth, his tongue, his questing, inflammatory hands and, at long, long last, struggle as she might, with the thrusting mastery of his body.

When it was over Luc lay still, keeping her captive, while Emily lay beneath him, too exhausted to attempt escape, hating him for his superior strength, hating herself for her idiotic weakness, appalled at her stupidity in putting herself in a position where all this had been made possible. But above all she hated her despicable body. It had fought, up to a point, but it had lost. And, worst of all, it had enjoyed the process of its defeat to a degree which made her squirm to think of it. Tears of mortification rolled from the corners of her eyes, and Luc, immediately responsive to the movement of her body beneath his, opened his eyes to see the tears sliding from beneath the closed lids. Instinctively he kissed away the tears, sliding his mouth down her nose to her rebellious mouth—and then, to Emily's disbelief, it was all happening all over again, except that this time there was far too little fighting and regrettably more submission. And deep, deep down in the far recesses of her scarcely functioning mind was the knowledge that this time there was a response it was utterly useless to ignore.

CHAPTER FOURTEEN

EMILY'S eyes opened unwillingly as the early morning sunlight poured through the thin white curtains. She moved a little and found that an unaccustomed feeling of restriction was caused by a hard encircling arm around her waist, and a long bare leg thrown over hers. She lay perfectly still, flatly refusing to think of the events of last night; no 'use in crying over spilt milk. Thinking of milk reminded her of Jamie. There was no sound from next door, but it must be well past time for her to investigate. Cautiously she freed herself from Luc's unconscious embrace, looking at his face with an impersonal scrutiny as she slid out of bed. He lay relaxed, his sleeping face younger, less marked with care and responsibility than when awake. The blue silk dress still lay on the floor in a heap, accompanied by Luc's clothes, tangled wildly with her feathered stole, which looked unlikely to recover from the experience.

She bent wearily to pick up the dress, only to find herself scooped up and restored summarily to her former place, with her husband propped on his elbow looking down lazily at her embarrassed, indignant face. She struggled upright determinedly, avoiding his eyes.

'I must go to Jamie.'

Luc glanced at his watch.

'It is past ten, *carinha*,' he said, amused at the sudden horror on her face. 'He will be in the garden with Dirce by now, so you may as well stay where you are.'

Emily flung out of bed, diving for her dressing gown.

'Thurza will wonder what's become of me,' she muttered, wrapping it round her. 'I must——'

'My dearest wife,' drawled Luc, reclining against the headboard, his hands behind his head, 'no one will think it strange if I wish my wife to remain in bed a little late with me on the only morning of the week I am free to enjoy her company. After all, it was exceedingly late before we finally got to sleep.'

Emily turned on him hotly.

'Look here, Luc Fonseca, last night you—well, you took me by surprise. You needn't imagine it was an experience to be repeated. I meant what I said about not sleeping with you. . . .'

'Ah, but you did—eventually.'

'I know, but only, but only because——'

'But only because you were so exhausted with my lovemaking that you couldn't help but do so.' Luc's eyes gleamed maliciously. 'And now you are going to tell me you detested the experience so much you never wish to repeat it. *Que vergonha!* For shame.'

Emily stared at him mutely. The hateful knowledge in his eyes precluded all possibility of denial. He knew all too well, and so, unfortunately, did she, that what had passed between them last night had been no unbearable experience. Far from it. After the first instinctive resistance there had been nothing she could do to prevent the surge of response that had risen to make their lovemaking a very mutual satisfaction.

'It was just sex,' she said flatly.

'A very natural process, but you do not wish it to happen again?'

'No, thank you.' Emily moved to the door. 'Without love it's just animal.'

'And you do not love me, Emily.' Luc lay watching her broodingly.

'No—no, I don't,' she choked, and fled to the bathroom away from his disturbing black gaze that seemed to see right into the secret places of her mind.

For the next few days life went tranquilly on at the Casa d'Ouro. Emily's visit to the doctor was postponed when he was called away on an emergency, and another appointment made for the following week. She spent her time almost exclusively with Thurza and Jamie, as Luc took to arriving home later and later, and on the plea of mounting paperwork, spent his evenings after dinner in the study, coming to bed long after Emily. Jamie thrived in his new environment, causing great excitement one morning by taking his first steps unaided, to the adulation of his great-grandmother and the maids, all of whom behaved as though no child had ever achieved such a feat before.

'You must admit that ten months is very early,' said Thurza. 'I remember Luc was just as forward, though.'

Emily smiled fondly at her excited, triumphant little son, prey to a lethargy which had increased since the party.

'I feel quite guilty at how little I do here,' she said idly. 'I'm less use than those macaws. We both inhabit a gilded cage of sorts, but at least they have *some* function as warning signals. I'm quite useless. At home—I mean at the Dower House there was always so much to get through in a day, but at least Jamie was in a playpen. How I would have managed once he started walking I can't imagine.'

'Don't try. Enjoy your present leisure and concentrate on getting yourself more robust. Perhaps giving a party so soon was a bad idea.'

'Nonsense! I enjoyed it very much. Besides, I'm fully aware of your reason for doing so.'

Thurza smiled at her smugly.

'Now everyone knows that I fully endorse your presence here. They were able to see Luc's wife as a member of the family, not a little outsider we were obliged to take in merely to gain possession of Jamie.'

Emily grinned at the old lady's candour.

'Yes. And I appreciate it. I realise you must have been very reluctant to have Luc marry some little nobody who had—to be blunt—produced an illegitimate child. Jamie was the sugar on the pill I represented.'

'True,' admitted Thurza. 'But after one look at him it was only too obvious that you weren't passing off another man's child as Luc's.' She held up a restraining hand at Emily's involuntary protest. 'Besides, Emily, you obviously came here to Brazil under protest. I'm not so geriatric yet that I can't see that your marriage is causing you both a great deal of turbulence. Sometimes I think you're on the point of harmony, and then suddenly you are both formal and distant again, but, somehow, never indifferent.'

Emily laughed ruefully.

'Nothing gets past you, does it? Nevertheless, we are trying to make a go of things, if only for Jamie's sake.'

Thurza snorted.

'For Jamie's sake! Emily, when are you——'

Whatever else she intended to say was lost as Maria came out to announce something to Thurza. Apparently the Machado sisters had come to call.

Emily inspected her son quickly and deposited him in the playpen, glad that she was wearing a favourite dress that morning, a thin coffee-coloured lawn with a trail of yellow-centred white daisies wandering down the full skirt. Thurza greeted the two girls in local style with kisses on both cheeks, and sent for coffee as they turned to greet Emily. Analha Machado, in a demure yellow cotton dress, smiled warmly at Emily, taking her hand and wishing her a shy good morning. Teresinha, dressed in skin-tight pink trousers and much unbuttoned silk shirt, acknowledged Emily briefly, her attention immediately fixed on Jamie, who smiled at the visitors with an expression so like his father Emily felt regrettably smug at the look on Teresinha's face.

'Very like Luc, is he not?' Thurza smiled indulgently as Analha went on her knees alongside the playpen and touched Jamie's hair, making the type of baby noises that are universal. Teresinha stood still, looking at the child with something almost akin to hunger in her vivid face.

'*Nossa Senhora!*' she muttered. 'He is the—image, I think

you say—of Luc, Senhora Fonseca.'

Unsure which Senhora Fonseca was being addressed, Emily remained silent until the other girl looked towards her.

'You are to be congratulated.' Teresinha subsided gracefully on the sofa beside Emily, accepting the cup of coffee Thurza handed to her. 'You have a beautiful son. How very fortunate that he resembles Luc so closely.'

Emily took a cup from Thurza and handed it to Analha before replying.

'It certainly pleases Luc very much,' she answered quietly.

'May I pick him up, Emily?' entreated Analha. 'I may call you Emily?'

'Of course. Do take him out of the pen if you like. Perhaps he will demonstrate his new accomplishment.'

With a little coaxing from Thurza, and a great deal of encouragement from his mother, the little boy took three unsteady steps unaided before plopping down on his bottom with crows of triumph, his face alight as he saw a tall figure coming towards him.

'Da-da!' he said joyfully, and Luc came forward swiftly to pick up his son and greet the visitors, his free arm held out to Emily. She went to him with unusual alacrity, lifting her face for a kiss that proved more lingering than the occasion warranted. Luc kept her close as he chatted with Teresinha and Analha, and Jamie once again proudly showed his walking ability to his father, provoking laughter from Luc as he tossed his son high in the air to screams of delight.

Such unbridled domestic felicity proved too much for Teresinha, and firmly refusing pressing offers of lunch, she shepherded a disappointed Analha away from the sight of Lucas Fonseca in the role of proud father.

The visit left Emily much more happily disposed towards her husband and their relationship, if not completely to Luc's liking, was a great improvement on the barely concealed hostility that had prevailed since the night of the party.

One evening they dined with Bob McClure, as promised, with John Trelaur and Tom Enys as the other guests, and despite being outnumbered four to one, Emily felt no constraint in the all-male company. She was happy and relaxed in the convivial atmosphere, able to contribute to the conversation herself owing to Bob McClure's fascination with antiquity. Under Luc's encouraging gaze she talked at some length of Compton Lacey, her listeners genuinely interested in her account of its history. When they returned to Casa d'Ouro afterwards Emily lingered companionably with Luc over a nightcap, and for once prepared for bed minus the feeling of constraint that was usual when she and Luc retired at the same time.

Emily found her visit to the hospital to see Dr Ferreira less trying than expected. Thurza accompanied her and went round the pleasant little building with her before settling herself in a waiting room while the doctor subjected Emily to a thorough examination, took samples of blood and urine, and asked a variety of questions.

When Emily was dressed and sitting in front of his desk once more he raised an eyebrow and smiled at her across his clasped hands.

'I'm sure you realise there is every probability that you are once more pregnant, Senhora Fonseca.'

Emily nodded, smiling back ruefully.

'I've been telling myself for some time that it was merely the different way of life, but of course I'd accepted the possibility. With Jamie I was very sick, but this time I merely feel a bit languid, with an overwhelming desire to sleep all the time.'

'You are probably a little anaemic; we shall see. And, of course, until the report on your urine sample is confirmed it is not official. However, other signs all indicate that you will present your husband with a playmate for your son in, I should say, seven months or so. You agree?'

'Oh yes.' Emily gave a funny little smile. 'A small Christmas present, I expect.'

She rejoined Thurza thoughtfully, deciding it was only just to inform Luc of her news before telling his grandmother. After lunch, or perhaps after dinner would be better. She listened absently to Thurza extolling the virtues of Dr Ferreira, wondering how Luc would react.

Luc failed to appear for lunch. He had left a message with the maids to the effect that he was going down the mine to investigate the possibility of a new lode.

'A vein of ore,' explained Thurza.

'Bob McClure said something about it at dinner the other evening,' said Emily. 'I must ask Luc to explain it all to me properly, so that I know exactly what happens. I can't help feeling a bit apprehensive at the thought of men working so far beneath the ground.'

'I used to be at first,' admitted Thurza, a faraway look in her eye, 'but it is an experience you will never be able to share with Luc. Our miners are a superstitious breed, they won't allow a woman down the mine; even a priest is tabu because of his cassock. Yes, Maria?' She broke off as the maid came along the verandah with Bob McClure hard on her heels.

'Forgive the lack of ceremony, ladies,' he said, his kind face full of distress. 'I'm sorry to be the one to have to break this, but——'

Thurza rose to her feet automatically, her back as straight as a lance.

'What has happened?'

All the blood drained from Emily's face and her heart missed a beat, then resumed, pounding heavily in her breast like a drum.

'Now there's no need to get uptight,' began Bob miserably.

'Get on with it, man!' rapped Thurza.

'My findings have confirmed a lode present at a deeper level, and Luc went in to inspect the tunnel we're mining to meet up with it.'

'Please, Bob!' implored Emily.

'Luc went in with Zé Villela, the assistant to John Trelaur, plus the shift boss and about half a dozen men. There was a rock burst, and I'm afraid they're trapped behind an extensive rockfall.'

Thurza sat abruptly, looking for once every minute of her age, and Emily swiftly sat beside her, taking a cold hand in her own, chafing it gently, her eyes fixed on Bob McClure's.

'Was anyone injured?' Her voice seemed to be coming from a long way off.

'We don't know. But there has been some communication by means of hammering on the steel-compressed air mains.' He went down on one knee in front of them, his face urgent. 'Please try not to worry too much, they should be able to bleed off compressed air for oxygen if they need it, and they have their cap lamps for light. If they use them sparingly they'll have light until we get them out.'

Emily stared at him in dismay.

'How long will you take to get them out—hours? Days? What's being done to get them out—aren't you pulling the rocks away?'

'It isn't that simple, honey,' said Bob gently, and Thurza straightened, squeezing Emily's hand tightly. Bob swallowed, and went on unhappily, 'It will depend on the extent of the fall. They can't go at the clearance like a bull at a gate, you know, they have to clear the fall slowly, shoring with steel arches and timber as they go. This has to be done with great care. I'm sure neither of you, and certainly not Luc, would want further injuries in a reckless dash to get them out. It could take anything up to a day or two, maybe longer.'

'Thank you for letting us know personally,' said Thurza, pulling herself together. 'I'm sure you must be needed, so we'll let you get back.'

'Don't worry yourself sick now, Emily.' Bob was obviously at a loss to know how to comfort the white, still girl.

Emily smiled faintly.

'Don't ask the impossible, Bob, but thank you again.' She walked to the door with him, then returned to sink down on a chair, staring unseeingly in front of her.

'I had a piece of news to give him today, Thurza,' she whispered, dry-eyed. 'The doctor confirmed my suspicions this morning. I'm pregnant.'

'Oh, my dear!' Getting up resolutely, Thurza gave Emily her hand. 'In that case, I'll ring for lunch. You need feeding up more than ever now. I might have known that was why you were so peaky-looking. We'll eat in peace while Jamie's still asleep.'

The thought of food made Emily's gorge rise, but she sat at table obediently and drank some clear soup, then gave up.

'It's no use, Thurza,' she said after a while, laying down her knife and fork. 'I just can't swallow. The stuff won't go down. I keep thinking—imagining——'

'Well, stop it,' said Thurza roundly, pushing her own plate aside impatiently. 'We won't help matters by getting morbid.'

'No,' agreed Emily, then, unable to keep back the thought obsessing her, 'What if he's injured!'

Thurza's breath drew in sharply.

'We have no way of knowing, of course, but remember they wear protective helmets and have enough sense to get out of the way at the first sign of trouble. And don't forget, they *have* been in communication.'

'I'm sorry,' said Emily in remorse. 'I'm no help at all, am I, and you must be more worried than I am.'

'I believe you are a great deal more attached to Luc than you allow yourself to admit,' said Thurza, her old eyes shrewd. 'Isn't it time you let him know?'

Emily swallowed hard.

'If I'm given the chance I'll do my utmost to put things right between us,' she said huskily, her mouth dry at the possibility that the opportunity might never arise.

They got through the day somehow. Feverishly Emily played with Jamie, pushed him round the garden in his chair, and insisted on giving him his bath and his supper herself in the kitchen. The maids were so stricken about their master that they were no company for the little boy. Jamie, blissfully unaware of the cloud hovering over Casa d'Ouro, insisted on feeding himself, and the ensuing mess took everyone out of themselves for a while in helping to clear up.

Twice the phone rang. Thurza had stationed herself in the morning room alongside one extension, and Emily left Jamie to Dirce, flying to the old lady's side. The first time it was John Trelaur, the Mine Captain, assuring them that rescue operations were well under way, and that they were in regular communication by means of knocking on the air mains. The second time it was Bob McClure, reporting on the further progress of the clearance operation, which to Emily seemed to be proceeding at a snail's pace.

'It's the only way, Emily,' said Thurza sternly. 'Any faster and it could result in a further fall.'

Emily flinched.

'Luc must be hungry,' she said, changing the subject hurriedly.

'Thirst is more of a problem, I expect. But eventually they may be able to pass canteens of water through before the fall is cleared completely.' Thurza's eyes softened as they rested on Emily's white face. 'Now go and bring Jamie in here to play for a while before he goes to bed.'

Emily obeyed like an automaton. She felt cold right through to her bones. Ever since Bob had arrived with the news a chill seemed to have permeated through her entire body, and even hugging Jamie to her fiercely did nothing to alleviate it. She took Jamie along to where Thurza was stationed in the morning room, and both women derived a little comfort from watching him crawl around the room, pulling himself upright on the furniture and reminding them forcibly that, whatever their inner torment, life must go on outwardly normally, for Jamie's sake.

It was after the baby was settled down for the night that the waiting became agony. Neither made any attempt at dinner and settled for incessant cups of coffee and tea brought in unasked by a wan, subdued Maria. To pass the time Thurza began to reminisce about days gone by at Casa d'Ouro, telling Emily of receptions given that far outshone the modest affair of the previous week.

'At one time,' related Thurza, a faraway look in her eye, 'we had many more British people here in key positions, and it was possible to make up a cricket eleven. One of the social events of the year was a visit from Rio Cricket Club for a weekend. We'd put up the visitors here and, apart from the match, there were lunches and dinners and a fancy dress dance. . . .' She smiled naughtily. 'I enjoyed myself enormously at those affairs. Comes from having a basically frivolous nature, I suppose.'

'You—frivolous?' Despite her anxiety Emily couldn't help laughing.

'Oh yes.' Thurza's eyes twinkled. 'I haven't always been a wayward old tartar, you know. At one time I was a gay, giddy girl just like everyone else. It used to cause trouble with Jaime on occasion. He used to say I liked nothing better than chattering away at cocktail parties, a glass of wine in my hand, flitting from group to group like a butterfly.'

Emily felt wistful.

'I don't think I've ever been a gay and giddy girl,' she said quietly.

Both women were abruptly quiet. They gave up any

pretence of being cheerful and sat, tense, their whole energies given over to the sheer torture of waiting.

'Couldn't we have gone down to the mine?' burst out Emily at one stage.

'No.' Thurza shook her head decisively. 'We'd be no use, only in the way, and someone would feel they had to look after us.'

'Yes. Yes, of course you're right.' Emily subsided into silence again, uttering a silent, fervent prayer that God would allow her to see Luc again, unharmed and able to listen to her.

I hope he'll want to listen, she thought bleakly. I want him to know that I love him, if he's still interested. He had to be interested, surely, to make love to her like that the other night. But then it was he who had told her it wasn't necessary to love in order to make love. She stared blindly at her tightly clasped hands. She knew now that she had never stopped loving him, though until today she had been too stupid, or was it stubborn, to realise it. Her love for him hadn't died at all, it had merely been shut up in some sort of mental deep freeze waiting for the key to unlock it and set it free again, very much alive. Alive! At the thought Emily was gripped with despair. Please let him be alive, let him know that she loved him, had never stopped, only she was too hurt, too stiff-necked to admit it, even to herself.

'What is it, Emily, do you have a pain?' Thurza was watching her with anxious eyes.

'Nothing I can take a pill for,' said Emily apologetically, 'it's just this interminable waiting. How long have they been down there, Thurza?'

'Since nine this morning, according to John Trelaur. Twelve hours.' Thurza rose to her feet. 'Come, Emily, let's have a look at Jamie, move around a little. We shall easily hear the telephone if—when it rings.'

Emily obeyed, and for a while they paced along the verandah, looking up at the brilliance of the stars. It was a terrible thought that they were up here in the balmy, perfumed night, breathing in the soft air, watching the glittering pinpoints of light in the velvet sky, when somewhere far below them Luc and the other men were shut away in a dusty tomb.

The maids were huddled together in the kitchen instead of in their own quarters when Emily volunteered to make more tea. Glad of something to do, they hastily provided a tea-tray, Dirce insisting on making some dainty little crustless sandwiches filled with cucumber and prawns. Listlessly both women managed a couple of these, washed down with several cups of tea. As Emily was pouring out the second cups the telephone rang. The teapot slid out of her nerveless fingers on to the tray, splashing them with scalding tea as Thurza seized the instrument and listened intently to the voice on the other end of the line.

'Thank you, John, thank you very much for letting us know so quickly,' she said after a couple of interminable minutes. 'Please convey my grateful thanks to all those who are working so hard.'

'What is it, Thurza—tell me!' implored Emily.

'They've very nearly completed the rescue operation.' Thurza was suddenly white and limp. 'Another hour or so and the men should be out. Luc is perfectly all right.'

Emily dropped on her knees beside Thurza, buried her head in the older woman's lap and burst into tears. Thurza let her cry, smoothing the pale hair with a comforting hand for a while before reverting to her usual bracing self.

'Come along, Emily,' she said briskly, patting the bowed head. 'Up you get and go and wash your face. Luc won't want to come home to a wife covered in red blotches.'

Emily scrambled to her feet, sniffing loudly.

'No, you're right. Sorry. I'll go and do some repair work.' She looked back at the open doorway. 'Did Mr Trelaur say Luc was completely unhurt?'

'He just said he was all right. Now go along and do something to yourself, you look a sight. By the way, perhaps you'd better call Dirce in here. I feel suddenly too old and weary to totter to the kitchen.'

Emily's Portuguese was progressing, and a couple of halting phrases and a lot of arm-waving soon sped Dirce off to her mistress, while Emily went off to try to repair the ravages of her crying bout. When she returned Thurza was sipping brandy from a large balloon glass and waved to a similar glass on the small table beside Emily's chair. Emily made a face.

'Go on, drink it,' commanded Thurza. 'Do you good after the day we've spent. Unwind those tense nerves.'

Despite her dislike of the taste the fiery warmth of the brandy helped Emily considerably, permeating through her body and dispelling the frozen feeling that had chilled her since the news of the accident. The two women were able to chat quite normally, though neither troubled to disguise the fact that one ear was cocked, listening for the sound of Luc's jeep. Dica and the others were happily engaged in preparing a meal for the *patrão*, and the whole atmosphere of the big house was perceptibly different. Emily marvelled silently. All because of one man. It was gone two in the morning before the sound of tyres skidding to a halt on the gravelled drive outside the open window heralded Luc's return. They both hurried out on the verandah to welcome the tall, dusty figure coming wearily towards them. Luc's face was colourless with fatigue beneath the grime, his eyes glittering in a tired, triumphant smile. His grandmother reached him first, Emily, suddenly shy, hanging back as he embraced Thurza wordlessly. His head lifted and his eyes met hers, and Emily instinctively responded to the unmistakable appeal that drew her towards him like a magnet. He moved towards her simultaneously, and Thurza tactfully took herself off kitchenwards as Emily threw herself into Luc's arms, rubbing her face blindly against his, reaching up to touch his hair, his face, the tears flooding unchecked as his arms closed round her fiercely and his mouth met hers. For a long time they said nothing, each holding the other as though afraid to loosen their grip for an instant, a fraction, lest the other disappear.

When it was possible for her to speak Emily said unsteadily,

'I imagined you crushed, dead, suffocated—all sorts of horrors——'

He pressed her head against his chest protectively.

'It was nothing like that, *querida*. I'll tell you all about it tomorrow, but right now I need a drink, a meal and then bed.' He lifted her face to his. 'Though not necessarily in that order,' he muttered against her lips.

Suddenly Emily was euphoric.

'You didn't mention a bath in your requirements, Senhor

Fonseca,' she said gaily, 'otherwise I think your order of priorities was perfectly correct!'

'*Deus*, Emily,' he groaned, crushing her to him again, 'all I could think about these past hours was that smile!'

'Darling, darling,' Emily felt tears threaten again. 'Come. Let's go to Thurza. She's been wonderful. I don't think I'd have kept in one piece without her.'

They walked slowly along the verandah, arms round each other.

'Were you truly that worried, Emily?' There was no mistaking the undisguised longing in Luc's simple question.

'I nearly went out of my mind—Oh, Luc!' Anything further she might have said was stifled in an embrace that threatened to cut off her air supply altogether, succour arriving by means of a dry little cough from Thurza, who stood by the candlelit table on the verandah, watching them with a smile.

'Put your wife down for a moment, Lucas Fonseca,' she said dryly, 'and apply yourself to this steak. We'll join you; for some reason neither of us has had much appetite today.'

'Splendid idea, Thurza; that glass of beer looks like the answer to a prayer!' Luc seated himself with alacrity and allowed both women to wait on him hand and foot, anticipating his every wish, while managing to tuck into quite a substantial meal themselves. He told them a little about the accident, glad to report that beyond one broken arm and a fair amount of bruises and scratches, no one was hurt. Emily jumped up to pour coffee, as Luc consumed the final morsel of cheese, and leaned back in contentment to light a cheroot, running a caressing finger down her arm as she filled his cup.

'You needn't think this handmaiden bit is a permanent arrangement,' warned Emily, her smile incandescent. 'It's only because you gave us such a fright.'

'It almost makes it all worthwhile!' The glint in his eye made her toss her head.

'I'm sure it was all a ruse to attract sympathy, just like Jamie!'

'And how is Jamie today—any new accomplishments?' All the time he was talking Luc's eyes never left Emily's face, and she had difficulty in concentrating on her replies.

'No,' she said breathlessly. 'It's still three steps and down down on his bottom.'

Thurza watched them fondly, drank the last of her coffee and rose to her feet. Luc instantly followed suit, bending his head for her goodnight kiss.

'Goodnight, Luc,' she said, patting his cheek fondly. 'Thank God you're safe. After all this excitement I'm ready for my bed—and I should think both of you are, too.' With what looked suspiciously like a wink she bent to kiss Emily's cheek and left them alone.

'Was Thurza right, Emily?' asked Luc huskily, pulling her to her feet. 'Are you ready for bed? The same bed as your husband, *carinha*? I want very much to lie all night with you in my arms, to hold you and know that I'm not going to have nightmares about that black hole down there.'

Emily trembled.

'After you've had your bath,' she said, deliberately prosaic, refusing to look at him.

He took her hand and made off at great speed towards their bedroom.

'I will have the swiftest bath on record,' he promised, sweeping her along with him.

Emily giggled helplessly as he began to strip off his clothes before they had even left the verandah.

'What are you doing? What will the maids think?'

He turned on her fiercely, picking her up to hold her against his bare chest, that smelt unashamedly of sweat and dust.

'They will think I am a man impatient to make love to my wife—and they will be right.' He set her roughly on her feet inside their room. 'Two minutes.'

Luc was back in what seemed even less, a bath towel wound round his hips, his hair dripping.

'You're not even partially dry,' scolded Emily, frowning in mock disapproval.

'Do you mind?'

'No.'

'Why did you bother to put this robe on?'

'Instinct.'

'Have you any other instincts?'

'I—I think so.'

'Then show me, *querida*, show me!'

At the touch of Luc's skin against hers Emily discovered she had instincts hitherto undiscovered. The release from the tension of the day resulted in a euphoric outpouring of all the love and warmth in her nature Luc had demanded, so that the night was a wonder of revelation that left them shaken and unbelieving in each other's arms when finally the storm had passed and left them in a tangle of arms and legs that held each other fast, reluctant to let each other go even into the escape of sleep.

'Did I tell you I love you, Luc?' she murmured sleepily into his throat.

A tremor ran through his body.

'Repeatedly, *carinha*. Did you truly mean it, or was it just— the heat of the moment?'

His breath caught at the wickedness of her throaty chuckle.

'I had no idea I was capable of behaving like that, Luc! But I did mean it—I *do* mean it. I've never really stopped loving you really, but—well, I think I locked all the feelings for you away subconsciously when you left me alone, abandoned me, as I thought.' She laid a finger on his lips to stem his protest. 'Yes, I know it wasn't really like that, but I *thought* it was, which did the damage. Knowing you might have been killed today was the key that unlocked the door on my emotions. I didn't know how I could bear it if I—if you—if I never had the chance to tell you.' She pushed herself frantically against him, murmuring deep down in her throat as he kissed her and cuddled her close with comforting noises, as though she were Jamie. Jamie!

Emily pulled sharply away from Luc.

'What is it?' he asked instantly.

'I didn't go in to see Jamie before——'

'Before I chased you to bed.'

'I never gave him a thought,' she said, full of guilt.

Luc laughed delightedly and slid out from beneath the sheet.

'I will go and look at him. Don't go away.'

In a moment or two he was back, his naked body silvered by the moonlight through the window for an instant before he came in beside her and held her close once more.

'I was so absorbed in being a wife I forgot to be a good mother,' Emily said remorsefully. 'Is he all right?'

'Sleeping like an angel. And do not be so self-critical. You are a perfect mother.'

Emily was silent for a moment as she suddenly remembered her news.

'Just as well, really,' she said, wriggling closer to him.

'What do you mean?'

'Well, shall we say I've solved the problem about what to give you for Christmas.'

Luc propped himself on an elbow to look down at her, switching on the bedside lamp.

'It is April, Emily. Why are you thinking about Christmas?'

Emily gave him a smile of such pure happiness Luc's breath caught in his throat.

'That's when we shall have our next child, God willing.'

A blaze of delight flared in his eyes and he came down beside her again, holding her painfully tight. Then suddenly he held her away again slightly.

'But that is in only eight months' time . . .?'

Emily began to giggle.

'Precisely. Either we are more than ordinarily compatible, my darling husband, or those Fonseca genes of yours are frighteningly ruthless!'

Luc grinned at his tousled, flushed wife.

'Do you mind, *carinha*?'

'Not a bit. Besides, Thurza will be pleased. She wants to fill the place up again, she says. You can't deny we're off to a good start!'

He pounced, crushing her to him, frantically kissing her in every place he could reach, heedless of smothered, laughing protests.

'Hey!' she gasped with difficulty. 'You're supposed to treat me like a piece of Dresden china now I'm in a delicate condition—like they do in books.'

Black eyes glinted down wickedly into blue ones.

'I'll start tomorrow!'